NOWHERE BOYS

D1402288

For Cassidy

EGMONT
We bring stories to life

First published by Hardie Grant Egmont, Australia 2014
This edition published in Great Britain 2015 by Egmont UK Limited
The Yellow Building, 1 Nicholas Road, London W11 4AN

Text copyright © 2014 Elise McCredie, based on Nowhere Boys TV series,
created by Tony Ayres © Matchbox Pictures.
Cover photography by Ben King

ISBN 978 1 4052 7568 2

www.egmont.co.uk

59005/1

A CIP catalogue record for this title is available from the British Library.
Printed and bound in Great Britain by the CPI Group.

NOWHERE BOYS

ELISE McCREDIE

EGMONT

felix: into the woods

Felix's fingers thrashed at the strings of his electric guitar as if he were trying to do it damage. The chords screeched out of his amp in ragged harmony with his vocals.

> *'Water, fire, earth and air,*
> *Elements that we all share.'*

As Felix sang, he kept his eyes on his closed bedroom door, willing it to stay shut. From the lounge room he could hear the muffled sound of his parents' raised voices. He turned up his amp to cover the sound. He didn't have much time.

> *'Water wash our sins away,*
> *Earth guide us to a place.'*

He was pretty sure he had it right now. He looked at the black foolscap diary that lay open on his desk – his Book of

Shadows. Anything macabre or interesting went in there: pictures he'd downloaded from the net, stories about weird happenings, poems and, of course, the lyrics for this song.

> *'Wind brings with it fear,*
> *Flames of fire we must face.'*

He shut his eyes. He'd been working on the song for weeks and knew it off by heart. His skin prickled in anticipation as the guitar screeched to its climactic finale.

> *'Walk upon this earth again,*
> *Walk upon this earth — '*

An almighty banging on the door cut Felix off.

His dad put his head into the room, the stress clear on his face. 'Jeez, mate. Can you keep it down? Have you seen your mum's car keys?'

Felix stopped the recording on his phone and sighed. At least he'd made it to the chorus. 'Nah.'

'We need to get Oscar to hospital. Come and help us look.'

Felix switched off the amp and put down his guitar. He shoved the Book of Shadows into his schoolbag.

Ever since his brother's accident, his parents had been on a knife edge. If Oscar got even the slightest temperature they'd freak out. Oscar being in a wheelchair meant that if an infection took hold it could have severe consequences. Felix tried not to dwell on what that might mean in non-doctor speak. Oscar was never going to walk again. How much more severe could the consequences get?

Grabbing his bag, Felix headed into the cluttered lounge room. His mum was pivoting around like an oversized spinning top. 'I've even checked the flowerpots. Ken, you must have taken them in your suit to the drycleaners.'

In the middle of the maelstrom, Oscar sat in his wheelchair looking flushed but calm, a thermometer stuck in his mouth.

He looked up at Felix and rolled his eyes. 'Don't tell them,' he muttered, 'but I'm actually just hot from the 10k run I did this morning.'

Felix smiled. Oscar was amazing. Here he was, stuck in a wheelchair, and he could still make jokes about it.

'I liked your song,' Oscar added. 'Very goth metal.'

'Thanks, bro,' said Felix, trying for lighthearted to match Oscar's tone.

'Ken!' snapped their mum. 'Did you hear me?'

'Felix!' snapped their dad. 'Don't just stand there. Help your mother!'

Felix sighed and headed over to his mum's handbag, which was sitting on the lowboy. He idly looked inside. There at the bottom – surprise, surprise – was a set of keys.

'These what you're looking for?'

'Thank God,' said his mum, snatching them off him and wheeling Oscar out the front door. 'Let's go! You start the car, Ken.'

Felix watched his family tumble out of the house in a flurry of anxiety. He put his hand up in a gesture of farewell. 'Thanks for your help, Felix. No problem, Mum,' he muttered to himself.

His mum turned back and for a second Felix thought she was going to thank him after all. 'Oh, and Felix? Remember the dishwasher needs unstacking. And if we're not back by tonight the recycling needs to . . .'

Felix spotted the permission slip for his school excursion lying on the lowboy. 'You haven't signed my permission slip!' he interrupted, grabbing it and running after them. 'The excursion's today!'

In the driveway, his dad was lifting Oscar into the back seat while his mum stowed Oscar's wheelchair in the boot.

Felix watched them from the doorway. What was the point?

Oscar looked at him through the car window. He mouthed a melodramatic, 'Save me.'

Felix gave his brother a small smile and made his way back inside. The place was a disaster zone, but he didn't care. The dishwasher could wait. He had more important things to worry about.

He looked in the hall mirror. His dyed-black hair was

growing out and his mousy-brown roots were peering shyly through. He flicked his fringe across to cover them as much as possible, adjusted his lip ring, hoicked his bag over his shoulder and shoved his headphones in. His stomach rumbled. He hadn't eaten breakfast. But there was no time for that now. He couldn't afford to miss this excursion, no matter what.

Slamming the front door behind him, Felix hit play on his phone to listen to the song he'd recorded. It sounded good. Kind of powerful.

A hand grabbed one of his headphones.

Felix turned to see Ellen, his neighbour and best friend since forever. She was dressed in head-to-toe black, like Felix.

She fell into step with him as she shoved the headphone into her ear. 'Woah, metal as.' She grinned at Felix, her dark purple lipstick making the whites of her teeth look bright. 'You write it?'

Felix nodded, then produced his permission slip. 'Hey, can you sign this?'

Ellen looked at him for a beat. 'You're not serious.'

'Yeah, I am.'

'You've got an excuse not to go on the stupid bush thing, and you're not going to take it?'

Felix shrugged. 'I'm kinda looking forward to it.'

'You hate nature,' she said, looking at him closely.

Felix looked away. Did she suspect something? 'Yeah,' he said slowly, trying to come up with something convincing.

'But it's better than hanging around here.' He gestured back to the house.

Ellen looked sympathetic. 'Bad?'

'More than bad,' he said truthfully. 'Most days they don't even look at me.'

Ellen put up her arm and then, as though not quite sure what to do with it, she patted him.

He looked at her hand on his arm. 'What are you doing?'

Her arm fell to her side. 'Nothing.'

'I'm not a dog, y'know.'

Felix didn't want sympathy. He'd had enough of teachers and relatives all wanting him to 'talk'. Talking didn't make him feel better and it definitely didn't change anything.

'Give it, then.' Ellen held out her hand. She scribbled Kathy Ferne's signature and thrust the form back at Felix.

'Not bad,' said Felix. He could always count on Ellen.

'Yeah well, I should be using my skills for identity theft, not lame-o parental fraud. So hey, check out my boots. I bought them on eBay.' Ellen lifted her skirt to reveal black platforms with purple spikes protruding from the sides.

Felix smiled. 'Awesome.'

———

A large bus was parked out the front of Bremin High. Mr Bates, the year-ten science teacher, was piling orienteering markers into the luggage compartment. Felix felt the butterflies in his stomach start flapping around. He really should have eaten some —

Boof!

A ball hit Felix hard in the head.

'And it's a goal for Bremin!' yelled a voice.

Felix turned to see Jake Riles, leader of the school jocks, pumping his fist in the air. Felix scowled and rubbed his head.

Jake's best friend, Trent, stepped in front of him and grabbed the ball. 'Oops. Sorry, freak. You're so white and skinny I thought you were a goalpost.' Next to him, Jake cracked up.

'Then you didn't score a goal, did you, loser?' Ellen jumped in. 'You scored a point.' She turned to Felix. 'You OK? I've got some arnica if you want.'

'Aww, the she-freak's gonna look after da poor he-freak,' drawled Jake.

Felix bit his lip. Jake Riles wasn't going to get to him. Not today.

Mr Bates had scored a mini megaphone and was yelling into it. 'OK, everybody! Time to board. Please do so in an orderly manner. I'll need everyone to present their permission slips to me before getting on.'

Ellen nudged Felix. 'Check out the boy band.'

A Subaru had pulled up beside the bus and the three Conte boys – Sam, Vince and Pete – spilled out.

Felix watched as their mum blew Sam a kiss. For a brief

moment, he wondered what it would feel like to have parents that actually liked you.

Sam put his skateboard down and glided across to where his girlfriend, Mia, was waiting for him. She was the most beautiful girl at Bremin High. Felix turned away. Sam's perfect, shiny life was just a bit too much on an empty stomach. He and Ellen handed in their permission slips and made their way down the aisle of the bus. As usual, the back seats had been claimed by Jake and Trent's gang.

As Felix slid into a seat next to Ellen, he felt something hard and wet hit the back of his head. A spitball.

'When was the last time you rejects washed?' called Jake.

Felix ignored him. He looked around the bus, searching the faces to check everyone he needed was there. The bus driver started the engine and the doors swung shut.

Felix jumped up from his seat. They couldn't leave yet! 'Mr Bates?'

Bates was taking the roll on his clipboard. 'Yes, Felix?'

'We're not going right now, are we?'

'Bus leaves at 10 a.m. sharp.'

'But the freak needs to wee-wee, Mr Bates,' called Trent.

'That's enough,' said Bates firmly. 'You've got a problem, Felix?'

Felix thought quickly. He had to stall for time. 'It's just . . . I'm not sure that everyone . . .'

Out the window, he saw a figure running towards the

bus. It looked like a backpack with legs attached. As the figure got closer he recognised Andy Lau, the nerd who'd won the district science fair three years in a row. He was out of breath and weighed down by an enormous backpack, complete with sleeping roll, multiple water flasks, a flyswat and a fishing net. The bus doors hissed open for him.

Felix sat down, relieved. 'It's nothing, sir. All good to go.'

Ellen looked at him curiously. 'What was that about?'

'Nothing.' Felix looked away. He'd never actually kept a secret from Ellen before. They told each other everything. But this? Felix was pretty sure not even Ellen would understand this. Or if she did, she'd want to be part of it, and Felix couldn't risk that.

A drop of water hit the window. Great. One disaster avoided and now it was going to pour with rain? The whole excursion would probably be cancelled.

'Mr Bates?' Jake called out.

'Yes, Jake?'

'Looks like it's going to piss down.'

'Language, Riles.'

'Sorry. Looks like it's going to piss down, *sir*.'

Laughter filled the bus. Bates was not amused. 'The excursion will continue regardless of weather. You will be challenged to find a way to work with the elements to achieve your goal.'

Felix never thought he'd be grateful that Mr Bates was

the sort of teacher who didn't let anything get in the way of his plans. He was the kind of teacher who even turned up at school on teachers' strike days. Normally that was a massive bummer, but today – well, today Felix almost liked Bates. Almost.

The bus pulled out on to the road as Bates gave a rundown of the day's activities. 'On arrival you will be assigned into groups of four. This exercise is about team-building. Learning to work collaboratively with your peers.'

Ellen turned to Felix. 'If we're not together, I'm walking back.'

Felix looked at her for a beat and then looked at her boots. 'In those things? Good luck with that.'

She grinned and thumped his arm. Felix looked out the window. He wasn't sure she'd be smiling if she knew the truth.

'Each group will be given a map with checkpoints that your group must identify and mark off,' Bates continued. 'There are also a number of flora and fauna specimens that you must identify on this worksheet,' he said, waving it around in the air. 'A group leader will be responsible for the honest accounting . . .'

By the time Bates had finished giving instructions, the bus was pulling into the Bremin Ranges National Park.

The year tens piled out of the bus into the car park. Felix held his bag tightly, feeling tense. He watched carefully as Bates placed a stack of maps and worksheets on a picnic table.

Bates pulled out a sheet of paper. 'OK people, form groups of four as I read out your names.'

Felix gripped his bag tighter. This was it.

'Daniel, Alexis, Tammy, Mike,' called Bates. 'Mia, Trent, Dylan and Ellen.'

Ellen looked at Felix in horror. Felix did his best to look equally unimpressed.

'Felix, Jake, Sam and Andy.'

Bingo! His plan had worked. Felix moved quickly towards a dismayed-looking Jake and Sam.

Andy joined them, grinning cheerfully. 'Brains and brawn,' he said. 'Excellent choice.'

Jake stuck up his hand. 'Sir, I think there's been a mistake.'

'No mistake, Riles. Take a map and worksheet and get going. First group back here with all the requirements fulfilled will win a pass to the Ladbroke Ranges Science Expo.'

'That's a terrific prize,' said Andy. 'I went last –'

'I'll go get the map,' said Felix, cutting Andy off. He walked towards the picnic table.

Ellen appeared beside him. 'Come on, let's hitch back into town. I so can't spend four hours with those losers.'

Bates had the megaphone again. 'I heard that, Ellen. That's a definite no.'

Felix looked at her apologetically. 'Sorry. Let's meet at my place after for a debrief.'

Ellen shook her head unhappily and walked off.

Felix wanted to run after her, but he forced himself to focus. Ellen would be fine. He'd explain it all to her later. Once she knew the reason he was doing this, she'd understand, for sure.

At the map table, Felix grabbed a worksheet, but instead of picking up a copy of Bates's map, he quickly pulled out a hand-drawn map that he'd tucked into his Book of Shadows. He flattened it out.

As he walked back across the car park, a feeling crept up his spine like he was being watched. He turned sharply. Nothing. He turned the other way. And then he saw it: a woman standing among the trees. She was staring at him intently.

With a jolt, Felix recognised her. It was the woman who ran Arcane Lane, the magic shop. What was she doing here? Felix shoved the map in his pocket. Maybe she'd somehow discovered what he was up to. But how could she have worked it out? He'd been so careful.

'You got the map, freak?' Jake was calling out to him.

Felix turned. 'Yeah, sure.' He looked back to where the woman had been, but could only see trees moving gently in the breeze.

Spooked, he made his way back to the others.

'I don't know how we're supposed to win with these two netballers on our team,' Jake muttered to Sam as they headed into the bush.

Andy smiled nervously at Felix and, shouldering his heavy pack, followed the other two.

Felix took a deep breath. In the distance he could see Ellen hobbling awkwardly after her group. He watched Sam, Jake and Andy disappearing through the trees.

Everything had gone to plan, but something didn't feel right. There was still time to turn back. He didn't have to go through with it.

But then a gust of wind blew up out of nowhere and he was propelled down the path after the others.

'Wait up!' he called. And the moment when he could have turned back had passed.

andy: man vs wild

A shiny beetle with reddish-brown legs made its way across a piece of bark. Andy watched its progress carefully. It looked like a common furniture beetle but it also had some of the hallmarks of the carpet beetle. He'd have to check on their different habitats to be one hundred per cent sure. He tipped his pack off one shoulder and reached inside for his *Field Guide to Australian Insects*. He was about to open it when he heard a voice yelling at him.

'Get a move on, nerd.' Jake was jogging back down the path towards him.

Andy stood his ground. 'Mr Bates said we had to identify the fauna and flora.'

Jake grabbed Andy's field guide and shoved it back in his pack. '*Mr Bates, Mr Bates*. Who cares what Bates says? Jake Riles says if Trent Long beats him then someone's gonna pay.' Jake shoved Andy's backpack on to his shoulder and pushed him roughly back on to the path.

'If you'd listened to Mr Bates you would know that we actually can't win unless we've listed all the –'

But Jake was already out of earshot.

Andy sighed. Jake might be Bremin High's super athlete, but clearly his parents had taught him nothing about manners.

Andy adjusted the pack on his back and set off after Jake. He'd spent weeks preparing for this excursion by watching every available episode of *Man Vs Wild*. He'd watched Bear drink his own urine, kill wild pigs with sticks, and extract venom from a snake and then roast the carcass over hot coals.

'It's probably a good idea if we all stick together,' said Felix, falling into step beside him.

At school Andy spent most lunchtimes hiding in the library to avoid Jake and his friends. But Felix, with his pale face and strange piercings, frightened him even more. Andy smiled nervously.

Felix handed him the worksheet. 'We can try to do the flora and fauna stuff as we go, if you want.'

Andy looked at Felix suspiciously. Why was he being so friendly? Was he trying to lure him into a trap? Was he planning to suck his blood? Andy wondered how far ahead Jake and Sam were. He tried to sound relaxed. 'Do you know anything about the forest environment?'

'Well I know if it touches my flesh, my skin basically flakes off.'

Andy looked at him.

Felix shook his head, grinning. 'Joke.'

'Oh,' Andy laughed nervously. Felix was *really* not funny. Not funny at all.

'Come on, let's catch the others up.' Felix quickened his pace.

Andy struggled after Felix. His back was starting to ache and his new walking boots were giving him blisters.

Maybe his family was right. Maybe he shouldn't have come. His parents were terrified by nature. Probably because in Singapore it was a miracle to see a tree that hadn't been encased in concrete and surrounded by a shopping mall. They had only agreed to sign the permission slip when he'd promised to go adequately prepared for any crisis. He was starting to wonder if carrying a week's worth of food, insect spray, anti-venom, three changes of clothes and a pack of firelighters was a bigger challenge than facing the dangers of the Australian bush.

Andy stumbled. His pack seemed to be getting heavier with every step. He should have done some weight-bearing trials before he agreed to carry his body weight in survival essentials. He looked at the path ahead. Even Felix was out of sight now. He could feel the sweat pouring off him. He unlodged a flyswat from the side of his pack and whacked at the persistent cloud of mosquitoes that had taken up a roving residence around his head.

Jake rounded the corner and hurtled towards him. 'Right,

that's it. See through the trees? There, at the first checkpoint? That's Trent's team. He's beating us and he's got *real girls* on his team.'

Through the trees, Andy caught sight of a group of four moving off quickly from the first checkpoint.

'Girls aren't necessarily a handicap.'

Jake pulled Andy's backpack off his back. 'No, but you are.'

Sam and Felix jogged back towards them.

'What are you doing?' Andy asked, secretly relieved to have the weight off his back.

Jake unzipped the backpack and turned it upside down so that everything inside it spilled out on to the path. Jake, Felix and Sam stared at the contents of Andy's pack. Andy felt a rush of embarrassment. There really was way too much for a four-hour walk. Plus, he hadn't realised his grandmother had snuck in her floral poncho.

'Dude, what is all this?' asked Sam.

Andy looked nervously at them. 'Just basic essentials.'

'At least there's food.' Sam opened one side of Andy's lunch box, which was full of *xiaolongbao*. He poked at the dumplings suspiciously and then opened the other compartment and pulled out a chicken's foot. 'Oh man, even I'm not eating *that*.'

Jake held up the poncho. 'What's with the girly blanket with the hole?'

Andy felt the sweat trickling down his sides. He silently cursed his *nai nai*. 'It's a poncho. For when temperatures drop.'

He was relieved when Jake threw it into the bush without further comment.

Jake grabbed a thermos of herbs from Sam.

'Wait! They're from my *nai nai*,' said Andy. 'They keep the blood temperature steady.' But Jake had tipped them out.

Jake thrust the almost-empty backpack at Andy. 'Come on. We can still win.'

Andy slung the backpack over his shoulder. So light! His shoulders almost sighed with relief. They still had another three hours to walk. It would be much more enjoyable this way. After all, Bear Grylls always travelled light.

'Come on,' yelled Jake. 'They're probably at the second checkpoint already.'

Andy hesitated, looking uncertainly at his belongings lying on the path.

'We can probably pick it all up on the way back,' said Felix, appearing at his side. 'It's better if we all stay together.'

Andy looked at him curiously. That was the second time Felix had said that. Pretty odd, coming from someone who was always on his own or with his equally strange friend.

Andy took one last look at his supplies and then, grabbing a can of insect spray and a bottle of water, headed after the others. He felt guilty but strangely liberated.

Jake was at the first checkpoint when he caught up.

'OK,' said Jake. 'Here's the thing: we're going to have to sprint to the next checkpoint to catch up.'

Felix held up the map. 'There's a shortcut we could take.'

Jake clapped Felix on the back. 'Good one, Dracula. Lead the way.'

Andy didn't like that idea one bit. 'Wait. Mr Bates stressed that it was very important we follow the prescribed route.'

Jake rolled his eyes. 'Enough with the Mr Bates routine. The guy wears pink polo shirts, for Christ's sake.'

Andy looked at the map Felix was holding. It looked hand-drawn. He was sure the ones Mr Bates had were printed out. 'Maybe if I could have a look at the map?' he suggested.

Felix stuffed it quickly in his pocket and headed off the path into the bush. Sam and Jake followed him.

Andy considered his options. Something didn't feel right. Surely you should never leave the path when you were in the wilderness. Wasn't that Bush Survival 101?

But three against one meant he didn't really have a choice, and if Mr Bates got cross Andy could argue that the majority ruled. He looked around at the unfamiliar bush. The wind rustled the eucalypts. He took a deep breath and stepped gingerly off the path. He made his way through the undergrowth after the others. The bush closed in around him. He looked back but the path had already disappeared. He felt a small shiver of excitement as he pushed his way through the trees.

When he caught up with the others, they'd arrived at a small clearing. Directly in front of them was a steep drop, and they were surrounded on all other sides by dense, inhospitable bush. The wind had picked up and the branches swayed overhead.

Jake's mood had not improved, but now his anger was directed solely at Felix. 'Where are we, freak?'

Felix was looking at the map, concerned.

Andy moved in quickly to help. 'I can check the coordinates if you like.'

Felix stepped away, quickly hiding the map from view. 'It's all good. We just need to go a bit further east and then we should hit a stream, which –'

The map suddenly blew out of Felix's hand. It spun and whirled across the clearing towards the drop. Then everything happened at once: Felix chased after the map, but as he reached for it, he slipped on some loose rocks. Sam and Jake reached out to grab him but together they overbalanced, and before Andy knew it, all three of them had disappeared down the ravine.

Andy stood still, shocked. What had just happened? He could hear the boys yelling as they slid down, then suddenly all was quiet. He moved to the edge and peered down. He couldn't see anything. The ravine was dense with foliage. Maybe they'd been injured. What if one of them had broken a leg? He should turn back, find the path and get Mr Bates. But what would Bear Grylls do? Would Bear leave his mates alone in the forest? All right, 'mates' was probably too strong a word. These boys were rude, weird and unfriendly. But they were a team. And hadn't Mr Bates said they had to work together to solve any problems?

He heard a yell from below. 'Andy!'

They were conscious, at least. Andy hesitated. What would his family want him to do? Find the safe way home, of course. Well, maybe he wasn't going to do that. Maybe this was his one chance at adventure. He could slide down that ravine right into the arms of a wild pig. He could fight it with sticks, defy his family and be a man of the wild!

To truly know yourself, you had to test yourself against the elements. To survive, you had to dig deep into the catfish hole with your bare hands and pull out that four-foot fish, even if your flesh was pierced with venomous wounds.

Andy took a running leap and careered down the slope. He skidded fast, his backside scraping against mossy rocks, his arms getting scratched on fallen twigs. It was painful but exhilarating at the same time. His pack bounced against his back, eventually snagging in a tree branch as he made his descent. He landed on his back with an almighty *thump*.

Andy wasn't sure if he could move. He gingerly lifted his left leg and then his right. Seemed OK. He lifted his head.

The other three were sitting glumly on the ground. Andy followed their gaze. The slope they'd fallen down looked almost vertical from this angle. There was no way they would be able to climb back up.

Andy sat up. 'Did you find the map?'

Felix shook his head.

An eerie silence filled the bush. Andy noticed there was no birdsong. He looked around nervously.

'OK, so we call Mr Bates. He'll be able to track the call via GPS.' Andy pulled out his phone and stared at it. 'It should at least have SOS reception.'

The others all lifted their phones to show him their screens. They'd obviously already tried. Nothing. Not one bar of reception.

Andy stood up. Strangely, he didn't feel sore at all.

'So what do we do now, freak?' Jake asked.

Felix looked around, clearly unsure.

'What Bear Grylls would do is find running water,' Andy jumped in.

'So he can get naked and eat a slug,' sniped Jake.

'No,' said Andy. 'So he can follow it back to civilisation.'

Sam looked up at the darkening sky. 'I don't think running water is going to be a problem.'

As if on cue, deep rumbles of thunder sounded above them, and a bolt of lightning flashed through the dark sky. Rain began to fall in solid grey sheets.

The four boys stumbled through the thick undergrowth. Andy could barely see where he was going, so heavy was the downpour.

'Over here,' Felix yelled.

Andy followed his voice, pushing his way through the scrub to a small clearing. He stopped and looked around. Through the rain he could see the trees that bordered the clearing had strange objects hanging from their branches. Andy looked closer. The objects were clearly man-made. And bizarre-looking.

Jake shuddered. 'Where are we?'

'It's like some weird *Blair Witch* remake,' muttered Sam.

Andy touched one of the dangling objects. It was like a spider web made out of bark and wool. He'd never seen anything like it before. The sky suddenly cracked open and an angry gash of lightning lit up the boys' scared faces.

'We need to get away from the trees,' yelled Andy.

'There's a rock ledge over here,' called Felix, heading towards it.

The boys huddled together under the ledge. The rain still blew in around them, but they were at least slightly protected.

Sam shivered. 'Man, I'm so hungry I could eat my own arm.'

Andy shook his head. 'You can't eat your own flesh, it's indigestible.' He looked at the others, who were all staring at him. 'What?'

'Helpful information, dude,' said Sam.

'So what do we do now?' asked Jake.

'Bear Grylls would light a fire,' offered Andy.

'Good idea,' said Felix. 'If we could find some dry twigs.' He searched around for something they could use as kindling.

'They'll wait for us, right?' asked Sam.

'Bates will send a search party,' said Jake.

'Might not be till morning, though,' said Felix, making a little pile of leaves and twigs.

Andy looked around. 'Bear Grylls can get a spark going with a spindle. If there's a long stick around . . .'

Felix produced a plastic lighter and lit the twigs.

Jake looked at him, impressed. 'Good thinking, man.'

Andy felt put out. He'd actually had matches *and* firelighters in his backpack.

'We'll probably starve to death before we're found,' said Sam.

'We'll be like those footballers who crash-landed in the Andes,' said Felix, blowing on the twigs.

Jake looked at Felix. 'What footballers?'

Andy watched as the twigs finally caught fire.

'Oh, never mind,' said Felix.

'Come on,' urged Jake.

'You know. They got so hungry they were forced to eat each other,' said Felix.

Nobody said anything for a minute.

'Alive?' Andy whispered.

'No. The ones that were already dead.'

Sam looked at Andy. 'So you can digest other people's flesh, just not your own?'

Andy had never thought about that. 'Not sure. I'll have to ask my dad.' He looked into the small, weak fire and thought about his family. They'd been right after all. He'd give anything for his *nai nai's* floral poncho right about now, and as for the lunchbox of *xiaolongbao* they'd left lying abandoned on the path . . .

'How about a song to cheer us up?' Felix was holding up his phone. Without waiting for an answer, he hit play.

Andy listened in disbelief as the most miserable, tuneless song started to play.

'Water, fire, earth and air,
Elements that we all share.
Water wash our sins away,
Earth guide us to a place . . .'

Andy shuddered. He wasn't into modern music. He always listened to Schubert when he was studying and occasionally he'd listen to his dad's Wings LPs. But this? Could you even call this music?

'That's supposed to be cheery?' asked Sam.

But Felix had his eyes shut and was singing along.

'Wind brings with it fear,
Flames of fire . . .'

The song went on but Andy wasn't listening anymore. What had seemed like a great adventure was now just making Andy feel miserable and, honestly, scared. He wasn't sure if it was his imagination but it seemed like the storm had become even heavier since Felix had started playing his awful music. It was dark and wet. The wind changed direction and the rain sheeted down at the perfect angle to completely extinguish the fire.

felix: there's no place like home

Felix opened one bleary eye. Early morning sunlight glimmered through the trees. His whole body felt stiff and cold. He put his hand on his chest. His T-shirt was sodden. In fact, all of his clothes were completely soaked through.

He sat up with a start. It wasn't a dream. They really were in the forest. Lost. He looked around and saw the other three were still asleep. Andy had his mouth open and his shirt pulled across his face to protect himself from mosquitoes. Sam was curled up in a ball and Jake was sleeping sitting up, his head against the rock ledge.

Felix rolled into a sitting position and looked around. He was pretty sure he'd found the right place, but without the map it was hard to be absolutely certain. He knew it was down a steep ravine and that there was a clearing with a stone ledge and a ring of trees.

He looked up. Now that the sun was shining, the strange things dangling in the trees almost looked like budding flowers. They swung in the breeze. Felix took his charcoal pencil out of his bag and began to draw them. Somehow it seemed important to have a record. Surely they were a sign that he'd found the right place?

He stood up, accidentally bumping into an overhanging branch and causing a cascade of perfectly formed water droplets to land on Andy.

Andy woke up with a splutter.

'Sleep well?' asked Felix.

Andy took his shirt off his face and looked around. 'At least we weren't eaten by the panther that lives out here.'

Felix smiled. 'You really believe that story?'

There was a loud crack in the bush nearby. Felix jumped. Andy grabbed a nearby stick.

'What was that?'

'I don't know.'

There was another cracking sound, like a beast was moving towards them.

Sam and Jake woke up and jumped to their feet.

Jake rubbed his eyes. 'Oh man, I was hoping this was a bad dream.'

Felix looked around nervously. 'I think we should leave.'

'Why haven't they sent out a search party for us?' asked Sam.

'They probably have,' said Andy. 'Visibility is pretty low. We need to get to higher ground so the helicopters can see us.'

From somewhere in the trees nearby came an almighty splitting sound, like the earth was opening up.

'We need to get out of here. *Now!*' yelled Felix.

'How do we know which direction to go?'

'Doesn't matter.' Felix led the way out of the clearing as quickly as he could, knocking at branches to create a path. The sooner they got away from here, the better. 'Come on!'

The thought of a panther didn't scare him. But whatever was back there sure as hell did.

'Do we actually know where we're going?' grumbled Jake.

'Just out of here,' said Felix, without slowing down.

Sam looked up at the sun. 'My dad reckons if you point the twelve on your watch at the sun, north is halfway between the hour hand and twelve.' He looked down at his watch. It was digital.

Felix stopped and stared at Sam. 'Helpful,' he said, before returning to his bush bashing.

On the map there had been a dirt road not far from the clearing. He just had to find it. He wasn't sure they'd make it through another night out here with no supplies. He owed it to the others to get them home. Even *he* wanted to get home and, in all honesty, that wasn't something he'd felt for a very long time.

He pushed aside a branch and there it was. 'It's a road. Come on,' he yelled back to the others.

He could hear them whooping and yelling. Felix grinned.

They'd done it. Disaster averted. They would be home having hot breakfasts and even hotter showers before they knew it.

The others scrambled up behind him.

'OK,' said Felix. 'I'm pretty sure if we follow this east, it will take us into Bremin.'

'Where the news cameras will be waiting to welcome the heroes,' said Jake, pumping his fist in the air. Then he stopped dead.

Felix turned to follow Jake's line of sight. Down the road from where they were standing, a strange dust cloud was spinning. Only it wasn't a cloud. It was too close to the ground. And it seemed to be moving along the path towards them.

'What the hell is that?' asked Jake.

A sudden wind blew up around them. Sticks, leaves and small stones blew into the air. They formed strange patterns for a moment before falling to the ground like hard rain.

Felix felt paralysed by fear. The dust cloud was moving towards them. It whipped up into the air, spinning quickly, gaining intensity and speed like some strange sort of tornado.

He shook himself into action. 'Run!'

They turned and ran, with the twister or whatever it was now hurtling along the road behind them, as if it was hell-bent on sucking them up into its centre.

Felix's heart pounded in his chest. He looked over his shoulder, terrified. The thing was gaining on them, and still gathering speed. They could never outrun it.

'Off the road!' he yelled to the others. He careered off the road into thick bush. Branches quivered and cracked as he pushed his way blindly through them. He could hear the others not far behind so he knew they'd followed him. He had no idea where he was going, but he knew they couldn't go back by that road.

Bursting breathlessly out of the bush into a clearing, Felix found himself standing in front of a makeshift campsite. He stopped short. There was an old Holden car, a tent – and a wild-looking man standing in front of the tent brandishing a hunting stick. Felix froze. The others stumbled into the campsite behind him. The guy looked feral and mad. He waved the hunting stick in the air and stepped aggressively towards them.

'Don't attack us!' Felix put up his hands.

The man narrowed his eyes. 'You're attacking me, aren't you?'

Sam jumped in. 'No way, man. We're totally lost and we've just been chased by a tornado.'

The man lowered the hunting stick. 'A tornado out here? I don't think so. So still this morning I couldn't even get my wind farm working.' The man gestured to his system of mini windmills, their blades as still as the hands on a broken clock.

Felix was suddenly aware of how still it was. There wasn't so much as a breeze in the bush. Nothing. Just the sound of quiet birdsong filtering through the trees. What was going on?

'But there was a massive wind and this twister was chasing us down the road,' said Jake breathlessly.

The man grinned. 'Not everything out here can be explained, boys.' He put his hand out. 'Roland.'

The boys shook hands and introduced themselves.

'You fellas hungry?'

Sam, Jake and Andy happily sat down and gorged themselves on fried eggs laid by Roland's friendly brood of chooks. Felix kept his distance. He'd lost his appetite. How could a massive twister blow up out of nowhere and then completely disappear?

After they'd eaten, Roland offered the boys a lift back into town. They piled into the back of his old Holden and, after trying the ignition five times, Roland finally got the car started. They bumped back on to the road and towards Bremin.

Felix watched through the car window as the dense bush gave way to houses. The closer they got to Bremin, the better he felt. Everything was going to be OK. Whatever was out there in the bush was staying there. They had survived. Their families would be delighted to see them and he would never have to go back into the bush again. Ellen was right: he definitely did hate nature.

Jake rolled down the window and yelled at the top of his lungs, 'Bremin, I love you!'

Felix smiled. Nothing like a night of starvation and misery to make you love your home town. When Roland pulled up in the main street, Felix could have kissed him.

'All right, boys. Be good,' Roland called as they stumbled out on to the street, thanking him profusely.

They stood on the footpath and watched as the Holden shuddered off down the road. Felix looked around. Everything was utterly familiar. And yet –

'You'd think there'd be a welcome party. We've been missing all night,' said Jake, looking around. The people in the main street were going about their lives, completely uninterested in four bedraggled teenagers.

Sam shrugged. 'They're probably all out there, searching with choppers and stuff.'

That made sense, but still Felix couldn't shake his feeling of unease.

Jake pulled out his phone. He stared at it for a moment. 'Weird. I don't have any reception.'

The others checked their phones. Same.

'We should have reception now.' Andy held his phone up. 'Maybe they short-circuited each other in the electrical storm.'

Felix shoved his phone back in his pocket. 'I've got to go,' he said. He didn't really care if his phone was broken. He just wanted to get home.

'We can't just separate! We've had a bonding experience. How about a man hug?' said Andy hopefully.

'In your dreams, nerd,' said Jake. 'I'm outta here too. Have a good life, losers,' he called, walking away.

Sam clapped Andy on the back. 'Sorry, brainiac, I'm starving.' He turned to Felix. 'See ya, goth dude.'

'I'll see you at school,' said Felix to Andy.

Felix walked away fast. He had to get home. He started to jog. He couldn't wait to see his family. He couldn't wait to see if it had worked.

He reached his house and ran up the drive. There was Oscar sitting on the lawn playing with his remote-control helicopter. That was good. Whatever had taken him to hospital yesterday mustn't have been too serious. He jogged towards him. 'Hey, Oscie.'

Oscar looked up.

'How was the hospital?' asked Felix.

'What hospital?' Oscar got to his feet.

Felix stared at him and felt a surge of indescribable happiness. 'You can walk!'

Oscar looked at him strangely. 'Of course I can walk.'

'Oscar, that's amazing.' Felix couldn't stop beaming.

'How do you know my name?'

Felix's grin faded from his face.

'Who are you?' asked Oscar.

jake: o mother where art thou?

Jake sprinted through the streets of Bremin, desperate to get home. His mum would be out of her mind with worry. Last night the Bremin Bandicoots had played in the semi-final and they'd planned to go. It was their yearly ritual: pack a picnic, blankets and a thermos and cheer until their voices were hoarse. They'd done it every year since Jake could remember. Once, when he was really little, his dad had gone along with them. That was before they broke up. Before his dad had become an unemployed slob.

Jake shook his head. He couldn't think about that now.

He pulled his phone out as he ran. He had to call his mum and let her know he was OK. Still nothing. Bummer. It must've got water-damaged. He shoved the phone back in his pocket.

He hoped that loser real-estate agent Phil hadn't come back while he was gone. Real-estate agents would have to be the lowest form of life – always pressuring people for money and driving round in their fancy cars like they were more important than God. It wasn't his mum's fault they were behind with the rent. It was so unfair that his mum, who worked double shifts at Scaly Jim's fish-and-chip shop just to make ends meet, got harassed – while his dad, who never paid child support, got off scot-free.

Jake reached his street. There was his house. He'd never been happier to see it, even though it was kind of a dump. Some idiot had thought it was a good idea to cover the weatherboards with fake plastic bricks. Now they were peeling off, making the house look like it had a severe case of sunburn. But hey, it was home.

Jake pulled out his key, which was miraculously still in his pocket. He stuck it in the front lock. Didn't fit.

Huh?

He jiggled the key around. Still no luck.

'Mum!' he called out.

No answer.

Jake peered in the window. A massive Harley-Davidson took up most of the hallway. Where had that come from?

Jake went around the side of the house. The lounge room window was open. He hoicked himself up and pulled himself through.

His jaw dropped in astonishment. What had his mum done? Where were the green velvet couches she'd been saying she was going to re-cover for ten years? Where was the sideboard with her dolphin collection proudly displayed? Where were the photos of his football wins? His grandma's old clock with the too-loud chime? All gone. Instead, the floor was covered with old sheets. Wrenches and spanners lay on the sheets along with pizza boxes and a brand-new TV just out of its packaging.

There must be an explanation.

Then he realised: Phil had evicted them. In the short time Jake had been gone, Phil had thrown them out. He must have known he'd have a better chance if Jake wasn't around, because Jake sure as hell wouldn't have let this happen. Phil had probably organised for Jake to get lost so he could do this. The lying, conniving –

Jake heard footsteps coming down the hall. He quickly ducked behind a couch. The footsteps grew louder and heavier. Jake peered around the side of the couch. An enormous biker wearing a leather-fringed waistcoat with buttons straining over his tattooed stomach walked into the lounge room, cracking open a tinnie. He reached for the remote control to turn on the TV.

Jake shuddered. How was he going to let this dude know he was watching TV in the wrong house? He was totally into defending his territory and all, but against this giant?

The biker let out an almighty belch. Jake looked around for an escape route. If the biker saw him, he'd be cactus.

A mobile started to ring. Jake's hand instinctively went to

his pocket, but then with a curse, the biker made his way back down the corridor to get his phone.

Jake took his chance and reached the windowsill in one leap. He hurtled over it, landing awkwardly in a hydrangea bush. He raced back out on to the street. His six-year-old neighbour, Telly, was sitting on his broken fence, playing on his mum's phone.

'Telly! What the hell's going on?' Jake asked breathlessly. 'Have you seen my mum?'

'Huh?' Telly looked up, but his face was blank. Two rivers of snot ran from his nose.

'My mum? Did you see what happened?'

'Who are you?'

'Don't be an idiot.' Jake grabbed the phone from Telly's hands.

'Hey, give that back.'

'Shut it, OK? I need to make a call.'

Jake punched in his mum's number.

'The number you have called is not connected.'

He slammed the phone back at Telly. 'You must have seen something,' said Jake.

Telly just looked at him. The kid's BMX was lying on the ground beside him. Jake picked it up and rode off.

'Hey, that's mine!' Telly called after him.

Jake didn't care. He didn't care that Telly had started crying. He didn't care that Telly's bike was so small his knees were almost knocking his chin. What he *did* care about was the fact that not only had his mum been kicked out of their house, but she hadn't had the money to pay her phone bill.

Maybe he should go to his dad's? But the thought of going to his dad's seedy apartment filled him with dread. And besides, it was his fault they were in this mess. His dad never paid his mum a cent, and yesterday morning he'd even had the nerve to come over asking to borrow money. Jake had made his mum promise not to loan him anything, but he knew his dad could wheedle his way around her. She was too nice. She'd probably lent him fifty bucks and now her phone had been cut off. His dad was probably sitting on his couch watching the footy and drinking the money away in beer. There was no way he was going there – he'd probably end up punching the lazy douchebag.

Jake pedalled faster. Going uphill on this midget bike wasn't easy. He stood up and pushed hard on the pedals.

OK, so logically where would she be? Either out looking for him or at work. Yes, Scaly Jim's. He'd try there.

———

'Oil's not hot enough for orders yet, mate,' said Jim, the owner, looking up from the fryer.

'I don't want to order anything. I'm looking for Mum. She had a shift today.'

Jim looked at him. 'Your mum had a shift here?'

'Yeah. She always works Saturdays.'

'Just between you and me, mate, I'm not in the business of employing mature-age ladies. Got to keep costs down, you know, so –'

'But she works here every day.'

Jim looked at him strangely. 'What did you say her name was?'

'Sarah. Come on, Jim, this isn't funny.'

'Got a Sue, but if she was your mum she'd have had you at two,' he laughed.

Jake bit his lower lip. 'It's not a joke.'

'No mate, and neither is running a business, so unless you want to order something, clear off.'

Jake stormed out of the shop. Why was Jim playing games with him? Was there some joke he wasn't in on? Maybe his mum was cross with him for not calling last night. Though that really didn't make sense. She'd be more worried than angry.

He picked up Telly's bike. If Jim wasn't going to tell him the truth, he'd go and see Phil. Yep, that's what he'd do. He'd go and ask him directly why he'd chosen the night Jake was missing, possibly presumed dead, to throw them out of their house. God, his poor mum, having to deal with all of that in one night.

Jake barged into the mauve-and-grey reception area of Phil Mason's real-estate agency.

'Can I help you?' called the receptionist.

Jake walked straight past her into Phil's office. 'How dare you chuck us out?'

Phil, a balding man with a comb-over, jumped up from his reclining chair, thrusting his magazine quickly into a drawer. 'How can I help you?'

Jake clenched his fists. 'You can't just give our house away. You need to give us warning.'

Phil looked at him blankly. 'And your house is . . .?'

'You know our house. You've been there enough times, trying to scare Mum.'

Phil stood up. 'OK, kid. You need to calm down.'

Jake could feel his fingernails piercing into his palms. He was so angry he could . . . He took a deep breath and counted to ten in his head, like the school counsellor had taught him. He tried to speak slowly and calmly.

'You need to tell me where my mum is.'

'Mate, I've no idea what you're talking about.'

Jake unclenched his fists and grabbed hold of Phil's arm. He couldn't hold it in any longer. 'Listen to me, you fat freak. You tell me –'

The next thing Jake knew, Phil and the receptionist were dragging him out of the office and into the street.

Phil shook his head at him. 'Stay off the drugs, mate.'

Jake wanted to scream. What was going on? Why was everyone behaving like they had no idea who he was?

Jake got back on Telly's bike. The only thing he could think to do was report his mum missing.

It seemed pretty odd that he would go missing one day and then she would the next. Unless of course she went missing while looking for him, but how would that explain the biker? And Jim pretending he didn't know her? And Phil? God, his head hurt.

He climbed the steps to the police station and swung open the door. A young constable looked up from reception.

'Can I help you?'

Jake blurted it all out. He'd been missing in the forest overnight and he'd come home, only he didn't have a home anymore, and he couldn't find his mum and no one seemed to know her.

'All right, slow down,' said the cop. 'Your mum's missing. Have you tried calling her?'

'Obviously. But my dad borrowed money off her which meant she couldn't pay her phone bill, so it got disconnected which means –'

'OK, OK, back up a bit. First let's start with her name so we can check for admissions.'

Jake looked at him. 'Admissions? You mean, like, at the hospital?'

'Yep.'

'You think something bad's happened to her? An accident?'

'It's a formality, OK? What's her name?'

42

'Sarah. Sarah Riles.'

The cop stopped, pen poised above his piece of paper.

'Sarah Riles?'

'Yes.'

'You sure about that?'

'I think I'd know my own mother's name.'

'Any relation to Gary Riles?'

'They used to be married. He's my dad but there's no point calling him. He doesn't even have a phone.'

The cop put his pen down, then called over his shoulder. 'Boss? You might want to come out here.'

A moment later, Senior Sergeant Gary Riles appeared. He looked Jake up and down.

'What's your problem, kid?'

Jake's mouth fell open. His loser of a dad was a freaking cop?

sam: same sam but different

Sam was cruising. Man, it was good to have wheels again. A whole twenty-four hours on the soles of his feet? That was probably a record for him. His mum always joked that he'd skate from his bed to the fridge and back again, if only she'd let him.

His brothers, Vince and Pete, clearly couldn't have cared less when he got home. They hadn't even looked up from *Mortal Kombat* when he'd walked through the door. He'd had a hot shower, grabbed his skateboard, eaten whatever he could find in the fridge and, in all that time, the only conversation they'd had was to tell him his parents were at some cross-country thing.

He curved down a hill. It was good to be back. Although it was pretty random that his parents were out competing in a race when he'd been missing in the bush overnight.

Maybe they thought he'd stayed at Mia's? He hadn't told them he wasn't too welcome there after Mia's dad had caught them making out in front of *The Exorcist*.

Scary movies were such a turn-on. He smiled at the memory. Mia was such a hottie. He couldn't wait to see her. She was going to love hearing about his night in the bush – how it was just like being in a horror film, with all that crazy stuff hanging in the trees. Then there was the weird twister that chased them, and the mad hobo who tried to attack them. Yeah, that would make a much better story than Roland feeding them eggs and driving them home. Sam could be the one who fought him off and got everyone back safely. Girls loved a hero, right?

He looked down at the friendship bracelet on his wrist. Mia had given it to him the day before to celebrate their one-year anniversary. He actually hadn't remembered, but Mia was cool with that. She knew he had other things on his mind. He'd had to get his application in to the Big Break Competition that morning. He wondered when he was going to hear back about it. If he was a finalist he'd get to compete at the skate trials in Sydney and then maybe go to Brazil for the internationals. Man, his skills were way too big for Bremin. He was going to take on the world.

He barrelled under the railway bridge, streaming up the other side in a perfect arc. He was on the edge of town, where the houses gave way to the forest. Sam did an ollie up on to the footpath and flicked up his board. It was a bummer but he'd have to walk this last bit.

He pushed through the scrub. He hadn't expected to be back in the forest this quickly but he wanted to see his mum and dad and tell them he was OK.

Sam reached the old fire track and tucked his skateboard under his arm. He knew that the cross-country finish line was next to the old viaduct. He and his brothers used to come out here all the time as kids and dare each other to jump off. Vince had broken his arm once, and Sam had caught Pete kissing Fiona Press one summer's night. He'd thought that was pretty gross at eleven but maybe Pete had had the right idea. Coming here would be way better than being booted out of Mia's house by her pissed-off dad.

Sam stopped. There was the crumbling bridge and the finish line. He could see his dad doing calf stretches. He looked around for his mum. She was probably still racing. She wouldn't be happy to be beaten by his dad. Even when they were training, his parents were crazy competitive, especially with each other. Probably where he got it from.

'Hey, Dad!' Sam called.

His dad lifted his arms and stretched out his shoulders.

Sam called again. No response. Probably couldn't hear him. He jogged down towards his dad and put his hand on his shoulder. His dad turned in surprise.

'I'm home!' said Sam, with a big grin.

His dad did a double-take. 'Er . . . are you racing?'

What kind of a question was that?

'After the night I had? I don't think so.'

'OK, well you might want to move away from the finish line as we've still got competitors coming through.'

Sam was taken aback. 'Nice welcome home, Dad.'

His dad looked at him oddly, then turned to cheer on Sam's exhausted-looking mum, who was nearing the finish line.

'Come on babe, get that PB!' yelled Sam's dad.

Sam crossed his arms. Sure, being obsessed with sport was great, but if your son had been missing all night, wouldn't you be just a tiny bit worried?

His mum crossed the finish line and bent over in exhaustion.

Sam ran to her. At least his mum would be pleased to see him. 'Mum!'

'Sorry?' she said, looking confused and still trying to catch her breath.

Sam went to hug her. 'I'm back! I'm OK.'

His dad quickly intervened. 'You OK, babe?'

Sam's mum had gone very pale. 'Just . . . feeling . . . a bit . . .'

'Maybe you should sit down.'

She staggered, and Sam and his dad both moved in to support her.

His dad moved Sam's hands away. 'We're fine here, thanks.'

'But Mum looks terrible,' said Sam.

His mum's breathing was now coming in short, raspy bursts. 'I'm . . . not your mum,' she said.

Sam looked at her. *What did she just say?*

'Look, just back off, OK, kid? She's not your mum,' his dad said firmly.

Sam stared at them for a moment, then started to laugh. 'Very funny, guys. Did Pete put you up to this?'

But Sam's mum started to gasp for air. She clung to his dad.

Sam stopped laughing. She looked seriously bad. He reached for her again. 'Mum!'

Sam's dad pushed him away, more forcefully this time. 'Look. She is not your mum, and I am definitely not your dad. Now get lost, before I call someone.' He helped Sam's mum walk away towards their car.

Sam watched them, feeling like he'd been hit hard in the guts. What was happening? How could his mum and dad not know who he was?

Sam raced back down the fire track. He had to get out of the bush.

He'd thought his family would welcome him with open arms, but they didn't even seem to know who he was.

Sam ran faster. He burst out on to the road and put his skateboard down on the hard surface.

OK. Breathe, Sam. Breathe.

He looked around. Everything looked normal. An old dude was mowing his lawn. Some kids cruised around on their bikes. Bremin seemed the same as ever. He put his foot on his skateboard.

Solid. Good.

This he knew. He just had to stay on hard surfaces. Everything would be fine. His brothers hadn't rejected him, so everything was OK. His parents probably had exercise fatigue. That could happen, right?

He pushed himself along on his skateboard. As he moved, he began to calm down. His mind was playing tricks with him, that was all.

He skated back into town, keeping the board on a nice, easy line. Keep it steady and his mind would stay steady. He'd go to the skate park. That's what he'd do. Everyone knew him there. He was Sam the Man.

He eased his way into the main street of Bremin. He passed the supermarket, the police station, the wholefood cafe – everything in its rightful place. And there, in the main street, was the skate park. A few kids were flipping boards on the half-pipe. Pretty lame moves, Sam noted. Then he saw her: Mia. She was sitting on a bench with her laptop open.

Thank God.

He spun his board across the concrete and collapsed into the seat next to her.

'I have never been so glad to see you in my entire life.'

Mia looked up from her laptop. 'Sorry?'

'Weren't you worried? We were, like, missing for twenty-four hours. What did Bates say? Man, I bet he got in so much trouble.'

Mia held his gaze. 'Do I know you?'

'Mia, don't mess with me, babe. It's me, Sam.'

'I'm not messing with you. I've never seen you before in my life.'

Sam felt the air go out of him. 'But I'm your boyfriend.'

Mia laughed. 'You've got to be kidding me.'

Sam looked away.

So, this wasn't a bad dream, a hallucination, something he'd eaten. Mia didn't know who he was and neither did his parents. But his brothers did. Or did they? Now that he thought about it, they hadn't actually *looked* at him when he'd come home. He felt his head begin to spin. God, what was happening to him?

Mia reached up to shut her laptop. 'Listen, I've got to . . .'

Sam saw the leather bracelet on her wrist, and grabbed her arm. 'Wait. That thing on your wrist. Look!' He pulled up his sleeve and showed her the identical bracelet he was wearing.

Mia looked at it curiously. 'But I made that.'

'I know. Of course you made it. You gave it to me for our anniversary.'

Mia grabbed her laptop and stood up. 'I don't know how you got that bracelet, but it wasn't made for you. I made it for my boyfriend.' She slung her bag over her shoulder and walked away.

Sam jumped up and ran after her. 'Mia! Wait!'

Mia had reached the street. Sam grabbed her again. 'Listen to me. I *am* your boyfriend.'

She pulled her arm away. 'Let go of me.'

'Mia, please. Just listen to me.'

Mia turned on him. Her eyes flashed with anger. 'No! You listen to me. You are *not* my boyfriend. So stop freaking me out and leave me alone!' She turned and walked off down the street.

Devastated, Sam stood on the footpath, staring after her. Shoppers and schoolkids moved around him like he wasn't there. Sam couldn't move. Couldn't take his eyes off his girlfriend, *his* girlfriend, walking away from him like he didn't exist.

'Same thing happened to me.'

Sam dragged his eyes off Mia's retreating figure and saw Andy sitting on a bench, watching him.

'When I got home, I went to my room,' said Andy. 'Only it wasn't my room anymore. It was my sister, Viv's, and she'd re-decorated it with posters of Pink and Lady Gaga. She threw a lamp at me and then my *nai nai* chased me out of the house with a meat cleaver.'

Sam stared at him. 'So . . . what? *None* of your family knew who you were?'

'My sister called me a stalker,' Andy said bitterly. 'Like anyone would want to stalk her.'

Sam didn't know whether to be relieved or terrified. 'My parents don't know who I am either.'

'My dad once told me about an order of monks who had mass delusion and thought they were possessed by lizards.'

Sam looked at Andy blankly. What the hell was he talking about?

'I think the same thing has happened to our families. The stress of us going missing has caused them to have mass delusional hysteria, resulting in collective amnesia.'

'What about the others?' asked Sam. Andy made no sense at the best of times, and right now the last thing Sam wanted to hear was theories about monks and lizards.

Andy shrugged. 'If this is happening to us, it's probably happening to them too.'

Jake was picking up a tiny bike outside the police station when Sam and Andy found him.

Sam watched him, wondering how you ask someone if their family has forgotten them. Not exactly something you ask every day.

'Hey, Jake.'

Jake glanced up defensively. He didn't look great.

'Is everything OK?' asked Andy.

'Why wouldn't it be?'

Sam and Andy looked at each other.

'We were just wondering if you'd found your parents,' asked Sam carefully.

Jake turned away. 'I'm looking for my mum.'

Sam felt his stomach turn. 'So, you haven't seen her since we got back?'

Jake shrugged. 'She's probably just shopping.'

'What about your dad?' asked Sam.

'What's he got to do with anything?' Jake snapped. 'I just need to find my mum.' He straddled the bike and went to push off from the footpath.

Sam stopped him. He had to give it to Jake straight. 'Listen, Jake. Andy and me? When we found our parents, they didn't know who we were. It's like we were complete strangers.'

Jake looked at him like he was crazy. 'What are you talking about?'

'And it's not just our parents. Mia didn't know who I was either.' Man, it hurt to say that out loud.

'My theory is that our families are experiencing mass delusional hysteria caused by –'

'Does anyone ever understand a word you say?' Jake interrupted Andy.

'My family do. Or did,' Andy corrected himself.

'Yeah well, sad story, guys, but I've got to find my mum.'

'When you do find her, I'd say there's a seventy to eighty per cent chance she'll have no idea who you are,' said Andy. But Jake wasn't listening. He was staring at a woman walking down the footpath on the other side of the street.

Sam followed his gaze. The woman was wearing a smart suit and high heels. She zapped open a black BMW nearby.

'Mum!' called Jake.

Sam did a double-take. That was Jake's mum? Sam had only ever seen her driving a beaten-up Nissan and wearing a tracksuit or her fish-and-chip shop uniform.

The woman opened her car door and got in.

Jake pedalled across the street to reach her car. 'Mum! Wait!'

The woman ignored him. The BMW pulled out on to the road and Jake set off after it.

Andy shook his head. 'That's not going to end well.'

Sam felt ill. Jake's mum clearly didn't recognise him. So that was three of them.

He turned to Andy. 'We need to find Felix.'

felix: it's a miracle right?

Felix's mum came out of the house, the screen door banging behind her. She was carrying a tray of fairy bread. 'Here you are, boys.' She placed the tray in front of Felix. 'Would you like something to drink? Fergus, wasn't it?'

Felix smiled uncertainly. 'Felix, actually.'

'It's so nice for Oscar to have a friend over for a play date.'

'Mum,' Oscar growled. 'Play dates are for two-year-olds. And we don't even know each other.'

'I didn't think I'd seen you before,' said Felix's mum. 'Are you at Bremin High?'

Felix took a deep breath. As soon as his mum had seen him in the driveway she'd demanded he come and 'play' with Oscar. That was weird enough, but it was even weirder when she introduced herself as Mrs Ferne. And now here she was, feeding him and smiling at him. Clearly, she had *absolutely* no idea who he was, which was seriously freaky. But it was better than her hating him, right?

Felix figured the safest route for now was just to play along. 'Not yet. We've just moved here.'

'Oh really? Where fro–' She suddenly sneezed. 'Goodness me, my hayfever's starting early!' She held a hand up to her nose. 'Excuse me a mo.' She opened the screen door and disappeared inside.

'Mum's a bit intense,' Oscar said apologetically. He looked at Felix for a moment, as if trying to work him out. 'So, what's your story? Do you normally just appear in people's front yards wanting to hang out with kids you don't know?'

Man, Oscar was defensive. Felix picked up a piece of fairy bread. He suddenly realised how starving he was. 'I only do it for the food.' He shoved the fairy bread in his mouth. It tasted delicious.

Oscar picked up a piece and looked at it with disdain. 'How old does she think I am?'

'Yeah, well, she does like to baby you,' said Felix, shoving a second piece in his mouth.

Oscar looked at him strangely. 'How would you know that?'

Felix stopped himself. He had to be careful. If he said too much, Oscar would think he was utterly nuts and his mum would probably throw him out on the street.

'Oh. I don't. It's just, that's what mums do with the youngest. I mean . . . with kids.'

'I guess.' Oscar shrugged and stood up. 'Well, if you're

not gonna tell me anything, do you at least know how to play chess?'

'Sure,' said Felix, taking a third piece of fairy bread.

He watched Oscar walk across the porch. A warm feeling went through him. His brother wasn't going to spend the rest of his life trapped in a metal chair with two wheels. He was going to walk to school and play sport and get a girlfriend like everybody else. He wouldn't have to wear the 'disabled' tag, and his parents weren't going to spend their rest of their lives stressed about money and caring for him.

OK, so his family didn't know who he was, but he could live with that if it meant that Oscar had a second chance. That's what he'd wanted, after all. Maybe it was like in those fairy tales where you get what you want but lose something else. Like that mermaid who got to have legs, but whenever she walked it felt like she was walking on knives. He'd do that for Oscar. He'd pretty much do anything.

Oscar came back with the board and started to set up the pieces. The screen door opened again and Felix's mum put her head out. 'Oscie, you've got some more friends over. Mr Popular.'

Oscar cringed.

Felix looked up to see Sam and Andy come out of the back door. His mum ducked back inside. What were they doing here? How did they even know where he lived?

'Ah, Oscar. This is Sam and Andy.'

'Are they friends of yours?'

'Er, yeah. Kind of.'

'We need to talk,' Sam said to Felix. He looked pale.

Getting the message, Oscar stood up. 'I'll go get drinks.'

Sam and Andy stared in disbelief as Oscar walked to the door and opened it.

Andy turned to Felix. 'Your brother can *walk*?'

Felix wasn't sure what to say. Maybe now would be a good time to tell them. *Thank* them. After all, he couldn't have done it without them. But all that came out was feigned surprise. 'It's incredible, right?'

His mum popped her head out of the door. She was holding a handkerchief to her nose. 'Fergus?'

'Felix, actually.'

'Sorry. Felix.'

Felix felt Sam and Andy's eyes on him.

'I was just wondering if you'd like to stay for tea? It's so nice for Oscar to have a new friend.'

'Sure, that'd be great,' he said.

She sneezed again and the door banged behind her.

Sam stared at him. 'Your mum doesn't know your name?'

Felix shrugged and looked away. Oscar walking was one thing, but how was he supposed to explain that his family didn't have a clue who he was?

'She just asked you to stay for dinner,' said Andy.

Felix took a deep breath. 'OK, they don't know who I am

yet, that's all. But Oscar can walk. It's a miracle, right?'

Felix looked hopefully at Sam and Andy. How could he make them understand that even though this family didn't know who he was, it kind of didn't matter right now? In fact, things were a lot better than the way they were before. Not only could Oscar walk, but his mum actually seemed to *want* Felix around. He felt like a human being in her presence again, not the loser son who'd ruined everybody's lives.

'Yeah, Felix, it's a real miracle that none of our families have a clue who we are,' said Sam bitterly.

Felix took a moment to process what Sam had just said. *None* of their families?

Sam was struggling to keep it together. 'My parents think I'm a nut job, Andy's grandma chased him with a meat cleaver and Jake's mum is *nothing* like Jake's mum.'

Felix stared at him.

'And your mum thinks you're called Fergus,' added Andy.

'So that means the same thing has happened to all four of us,' continued Sam.

'Which means it has to be connected to what happened in the forest,' said Andy.

Felix felt a wave of panic. *Oh God.* What had he done?

He was saved by Oscar reappearing with a jug of cordial and some cups. 'We've only got sugar free, so you have to drink three times as much.'

'Sam and Andy were actually just leaving,' said Felix.

He had no idea what was going on, but whatever it was, he couldn't discuss it now. Not in front of Oscar.

Sam leant in. 'Something happened out there, Felix. We need to work out what it was. Find out how to fix it.'

'What happened out where?' asked Oscar curiously.

Felix shook his head at Sam. Couldn't he get the hint? 'I'll catch up with you guys later, OK?'

Sam was looking more and more upset. 'Dude, this can't wait. We need to be together. Work out –'

'Later. OK?'

Sam shook his head in disgust. 'You really are a freak.'

Felix watched Sam and Andy walk down the back steps and away from the house. He knew he was acting like a jerk but he didn't know what else to do. He needed to buy some time. Think things through.

Oscar looked at him sympathetically. 'Don't worry, I get called a freak all the time. It's your move.'

Felix smiled at him, and pretended to consider the chessboard. Oscar could walk. That was what mattered.

Felix made an arbitrary move. His thoughts couldn't have been further from the game. None of their families knew who they were? How could that be? That was never part of the plan.

Oscar looked at Felix's move in disbelief. 'That's just opening your left field up to –' He stopped himself. Something had caught his eye. 'Oh no. Quick, we've got to hide.'

Felix turned. 'What?'

'Come on. Quick.'

Felix looked behind him again. Walking down the path at the side of the house was a girl in a pink-and-white sundress. A small dog cantered at her heels.

Oscar had slid off his chair and was inching across the porch on his behind. Reaching the back door, he opened it and slipped inside.

Felix watched the girl getting closer.

Was that . . . ? No. It couldn't be. And yet . . .

He jumped off his chair, letting it land with a bang. He raced down the steps of the porch. 'Ellen!'

The girl stopped. She looked him up and down. 'Who are you?'

Felix froze. It felt like his insides were rearranging themselves. It wasn't just their families that had forgotten them, then. It was everybody. That wasn't good.

'Sorry, my mistake. I just thought you were a friend.'

Ellen frowned. 'You knew my name?'

'Did I?' Felix thought fast. 'I was just saying *'ello.*'

Ellen screwed up her nose. 'You're freaky.'

Felix couldn't help himself. 'And you're not?' Seeing Ellen dressed like a pink-and-white extra from a Disney movie was out of control. *Grey* was normally too cheery for Ellen.

'That's rich coming from a wannabe emo.'

Felix looked away. That hurt.

61

'Is Oscar home?' asked Ellen.

'Ah, I think he's busy.'

'What? Playing Ninja Turtles?'

'Actually, no, he's more into chess these days . . .'

Ellen rolled her eyes. 'Whatever. Just tell him he brought in the wrong bin *again* and he needs to return ours, pronto.'

Felix stared at her. How could this be Ellen? His best friend? She turned on her heel and flounced off.

On impulse, Felix called out, 'Here, Wikileaks.'

Ellen's Jack Russell turned immediately and bounded back towards Felix. Ellen stopped and stared at him. 'How did you know my dog's name?'

Felix shrugged. 'Just a guess.'

Ellen took Felix in. For an instant, he thought he saw a glimmer of recognition. But just as quickly as it was there, it was gone.

'Come on, Wiki. Walkies.'

The little dog turned and ran after her.

Felix watched his best friend walk away. This seriously wasn't good. With everything that was going down right now, the one person he really wanted to talk to was Ellen. *Real* Ellen.

Oscar resurfaced. 'Has she gone?'

Felix sighed. 'Yep. Well and truly.' He turned back to the house. 'Come on. Whose turn is it?'

'Oh. Mum wanted me to tell you she's not feeling that

great, so we'll have to cancel dinner.'

Felix felt gutted. 'Really? Well we can still play, yeah?'

Oscar shrugged. 'Actually, I have to do my homework.'

Felix looked away. 'Right.'

'Sorry. It was really nice to meet you.'

Meet you? Those words stung, but Felix put on a brave face. 'Yeah, you too.'

Felix watched the rickety screen door slam behind Oscar. There was a finality to that slam. It was definitely keeping Felix out.

He walked down the side of the house and stood in the driveway, feeling utterly alone.

Oscar could walk. That was good, right? The spell had worked – kind of. Nothing else really mattered. Except . . .

He stood there, uncertain. Except now what was he supposed to do? He couldn't open that door and walk inside like he did every day of his life. He didn't belong there anymore. He thought about the others. Were they all feeling this way? Wanting desperately to enter a door that they couldn't?

The wind picked up and started shaking the branches of the old elm tree. Felix looked up. He hated that stupid tree. He fought back an urge to kick it and shout, *This is all your fault!* But it wasn't true. It was his fault. Everything was. First Oscar's accident, and now this.

Felix made his way down the driveway to the street. He had to find the others. Find out what was going on. He reached the street and turned left into town. The wind gathered force and he heard a strange noise above him. He looked up and saw the powerlines vibrating, like bars of music come to life. He listened carefully. Were they singing to him?

He looked back at the street. It was strangely empty. No people. No cars. He started to feel uneasy. He needed to be with people, not here alone. He began to run towards town.

He wondered where the others would be. He scanned the main street. Up ahead was a tall guy, riding a tiny bike. *Jake.*

'Hey Jake! Wait up!'

The bike stopped and Jake turned. When Felix caught up, he saw the defeated expression on Jake's face. 'You OK?'

'Not really.'

Jake looked as if the air had been completely punched out of him. Felix almost wished he would throw a ball at his head.

Jake gestured to the skate park. 'They're probably there.'

Sure enough, Sam was sitting on top of the half-pipe. Andy was on one leg, reaching his mobile into the air.

'Even if you get a signal, who are you going to call?' asked Jake as he slumped down next to Sam.

'Didn't go well, huh?' said Sam.

'You were right. She didn't have a clue who I was.'

Felix moved uncertainly towards them.

Sam looked up. 'What's the go, man? Your mummy not

tucking you in for the night?'

Felix shrugged. 'Guess they didn't like me that much after all.' He sat on the other side of Sam.

No one spoke. Felix tried to find the courage to apologise. 'Listen, about before . . .' he began. 'I just . . . it's a lot to take in and –'

'Tell me something I don't know,' said Sam.

Felix tried again. 'You were right. What you said. We need to stay together. Work out what's going on.'

'And how do you plan on doing that?'

Felix wished he had an answer, but the truth was he had absolutely no idea.

'Well, we can't stay here all night,' said Andy eventually. 'Two nights out in the open and we'll probably get a pneumonic infection.'

'What do you suggest, Bear Grylls?' snapped Jake. 'Build a shelter from the bones of tree frogs?'

Felix looked up at the rapidly darkening sky. He needed to take control. He was the one that had got them into this mess, so he had to get them out of it.

'There's an old abandoned shack in the bush,' he said. 'If it's still there, maybe we could make camp.'

'What about food?' asked Sam.

Jake shrugged. 'There's an apple tree at the back of the footy oval?'

Sam sighed. 'All right, then, let's do it.'

The shack wasn't all that far from Felix's house. He led the others along a couple of quiet suburban streets that backed on to the bush, then down a grassy slope towards a bush track. The four boys walked along the track, devouring apples. Night was falling and the deepening shadows made it hard to see where they were going. Felix held his mobile phone held out in front of him like a torch. At least it was good for something. He hoped against hope that the shack was still there. When he and Oscar were kids, their dad had brought them out here to fish. He'd taught them to swim in the river and they'd made campfires and spent hours playing spotlight in the bush. But they hadn't been here for a long time. Two years and three months, to be exact.

But the track came to an end and there, in a clearing, was a dilapidated bushman's shack. 'It's here!' said Felix, relieved. He ran to the door, and the rusty lock came off easily in his hands. The door creaked open and the boys stepped inside.

Miscellaneous junk – ropes, hessian bags, old boating equipment – dotted the floor.

The others looked less than impressed, but Felix didn't care. 'We can use the bags as blankets. And there's a river close by for fresh water.'

He rummaged around at the back of the shack, and returned with an old gas lantern. He lit it with his lighter and placed it in the middle of the space. 'Ta-da!'

'Think I preferred it when I couldn't see it,' Jake mumbled.

'Shelter is essential for survival,' said Andy. 'Good idea, Felix.'

'Don't suppose there's anything here to eat,' said Sam, looking through an old cupboard.

Nobody felt much like talking. As the night turned black, they covered the floor in old hessian bags and lay down, exhausted. Eventually, Felix heard the rise and fall of their breathing as they slept. But Felix couldn't sleep. His mind raced. What had he done? He'd meant to make things better, not worse. Quietly, he picked up the gas lamp and went to sit by the window. He was going to fix this. He had to.

He slid his Book of Shadows out of his bag and laid it reverently on top of an old crate. He turned the pages until he came to the spell he'd written out and recorded. What had gone wrong? There had to be a clue. If he could work out what it was then maybe he could find a way to change it. He'd be able to do that. He was sure of it.

As he re-read the spell, the hairs on the back of his neck prickled. He turned around. The others were still fast asleep; Sam snoring like each breath was his last. He turned back to the window, allowing his eyes to adjust to the darkness. The air was still, but there was a small movement behind a tree.

Was something out there? Was someone watching?

And then, as if a switch had been flicked, the gas lamp went out.

jake: to be or not to be

Jake squatted behind a parked car. From here he had the perfect view of an attractive two-storey house.

How often had he and his mum talked about their ideal house? Big, white, a view of the river. He'd wanted a basketball hoop in the front garden. She'd wanted a pergola covered in purple flowers. And here it was. Everything they'd ever dreamt of together.

Only they weren't together. Jake bit his lip. He imagined that record-scratch sound they always did in movies when the fantasy gave way to the grim reality. Sure, his mum had the perfect house, but what did he have? A falling-down dump and three stinking shackmates. He sighed. Coach Wilson would definitely call that a bad trade-off.

A BMW pulled into the drive. Jake watched as his mum got out of the car and popped open the boot. Yesterday he'd chased her car for five blocks and then blundered up to her, full of certainty. He was her son, surely she could see that?

Today he knew better. She didn't recognise him. She didn't *need* to recognise him. In this world, she had a whole new life. A new house, new wardrobe, and . . .

Jake's thoughts were interrupted as he saw a man walking out of the house towards his mum. A poodle barked at his heels. The man had a confident stride and wore a pale-pink polo shirt.

His mum bent down and picked up the yapping cotton-wool ball. She smothered it with kisses before putting it down and wrapping her arms around the man who, now that he thought of it, looked a lot like Mr Bates.

Jake's jaw dropped. It *was* Mr Bates!

Jake shook his head. No. There's no way his mum would be with his bossy, annoying knob of a science teacher.

But she started to kiss him. Jake wanted to look away but he couldn't. His mum was kissing *Bates*?

They broke apart and Bates reached into the boot to help his mum take out some heavy-looking boards. He placed them beside the car. They were real-estate boards, and emblazoned across the top of them was a picture of his mum and the words SARAH BATES REAL ESTATE.

Sarah Bates? They were married? His mum was a real-estate agent? This couldn't be happening. This wasn't right.

Without thinking, Jake suddenly stood straight up from his hiding place.

Bates looked over at him as he slammed the boot of the

car. 'Who the hell are you?'

Jake was totally sprung but he didn't care.

He turned to his mum. 'You're married to *him*?'

His mum took a step towards him.

'Careful, Sarah, he could be dangerous.'

'It's fine, Brian.' She looked carefully at Jake. 'Why are you here again?'

'*Again*?' said Bates, exasperated. 'Is this kid harassing you?'

She shook her head. 'No. Well, we did meet yesterday in rather odd –' She grimaced, and her hand flew to her head.

Jake watched her, concerned. She'd done the same thing yesterday. 'You OK, Mu–' He stopped himself.

'Who are you, kid?' demanded Bates.

'Good question. Maybe I can get back to you on that.'

'Don't be smart. I've every mind to call the police.'

Jake almost smiled. That he'd like to see. His dad arriving to protect his mum. That would sure be a first.

Bates wasn't going to let it go. 'What are you doing, hiding there?'

Jake wanted to yell back, *What are you doing married to my mum?* But he knew it would just make things worse. He gestured to Telly's bike lying on the road. 'Got a flat.'

His mum staggered slightly.

'Sarah, you all right?' Bates asked, concerned.

'Just a migraine coming on.'

That wasn't like her. She never got sick. Ever.

'You don't get migraines,' said Jake.

'You're right,' she said, surprised. 'I don't. How did you –'
She staggered again.

Bates supported her and turned back to Jake. 'Take your
bike and clear off. I don't want to see you around here again.'

Jake stood there hopelessly, watching Bates lead his mum
back to the house.

What was his mum thinking? His dad was bad enough,
but *Bates*? How could she see anything in that uptight
schmuck?

Jake rode to his old neighbourhood. He didn't need the bike
anymore. There was nothing left to chase after.

He found Telly, dressed in a Superman outfit, jumping
off his garage roof and pretending to fly.

Jake dumped the bike. 'Thanks for the loan,' he called.

But Telly was too busy extracting himself from a pile of
mulch to respond.

Jake took one last look at his house. He'd always been
ashamed of how povvo it looked. Most of the footy team
didn't even know where he lived. He was too embarrassed to
tell them. But right now he'd give anything to open the front
door, go inside and for everything to be exactly the way it was
before. It didn't matter that he and his mum would never be
able to afford a big, white house. He'd be happy just to curl

up on the ratty old couch in the lounge room and admire the view of the neighbour's brick wall.

But if he went anywhere near his front door he'd probably get bludgeoned to death by that hairy biker. He took a deep breath and walked determinedly in the other direction.

———

In town, Jake found the others standing beside two large dumpsters at the back of the Mini Mart.

'Where've you been?' asked Sam.

He shrugged. He couldn't tell them about Bates. Couldn't cope with the humiliation. Sure, the others had their own problems, but at least their parents were still married to each other.

'Felix is instructing us in rubbish-eating,' said Andy brightly.

Felix sighed in frustration. 'It's not rubbish, OK? Food gets thrown out when it reaches its use-by date. It's perfectly edible.'

'So, what do we do?' asked Jake.

'They call it dumpster diving,' said Felix. 'You basically just take anything that's edible.'

Jake suddenly realised how long it had been since he'd eaten anything other than apples. 'I'll do it,' he said. 'Give me a leg up, Sam.'

Sam looked surprised, but linked his hands.

Jake pulled himself up. He rolled the lid of the dumpster back and threw one leg over the metal side. It stank like hell in there. He lifted his other leg over and landed with a thump in a foul, moist mess of rotting food. But Jake didn't care. It was a welcome distraction. It took his mind off his mum kissing Bates, and her whole new perfect life. Plus he could avoid the others asking him questions. They'd find out soon enough, but for now he wanted to keep it to himself. He didn't like talking about personal stuff. When his mum and dad split up, everyone wanted him to talk about it. He hated that.

He checked out a box of doughnuts. Only two days past their use-by date, with a little bit of mould. He chucked them out to Felix and scrounged around some more. A carton of custard. He threw it over the side.

Jake reached deeper into the dumpster. This was why they must call it diving. To get the really good stuff you had to dig deep. He pulled out a packet of unopened biscuits, some yellowing broccoli and a bunch of black bananas. Over the side they went. He dug even deeper and emerged with some bread and squashed jam rolls. He tossed them over the side and could hear Andy, Sam and Felix cheering.

Suddenly the laughing stopped and Jake heard a voice.

'What the hell's going on here?'

Jake peered over the side of the dumpster. A man was standing at the back door of the Mini Mart.

'Holy crap, it's Dad,' said Felix.

73

'This is private property,' shouted Felix's dad, moving towards them.

Felix hesitated for a second, then yelled, 'Run!'

With a quick pull-up, Jake was out of the dumpster and taking a flying leap from the top. The others grabbed as much loot as they could carry and all four of them bolted off down the street.

They sped down the back streets of Bremin. Felix's dad soon gave up the chase and they found themselves running down the street behind Bremin High.

'The oval,' panted Jake. 'No one will be around on a Sunday.'

They ducked under the fence and, dumping their stash of food, collapsed on to the grass.

Jake looked at all the food they'd salvaged. It wasn't a bad spread. Especially when you hadn't eaten properly for two days.

Sam gave Jake a friendly shove. 'Good diving, man.' He ripped open the pack of doughnuts and offered them around. He took a bite and chewed thoughtfully, as if he were a judge on a cooking show. 'It has a distinct aroma, with a certain intense rubbishiness.'

The others laughed and Andy picked up a bread roll. He took a small bite, considered it. 'Mmm, full of surprises. Chewy interior, slightly mouldy aftertaste, with a hint of cigarette butt.' He pulled a cigarette butt off the bottom.

'Oh, that explains it.'

Jake smirked. The nerd was actually quite funny when you got to know him.

Sam gulped his second doughnut down and reached for a third. 'I'm giving these three out of ten.'

Jake peeled a sloppy-looking banana. 'Definitely two for me.'

Felix picked up a doughnut and held it up. 'A big fat zero.'

The boys laughed. With their stomachs full for the first time in days, they lay back in the grass. The sun was shining and Jake felt the warmth spread through him.

'You know what really freaks me out?' said Sam.

'Felix's BO?'

'How everything is exactly the same,' Sam went on. 'Like, my parents are still fitness freaks, and Felix's dad still runs the supermarket and Andy's family still have the same restaurant.'

Jake felt the warmth disappear from his body. He sat up. Maybe things were the same for the others. But for him, everything had changed. His mum was married to Bates and his dad was a cop.

'Exactly the same. Except they don't know who we are,' said Andy.

'Yeah,' said Sam. 'It does my head in.'

'It's like we don't exist,' said Jake angrily.

Felix looked at him. 'We do exist.'

'Really?' sniped Jake. 'Then how come no one knows us?'

Sam reached over and pinched Jake's arm. Hard.

'Oww!'

'See? Proof of your existence.'

'Very funny.' Jake slumped over, putting his head on his knees.

'You know,' said Andy, sitting up, 'Jake's right. No one knows us. But if we had concrete evidence that we exist in this world, maybe our families would believe us. It could be the trigger to cure their amnesia.'

'Yeah, good one. And where are we going to get that from?' asked Sam.

Everyone was quiet for a minute or two as they thought.

That's it! Jake got to his feet and pointed at the school buildings. 'There.'

Sam shook his head. 'Seriously? You want to go back to school? The only good thing about this is not –'

'There must be proof at school!'

Andy looked at him. 'That's not such a bad idea.'

'There must be records of us on file,' said Jake.

'And how are we supposed to get in there?' asked Sam.

'I know the door codes,' volunteered Felix. 'At least, I used to.'

Jake felt a surge of excitement. If he could get hold of his school record, then he could show it to his mum. She couldn't argue with that. Her name would be on it as an emergency contact. *Relationship to student: Mother.* Surely if she saw that, she'd have to believe he was her son.

'The only person here on a Sunday is the janitor, and he does his rounds first thing and then again around five,' said Felix.

Everyone turned to look at him.

'I had a month of weekend detentions in year eight.' He shrugged. 'You pick up stuff.'

───────

The boys approached the front entrance of the school. Felix punched some numbers into the security pad.

To everyone's surprise, it buzzed open. Jake clapped him on the back. 'Nice one, freak.'

Felix sighed. 'Do you think you could stop calling me that?'

Jake considered it for a moment, then shook his head. 'Nah.' He made his way down the corridor, followed by the others. He knew what he had to check first: the photos in the gym. If he existed, he would still be there. They entered the gym and Jake looked at the photos along the wall.

SPORTS HOUSE CAPTAIN: TRENT LONG.

FOOTBALL CAPTAIN: TRENT LONG.

BEST AND FAIREST: TRENT LONG.

Jake turned away. That wasn't right. Trent was a deputy, a wingman. He was never a captain. He didn't have the leadership skills. That was Jake's domain.

Andy put his hand on Jake's shoulder sympathetically.

'It's OK. It doesn't prove anything except that Trent's a better player.'

Jake shrugged him off. 'And that's supposed to be comforting?'

'Come on,' called Felix. 'I know the code to the staff offices. We can check the student records there.'

When they got to the staff room, Felix punched in the codes and Andy quickly booted up the computer.

Jake watched over his shoulder. Part of him wanted to stop Andy. If he didn't actually check, then they could keep believing . . .

SAM CONTE, Andy typed in.

A window came up: NO RECORD FOUND.

FELIX FERNE, Andy typed.

Another window: NO RECORD FOUND.

ANDY LAU.

NO RECORD FOUND.

There was silence. Andy looked nervously at Jake.

JAKE RILES, he typed in.

NO RECORD FOUND.

The boys stared at the blinking cursor.

'We officially don't exist,' whispered Andy.

Jake turned and ran out of the staff room. He belted down the stairs. He burst into the gym, grabbed a basketball and hurled it at the hoop. This he knew: you pick up a ball, you bounce it, you throw it through a metal ring and then you pick it up again. Simple. Maybe if he could just keep bouncing the ball he wouldn't have to face the fact that he was officially a nobody.

He bounced the ball harder and threw it through the hoop. A perfect shot. He imagined the crowd roaring for him. The way they used to when he shot the winning hoop at the District Championships. How his team would pick him up on their shoulders, their captain, their hero.

He caught sight of Trent grinning from a photo on the wall. BASKETBALL CAPTAIN: TRENT LONG.

Jake picked up the ball and threw it hard at the picture. It fell to the ground, the glass smashing into shards. The ball bounced back and he picked it up again. He aimed it at the next picture of Trent and –

Crash!

It fell to the floor.

Sam, Andy and Felix burst through the doors as Jake picked up the ball again. He aimed it for the third time at Trent's smug face.

Smash!

To the floor.

'Jake, stop!' yelled Sam.

Jake picked up the ball again and was about to throw it when Sam wrestled him to the ground.

'Come on, man. You can't do that.'

Jake fought him back hard. 'Why not?'

'Yeah, why not?' Felix said from the doorway. 'Who's going to get us in trouble? Our parents don't even know who we are.' He opened a cage full of basketballs and they rolled across the gym floor.

'This is a real X-factor in my theory,' said Andy. 'It can't be amnesia if there's no record of us.' He clicked his fingers. 'I know. It's identity theft.'

Jake threw a ball at his head. 'Why would anyone want to steal your identity?'

Andy threw the ball back, hard. 'I object to that.' He launched himself at Jake and they wrestled.

Andy fought like he'd never done it before, snickering and giggling. Jake quickly pinned him to the floor.

Felix threw a volleyball net over them.

Sam grabbed the cleaner's trolley from the hallway and rolled into the gym. He jumped up on it like it was a huge skateboard. Then Jake and Andy freed themselves from the net and they took turns riding it around, yelling and whooping at the top of their voices, while Felix let off the fire extinguishers. Soon the whole gym was covered in a sheer white mist.

Jake perched himself on top of the gym wall ladder and looked down through the haze at the chaos below. Andy was being swung around in the cleaning trolley by Sam. Felix was throwing rolls of toilet paper around. The whole gym had been totally ransacked. What had once been Jake's inner sanctum, the place he trained every day, now meant nothing.

Jake felt glad it was trashed, glad that Trent wouldn't be able to train there on Monday, wouldn't be able to win a game. If he didn't have *his* life any more then it sure as hell wasn't fair that everyone else could keep theirs.

He was about to swing down on to a pile of gym mats when something caught his eye. A security camera bolted into the corner of the ceiling. He stared at its insistent flashing light. It was recording everything. He felt an instinctive wave of fear, but brushed it aside and leapt off the ladder with a huge roar. Felix was right. Who would the school report it to, anyway?

You can't get in trouble if you don't exist, right?

sam: mg 4 sc

Sam's dad sat at the head of the table, a lopsided party hat on his head and a big grin on his face. In front of him was a table laden with food. Barbequed lamb. Italian pork sausages, a fattoush salad. There were homemade dips, *batata harra*, pitta bread, and Sam's mum's *kibbeh*. Vince and Pete were shoving food in their mouths while simultaneously yelling at the World Cup on the TV. Sam wasn't watching. He was savouring every mouthful. He dipped his *kibbeh* in yoghurt sauce and felt the creamy garlicky taste spread across his tongue, followed by the moist tenderness of the spicy meat. He bit into a tomato drenched in olive oil, the sweetness exploding in his mouth. His brother Pete was yelling at him, 'Sam, Italy scored a goal, Sam!' But Sam didn't care. He took another bite of the tomato.

'Sam!'

Sam opened one eye. Andy was sitting beside him waving a bunch of weeds in his face. 'Sam, wake up. I've got breakfast.'

Sam rubbed his eyes and sat up.

Andy grinned at him triumphantly. 'I found these dandelions, which are very high in potassium, and I got some pigweed as well.' He held up a handful of dirty, fleshy-looking leaves. 'Very high in omega-3.'

Sam fell back to the ground. 'Please let *this* be a dream. Please.'

Andy took a bite of the dandelion leaves. 'Delicious,' he said, grimacing.

'You're not selling me, dude.' Sam got up and walked out of the shack. His stomach rumbled. He wasn't sure which was worse: being permanently hungry, or permanently forgotten. He walked across a small clearing to the river. Andy followed him, chewing on his leaves.

Sam pushed through the eucalypts by the bank. Jake was swimming and Felix was sitting on a rock with his head in his weird black book.

'Come in, guys,' Jake called to Sam and Andy.

Andy shook his head. 'Mum says it's not natural to go in beyond waist level.'

Sam gave him a friendly shove. 'Come on. Your mum's not here now, is she?'

Sam ripped his shirt off and, after a moment of hesitation, Andy did the same.

The freezing water was strangely exhilarating. Sam splashed at Jake, who splashed back harder. They both turned to Andy, who had only managed to go in up to his ankles. They reached their hands up to splash him but Andy took a huge breath and dived under.

Sam and Jake laughed. 'Woohoo!'

Andy surfaced, spluttering. 'I've never swum in non-chlorinated water before.'

'Come on, Felix,' Sam called.

Felix shook his head. 'I'm fine.'

'What's that book you're always writing in?' asked Sam.

'Just my diary.'

'Seriously, you're writing a diary?' said Jake.

'What's the point of writing a diary?' asked Sam. '*Got up. Got hungry. Stayed hungry. Went to bed. Still hungry.* That pretty much sums it up.' Sam didn't really get why anyone would keep a journal, but he secretly wished he had a sketch pad so he could draw.

Felix shut his book guardedly. 'Maybe it'll be a bestseller one day.'

Jake laughed bitterly. 'Yeah, a real feel-good read. The story of four boys who don't exist.'

Sam ducked his head under the water. He didn't want to hear any more that he didn't exist. He *did* exist. He knew that. He swam away from the others.

The river water was a dull brown. Sam flicked his eyes open underwater but he couldn't see anything. He swam slowly. He could hold his breath for almost a minute. Being dunked by his brothers had some advantages. If you just concentrated your mind, you could trick your body into thinking it didn't need to breathe. He felt his diaphragm expand, wanting oxygen. He let it contract and subside. See? He'd tricked his body. He didn't need to breathe.

Maybe that's all this was. Some kind of trick. Maybe all they needed to do was pull aside the magician's curtain, see what was really going on. Anything can appear to be a certain way when it really isn't.

He burst to the surface. He'd swum the width of the river. He could see Jake and Andy playing chasey in the water. Funny, from this far away, they almost looked like they liked each other.

He was about to swim back when he saw a flash of blue in the trees. He swam down towards it and pulled himself up on to the bank. There, covered haphazardly with a few branches, was an old upside-down rowboat.

Sam stared at it. He knew that boat. He and Mia had come here often last summer and rowed along the river. They'd shared their first kiss in that boat. He'd been so nervous that once they started kissing, he made the boat rock so hard she'd fallen in the water. How sketchy was that?

Man, if he could have her back, he sure as hell wouldn't do anything that dumb. He would hold on to her so tight. There was no way she'd go overboard.

He shook his head and was about to dive back into the

murky river when a thought occurred to him.

He and Mia had pledged their love for each other in that boat. He turned back to stare at it. Did he dare turn it over? Would knowing that he absolutely didn't exist be too awful to deal with?

He hesitated but then, in one swift move, he overturned the boat. And there it was, carved into the side: a love heart with the initials MG 4 SC.

He stared at it, too shocked to react. Then, slowly, a grin spread over his face. This was it. This was what they'd been looking for. They *did* exist. This was *proof.*

Sam dived back into the water and swam quickly back to the others. 'Hey!' he called as soon as they were in earshot. 'I've got proof we exist. In the boat.' He crawled up on to the bank, breathless.

Jake looked at him like he was crazy. 'Are you OK, dude? Did you eat some of Andy's dandelions? Because . . . you know?'

'I'm not crazy.' Sam grinned. 'Mia and I did a carving last year and it's still there. My initials. So I *have* to exist.'

The others looked at him doubtfully.

'Come on, this is good news, right?'

'Yeah, but you spoke to Mia and she didn't have a clue who you were, remember?' said Andy.

'Well, maybe this will trigger her memory.'

Andy nodded. 'That's true. And it could trigger a chain reaction, causing everybody's memories to return.'

Felix eyed him cynically. 'I thought you'd given up on your amnesia theory.'

Andy shrugged. 'It's worth a shot.'

'I have to show it to her,' said Sam.

Jake shook his head. 'Dude, there's no way you're gonna get her to come here with you.'

Sam's grin faded. 'Yeah, true.' But a moment later, he brightened up. 'So we take it to her.'

The other three stared at him.

'You want us to carry a boat through Bremin to your girlfriend's house?' Felix said slowly.

'Why not? If it proves we exist.'

'You can take it to her another way,' suggested Andy.

'How?'

'Take a photo of it.'

Sam looked at Andy, impressed. 'Finally, Bear Grylls has a decent idea.'

'Yeah, except all our phones are out of battery,' said Jake.

Sam thought for a second. 'I'll get my mum's digital camera,' he said, refusing to be deterred. 'My key still works. Come on.'

———

Sam was buoyant as he led the others up the path to his house.

They passed an open garage. Felix put his head in and saw it was full of sporting and camping gear. 'Do you think while we're here we could get some other stuff?'

Sam shrugged. 'Sure.' The boys looked around the garage. 'My dad's an outdoors freak. All the old stuff's over there. He won't notice if you take it.'

Jake picked up a Thomas the Tank Engine sleeping bag. 'Perfect for you, Felix.'

'Knock yourselves out, guys.' Sam left the others in the garage. He stepped up on to the porch. The sliding door was open and he could hear the monotonous sound of the Xbox from inside. Good. Once Vince and Pete were in front of that thing, nothing would distract them.

He dropped down low and scuttled across the floor to the kitchen. The tinny jingle of victory came from the TV and Vince stood up. Sam quickly hid himself behind the bench.

'All hail King Vince! Poor Petey. Must be hard coming second your whole life.'

In response, Pete lifted a butt cheek and let rip with some serious chemical weaponry.

Vince collapsed against the wall, coughing. 'Oh man, that is seriously rank.'

Sam seized the moment and reached across to open the second drawer. *Yes!* There it was. He grabbed the camera and put it in his pocket.

He was about to dart back to the door when Vince took a few steps towards the kitchen.

Pete called from the couch, 'While you're there, can you

make me a baked-bean toastie?'

'No way, man. D'you think I've got a death wish?'

Sam held his breath. Vince's feet were an arm's length from where he was squatting. His brother would see him for sure. How the hell was he going to explain being caught red-handed with a camera?

They'd call the police. He'd be locked up . . . and given three meals a day, a bed to sleep in. Sounded pretty good actually, except then he'd never see Mia.

Vince's feet moved closer – but then the sound of a new game started up on the Xbox. 'Hey, unfair advantage, loser!' Vince called, walking back into the lounge room.

Sam made a dash for the door, grabbing a bunch of bananas from the fruit bowl as he went. He hurtled down the steps to the garage.

Sam left the others at the shack 'making house' and headed back to the boat, eating a banana. He walked upstream to where the water was shallow, then took off his shoes and socks, and waded across. Even to his nose, his socks stank. He gave them a quick rinse and slung them over his shoulders to dry. No point approaching Mia if he smelt like crap.

He clambered barefoot on to the opposite bank and made his way back downstream towards the boat. God, he hoped he hadn't imagined it.

But no. There it was – as clear as day: MG 4 SC.

He pulled out the camera and lined up the shot.

Snap.

Perfect.

He took a few more, just to be sure. He let the camera fall to his side.

OK, he'd done it. He had proof.

The wind picked up and trees by the river swayed. Sam turned around quickly. He had the unmistakable feeling that someone was watching him.

'Hello?'

Maybe one of the others had followed him.

But there was no answer. Just the quiet creak of branches moving with the wind.

Sam shivered; this place totally gave him the creeps. Grabbing his shoes, he hightailed it out of there.

Mia was at the skate park with Ellen. Damn. Ellen's looks had totally improved, but her personality was exactly the same: annoying as hell.

As Sam approached, Mia looked up. Then she turned quickly to Ellen and whispered something.

'We're in the middle of a meeting,' Ellen said officiously.

'I just need to show Mia something.'

'Well, we're busy, OK?' Ellen snapped.

Ignoring her, Sam sat down next to Mia and pulled out the camera. He put the picture of the carving in front of her.

'There, see. The blue boat. Last summer. Remember?'

Mia looked at him. 'Of course I remember.'

Sam grinned. 'You do? That's great!'

'I did that carving with my boyfriend.'

Sam thumped the bench. 'Exactly! That's what I've been trying to tell you.'

Ellen stifled a laugh with her hand.

Mia spoke slowly and carefully. 'But you're not my boyfriend.' She gestured to a scowling dark-haired guy who had suddenly appeared at her side. '*This* is my boyfriend. Sammy.'

Sam stared at the boy. This was Mia's boyfriend? This wet-looking gimp?

'What's your deal, dude?' snarled Sammy.

'What's *my* deal?'

Sammy was staring at his board. 'Hey, that's my board. It got stolen from my house yesterday.'

'*Your* house?'

'Yeah.' Sammy reached out to grab the board and Sam saw a friendship bracelet, identical to his, on his wrist.

Sam flinched. A horrible thought had hit him. He quickly flipped his board and skated away.

'Hey, give me my board back, hack!'

Sam kept going. That kid. *Sammy*. What was he talking about? *His* house? *His* girlfriend? It wasn't possible.

Sam skated as fast as he could back to his house. He bounded up the steps to the porch. This time he didn't care who saw him. It didn't matter anymore. The screen door was locked. Sam pulled out his key, shoved it in the lock, and slid open the door.

Dumping his skateboard, he ran to the bookshelves. He ripped out a photo album and opened it. A photograph of *Sammy* smiled out at him from behind his tenth-birthday cake, his mum and dad in the background. *Sam's* mum and dad.

Sam felt sick. He didn't want to turn the page, but his fingers did it anyway. There was Sammy in his skate gear, holding a trophy after winning a skate comp, flanked by his proud older brothers – Pete and Vince. *Sam's* brothers. He flicked again. Sammy as a toddler, Sammy's first day at school, Sammy at Little Athletics, Sammy learning to surf.

Sam couldn't look anymore. He slammed the album shut. He couldn't breathe. It was like being underwater but with no possibility of hitting the surface. His diaphragm was contracting but no air was getting in.

He looked up. There on the wall was a studio portrait of his family: Mum, Dad, Pete, Vince and, dead in the centre, a smug, grinning Sammy.

Sam sucked air deep into his lungs and his throat opened up, releasing a desperate, ragged-sounding cry. He slumped down on the floor, trying to breathe.

Outside, there was the sound of a car door slamming.

Sam got up and went to the window. His mum was in the driveway. His beautiful mum. He watched her getting her easel and paints out of the boot. He'd got his love of drawing from her. She'd taught him how to make a situation better by looking at it a different way: by painting it or drawing it. She'd shown him how drawing could change things. She always understood everything. He had to talk to her, make her see.

He ran out of the house and down to the driveway. 'Mum!'

She turned sharply. 'Oh, you gave me a fright. Are you looking for Sammy? He should be home soon.'

'I'm not looking for Sammy. It's me, Sam!' He grabbed her arm and almost instantly she started to breathe raggedly. 'Mum, that boy Sammy, he's not your son. I am!'

His mum looked up at him, her breathing laboured. 'Sweetie, I'm not your mum.'

'You are. I promise you.' Sam wracked his brain. He had to convince her. 'Every birthday you make us a cheesecake. It's black cherry. The same cake that your mum used to make for you . . .'

She looked confused. 'What?'

'When you were my age you lived at the beach and were a junior surf champ. Uncle Noel still calls you Gidget . . .'

His mum bent over double, her breath rasping.

Sam kept going desperately. 'That's why I started skating.

To be like you.' He grabbed her arm harder. 'I miss you, Mum. Please, remember me!'

He took his hand away and in its place, a creeping bright-red rash made its way up his mum's forearm. She clutched at it and then collapsed, unconscious, on the driveway.

Oh God. What had he done? Had he killed her? Was it all too big a shock? He should have kept his big fat mouth shut.

He turned and sprinted back inside. He grabbed the phone and punched in 999. The impersonal voice of the operator came on the line. 'What's your emergency, please?'

Sam looked out the window and saw Sammy running up the path. He ran straight to Sam's mum. Sam watched as she slowly stood up. Sammy put his arms around her and helped her to sit in the front seat of the car.

'What's your emergency, please?'

Sam watched his mum smile and reassure Sammy. She tousled his hair affectionately.

Sam hung up the phone and stared at them through the glass. He'd been absolutely, unquestionably replaced.

andy: a very hungry ghost

'So, if by chance we stumbled across a wormhole, then we could have slipped through space and time into an alternate universe.' Andy was sitting on a Bob the Builder sleeping bag, trying to convince Felix and Jake of his latest theory.

Andy took a bite of pigweed and chewed it thoughtfully. He'd been going over and over this in his head. The only explanation that really made sense was that they were in a parallel universe. 'It's possible that large bodies of mass can move between dimensional planes –'

Andy's stomach made a terrible gurgling sound.

Felix looked up from his black journal.

'You're talking out of your arse, man,' said Jake, cracking himself up.

Andy ignored him. He needed to concentrate. 'An Einstein-Rosen bridge is a tunnel with two points in different space-time continua.' His stomach gurgled again, and he paused. Maybe Jake was right. 'Have we got any toilet paper?'

Jake laughed. 'Dude, we don't even have a toilet.'

Andy made a run for the door, barely making it to a tree in time. He crouched with his pants around his ankles, feeling the effects of a twenty-four-hour diet of weeds. It wasn't good. Even worse was only having a handful of gum leaves to finish the job. Bear Grylls must have the constitution of an ox. Andy Lau's bowels were more equipped for spicy pork buns than dandelion leaves.

He brushed away thoughts of his *nai nai*'s cooking. No point thinking about that now. He had a Lorentzian wormhole to find. If that was how they got here, then surely that was the way home. Only problem was, how do you find a wormhole? And even if you *do* find one, how do you keep it open long enough to transport four guys? That's a lot of mass.

Andy frowned. If they had got here via a wormhole then it must have been a total freak occurrence, so the chances of them returning the same way were infinitesimally small.

He sighed. He wished he could talk to his dad. *He'd* be able to explain what had happened to them using some complex mathematical formula that made utter logical sense.

When he was finally done, Andy staggered back towards the shack. He was going to have to hold off on the weeds for a while. But they needed food, and so far he hadn't had any luck catching fish. Bear Grylls sure made it look easier than it was.

He could try trapping some wild animals. Possums, maybe.

He opened the door to the shack. It was looking almost cosy. Camping mats lay on the floor. Jake had blown up an old li-lo, and some rickety camp chairs surrounded an old card table.

Home sweet home.

Jake and Felix were arguing. Felix had found fifty cents in the pocket of one of Sam's dad's old raincoats and Jake wanted to go and spend it straight away.

Felix disagreed. 'You can't buy anything useful for fifty cents. We should wait until we get more and then put it together.'

'How are we going to get any more? We can at least buy some gum. Remind our mouths what they're meant to be doing.'

Andy looked at the silver coin Felix was twirling in his fingers. He suddenly had an idea. 'We could get a really good meal for that!'

Jake looked up. 'No way, man. You're not on dinner duty *ever* again.'

Andy smiled. 'Trust me, this will be a dinner fit for a king.'

———

The boys made their way into town. Andy walked purposefully. This was the best idea he'd had in ages. OK, so it didn't involve a camel's stomach or boiling live crickets, but it did involve the stealth and ingenuity of a hunter. And if the end result was food, who really cared?

'There's Sam,' said Jake.

Sam was sitting on a bench next to the skate park, staring into space.

The boys surrounded him.

'You OK, man?' asked Jake.

'How OK can you be when your parents had another kid instead of you? And they called him Sammy and he's a pro skater and his girlfriend is . . .' Sam looked across the skate park at Mia.

Jake followed his gaze. 'That totally sucks.'

'Yep,' said Sam.

Andy had no idea what to say. He'd never had a girlfriend in his life, let alone lost one. But he did know one thing that would cheer Sam up. 'Do you want some food?'

Andy opened the door of the phone box and the four boys squeezed in. Andy nodded at Felix. 'OK, put it in.'

Felix reached up and pushed the precious fifty-cent coin into the slot. The stench of his armpit wafted into Andy's face.

'Ooh, that's really not good.'

Jake shrugged. 'I've tried to tell him, but does he listen?'

Felix scowled at them both, but Andy was busy punching in the number.

The phone rang twice and his *nai nai* came on the line. Andy had an overwhelming desire to tell her how much he missed her and loved her. But remembering the way she'd chased him out of the house with the meat cleaver, he stopped himself.

'Hello, Mrs Lau . . . yes . . . two serves of twenty-two, extra-spicy. Yep . . . four sixty-threes . . . and a fifty-four. Deliver to one-forty-four Acacia Court . . . Yes, in cash.'

Felix leant in. 'Get some lemon chicken.'

'Seriously? That's not even real Chinese.' Andy turned back to the phone. 'And a thirty-seven, that's all thanks. How long will it be?' Then he hung up.

Jake looked unimpressed. 'Now what? We kill the delivery guy?'

'The ninja must learn to wait,' said Andy cryptically.

The four of them waited on the street opposite Lily Lau's Chinese Restaurant.

Andy's sister Viv and his *nai nai* were struggling to unfurl a banner across the front of the restaurant, which said in bright red letters, FESTIVAL OF THE HUNGRY GHOST.

Every year Andy's *nai nai* forced him to make dumplings for the hungry ghosts. Apparently if they weren't fed they got angry – very angry.

Andy thought the whole thing was hocus-pocus, but Nai Nai insisted on the tradition. So every year, he and Viv made mountains of perfectly shaped dumplings that they never got to eat. He'd once snuck one off the pile for himself, and Nai Nai had whacked him across the shins with her rolling pin.

Andy sighed. Happy days.

An overweight man with a handlebar moustache came out of the side door of the restaurant, carrying some plastic bags.

'That's him. Kevin,' Andy whispered.

The man jumped on a moped with LILY LAU'S CHINESE RESTAURANT emblazoned on the side and started the engine.

'Come on,' said Andy, as the moped put-putted down the street.

At that moment, Viv spotted him. 'That's him again,' she yelled. 'The *stalker*!'

Andy and the others took off after the moped. This new version of Viv disturbed him. He'd never got on all that well with her, but now she'd had a personality transplant, he found himself kind of missing his old goody-two-shoes sister.

The moped made a right turn into the main street.

'OK,' said Andy, indicating for the others to stop behind a tree near the newsagent's. 'Kevin has a crush on the newsagent. Every afternoon he sneaks her over a little package of love dumplings. There he goes.'

Kevin drove straight past the newsagent's.

Andy's face fell. 'Maybe it's different in this reality.'

Kevin stopped at the post office, posted a letter and turned the moped around. He glided to a stop outside the newsagent's.

Andy grinned. 'OK, watch and learn.'

Kevin took a package out of the moped and walked into the shop.

Andy sprinted across the street. He grabbed the bags of food and was back with the others just in time to see the bewildered expression on Kevin's face as he discovered his delivery had disappeared.

———

The boys sat in the sunshine outside their shack. Andy unpacked the small plastic boxes and placed them reverently on the grass.

'Sixty-three: Phoenix Talons – steamed chicken feet. Twenty-two: Szechuan liver with snow peas. And fifty-four, the ultimate: Chu Kiok Chou – pigs' trotters in vinegar.'

Jake and Sam looked miserably at the display.

'Why didn't you order normal food, nerd?' muttered Jake.

Andy looked sideways at Jake as he reached for a pig's trotter. It was unbelievable. He'd provided enough food for all of them, which was a lot more than Jake had ever done. He squared his shoulders. 'Why do you keep calling me *nerd*?'

Jake almost smiled but quickly covered it by shoving a snow pea in his mouth.

Andy noticed Felix, who was looking somewhat dismayed. 'Oh, I nearly forgot . . .' He pulled out one more container and opened it with a flourish. 'Thirty-seven: lemon chicken.'

Felix smiled gratefully. 'Thanks, Andy.'

Andy picked up his chopsticks and began to eat. Eating his *nai nai's* food had a strange effect. Yes, it was delicious, but with every mouthful, Andy felt more and more homesick.

Every flavour and spice seemed to be related to a memory. Nai Nai hitting his knuckles for folding the dumpling dough the wrong way, his dad telling him bedtime stories about particle physics, Viv beating him at the science fair, and his mum making him wear three singlets to school when the temperature dropped below thirty degrees.

Funny how the things that drove you crazy about your family were the things you missed the most.

Andy felt a tear fall and quickly wiped his eyes. 'It's the chilli.'

Jake held his gaze for a moment. 'You did well, nerd.' Only this time he said 'nerd' with a smile.

Andy smiled back. He watched Jake, Sam and Felix gulping down the food. He might not be Bear Grylls, but this feast wasn't a bad effort.

A dark shadow suddenly passed across the sun and the bright day turned grey.

The boys looked up at the sky. From somewhere came the sound of a long, low howl. They looked at each other nervously. *What was that?*

'Probably just the panther come to get Andy,' said Jake,

trying to make light of it.

The slow, mournful howl came again. This time it sounded closer.

'We should go inside,' said Felix, putting down his chopsticks.

A breeze started moving in the trees around them as they got to their feet. The wind picked up, gathering force. It whipped around them in circles, lifting twigs and bark off the ground.

'It's the twister again!' yelled Jake, as the wind circled and howled.

Andy tried to move. He put a leg out in front of him, but the wind was so strong now it forced his leg back. The others were fighting against the wind too, trying desperately to reach the shack.

There was another spine-chilling howl. Louder this time, like it was right next to them. Andy's hair stood on end, and he turned to see a hooded figure standing motionless in the forest.

'There!' he yelled above the wind to the others. 'There's something there!'

The others turned to look, but the figure had gone.

Andy shut his eyes. He didn't believe in ghosts. Ghosts couldn't be proven. They weren't scientific. They were just imagined.

He opened his eyes again and this time, the figure was closer. A black hood shielded its eyes, but Andy knew what it was. The hungry ghost. He opened his mouth and screamed.

For a second, the wind died down. The leaves and twigs fell to earth and the strange figure disappeared.

'Get inside. *Quick!*' yelled Felix.

They bolted for the door of the shack. As soon as they reached it, the wind picked up again. Stones and sticks flew at them. Sam struggled with the latch. 'It won't open!'

Andy glanced over his shoulder, terrified. Another howl. So loud now it seemed to shake the roof of the shack.

Felix and Jake threw themselves at the door, and the catch finally released. They raced inside and Sam slammed the door shut. The wind hammered at it, almost like it was determined to get in. Felix and Jake pulled some old planks of wood across to hold it shut, while Andy and Sam piled every heavy object in the shack up against it.

The roof of the shack creaked and wailed with the wind. The eerie howling got louder and louder.

Felix lit the gas lantern and the boys huddled together on their sleeping bags. Andy stared at the flickering light of the lantern, trying to calm his thoughts. He didn't believe in ghosts. He only believed in the rational. The provable. It was just a storm. That's all it was.

The boys moved closer together, embarrassed by their fear.

'Man, this is so messed up,' said Sam, putting his head in his hands.

The whole shack started to shake as thunder boomed

overhead. Lightning flashed through the window, and in that second, Andy saw his own terror reflected on the others' faces.

'There's something out there,' Felix murmured. 'But I don't think it's strong enough to get in.'

'Gee, thanks dude. That's so comforting,' said Jake.

They all bunched closer together, too scared to say any more.

After what seemed like hours, the howling died down, replaced by the more comforting sound of rain beating steadily down on the tin roof. One by one, the exhausted boys dropped off to sleep.

Andy lay in his sleeping bag, thinking about how much he'd wanted adventure. How he'd pleaded with his family to let him go on the excursion. He'd longed to be stuck in the wild with only his wits to protect him. What a fool.

If someone gave him the choice now between being an over-protected Singaporean kid with a belly full of food, or being stuck out here in the bush with ghosts wailing outside – well, he knew which one he'd choose.

Andy woke to the sound of birds chirping. He opened one eye. His head was lying on a soft pillow. For an instant he thought he was back in his own bed under his solar-system sheets, with his mum delivering him congee and steamed buns on a tray. But no, the pillow was actually Jake's stomach.

And it wasn't actually that soft. Actually, it was a bit wet. Oh. That was his own dribble.

Andy sat up and looked around the shack. Sun was pouring in the window. Sam and Jake lay asleep on their camp mats, their faces drained. Felix was nowhere to be seen.

With a shiver, Andy remembered last night's storm. He couldn't believe he'd actually managed to fall asleep. Looking around now, it seemed like it had never happened.

Andy got to his feet and walked out into the sunshine.

Felix was standing outside, inspecting the ground, with his black book in his hand. Feathers, leaves and twigs littered the ground around the hideout. 'This isn't good.'

Andy tried to sound more confident than he felt. 'It's just from the storm, right? Things got knocked around.'

'I don't think so,' Felix said gravely. 'There's a pattern, see? It's like some sort of spirit has been here.'

Andy shuddered. *The hungry ghost.* He shook his head. Standing outside in the bright light of day, the idea of ghosts seemed ridiculous.

'Well, how else do you explain the storm, the howling, the figure in the trees?' asked Felix.

'So you saw that too?'

'Yeah, I saw it,' said Felix. 'I think something is after us.'

Andy looked around at the bark and feathers. They did seem to be arranged in a well-ordered way. He pushed his fear aside. There was bound to be a perfectly rational explanation.

'Could it have been the panther?' Andy tried.

Felix scoffed. 'Oh, come on. No one believes that.'

'Well, it would explain stuff being moved around, and the howling.'

'You're living in a fantasy if you believe that.' Felix noted something down in his black book and walked away.

Andy knew the panther story was nonsense. But nothing made sense about last night. The weird figure, the spooky storm. It was like some crazy dream.

Then something hit him. Maybe Felix was right. Maybe they *were* living in a fantasy. He thought back to when they'd fallen down the cliff. That's when everything had gone wrong. He remembered how he'd stood up and he wasn't injured or even bruised. But he should have been, right?

Maybe when they fell, they were all knocked unconscious, and this *whole thing* was a dream. That was it! Occam's razor: the simplest solution was the most obvious.

'We have to wake ourselves up!' said Andy suddenly.

Felix turned and stared at him like he'd completely lost it.

'We're still in the forest,' said Andy.

'Well, clearly,' said Felix.

'No,' said Andy. 'We're still in the forest where we *fell*. We're *unconscious*! Dying of hunger and thirst while we dream this whole thing.'

Felix shook his head. 'Yesterday you were chasing wormholes.'

'I know, but this makes much more sense. It's all a fantasy, a final attempt by our neural transmitters to cling on to life.'

Felix stared at him. 'You know, the more you talk, the less I understand.'

'Watch this,' said Andy, determined to make him see.

He ran hard at a tree and hit straight into it with a whack, then fell to the ground. He staggered up, holding his head. 'Not strong enough. I need something to really shock me awake.'

'Last night wasn't scary enough for you?'

But Andy wasn't listening. He had to think of something powerful enough to shock his body into waking up.

Suddenly, he knew what he had to do.

He checked his watch. The school bus went down Glenview Road at about this time every morning. If he could get to the road in time, he could run out in front of the bus and the shock would wake him up. That's how dreams worked, right? Just at the moment the worst possible thing could happen to you, your body automatically wakes up.

He sprinted along the track, through the undergrowth and burst out of the bush. Breathless, he scrambled up the grassy rise and crossed over a few quiet suburban streets until he came to Glenview Road. He heard an engine rumble and then saw the bus, coming towards him from about a hundred metres away. Andy took a deep breath and steeled himself.

This was it. He was going home.

Then he noticed a girl in a Bremin High uniform walking to school on the other side of the road. She was wearing headphones and was close to the edge of the road, not seeing the bus coming up behind her. Was it . . . Felix's friend, Ellen? She looked completely different.

He tried not to get distracted. He knew this was his chance. If he could just stick to his plan, he'd get out of this nightmare.

The bus came closer and Ellen stepped on to the road. In that split-second, Andy could see the driver had turned around to yell at some kids. The bus had swerved, and was headed straight towards her.

Without thinking, Andy hurled himself at her, pushing her off the road where they collapsed into a ditch. The bus flew past them in a blur and travelled on, oblivious.

Andy's heart was pumping madly, and he realised that he was lying right on top of Ellen. Her headphones had been knocked off by the impact of their fall.

She looked up at him with wide eyes, her expression a mixture of shock and awe. 'Oh my God,' she gasped.

Andy was stunned. He felt her warm body pressed against his. Her shampoo-fresh scent filled his nose, and her breath was on his neck. He got off her as quickly as he could. 'Sorry.'

'What?' She laughed in disbelief, and sat up. 'You – you just saved my life!'

She was *beautiful*. And Andy had no idea what to do.

felix: bee warned

Felix walked away from the shack, deep in thought. First there was the twister, and now this freak storm had left stuff scattered all over the place in mysterious patterns. He climbed up a small rise, then turned to look back.

He took in a sharp breath.

With a bit of distance, the patterns formed by the twigs, bark and leaves were clearly defined. Very specific spiral formations pointed towards the shack as if it were the bullseye. Felix shuddered. That wasn't just a storm. Whatever had come last night was targeting them, and the flimsy shack had only just protected them.

On the corrugated tin roof was a swirling pattern, kind of like a giant drill had tried to bore its way through. Whatever – or whoever – this thing was, it was hell bent on getting at them.

Felix sat down on the rise and opened his Book of Shadows.

He began to draw. His hand moved quickly, almost as if he was not controlling it. Just like the urge he'd felt when he'd drawn the strange objects hanging in the trees, he wanted to record these patterns and find out what they were. If he knew what was after them, maybe he could find out what had happened.

He filled pages with drawings. Spirals upon spirals upon spirals. He drew until his eyes hurt. He let his hand fall to his side. What was the point? He was just going around in circles – literally. How was he ever going to find out what happened to them? It was like trying to solve his dad's diabolical sudoku without knowing the rules. No, wait. It was worse than that. It was like trying to solve a sudoku without even having a newspaper.

He sighed and was about to shut his book when something stopped him. He stared at the spiral pattern he'd drawn over and over. There was something familiar about it. Had he seen it before? And then it clicked: these spirals were like the ones he'd seen in the Book of Shadows that he'd found when he'd sneaked into the back section of the magic shop, Arcane Lane. God, that seemed like a lifetime ago.

And that creepy hooded figure last night – the way it had stood among the trees staring at them. It reminded him of the woman he'd seen in the trees on the day they'd gone missing. He hadn't thought about it since, but it had been so weird, seeing the woman from Arcane Lane in the forest. What was her name? Penelope? Poppy? Phoebe? Yes, that was it. Phoebe.

What had she been doing there? Was she following him? There had to be a connection.

He shoved his own Book of Shadows in his bag. Did Arcane Lane even exist in this reality? He had to go and see if it was still there. If it was, he could get another look at that original Book of Shadows. It might tell him what the spirals meant. And maybe it would give him a clue as to who or what was after them. At the very least, he owed the others that.

Felix made his way at a jog through the forest towards town. On the path, he saw Andy walking towards him, looking bewildered. 'You woken up yet?'

Andy's face went a weird shade of pink. 'Actually, I think wormholes are a more likely explanation.'

'Yeah, well, good luck with that,' Felix said. He didn't have time to discuss quantum physics, not that he understood it anyway. And besides, he had his own plan.

———

In town, Felix veered down a side lane. He climbed the dozen or so steps behind the car park and stopped, breathless. Arcane Lane was still there. Exactly as he remembered it.

Last time he'd sneaked into the back room when Phoebe was distracted by Mia wanting her advice about making friendship bracelets. He'd found her Book of Shadows in a drawer and had flicked through it, looking for a spell that might help Oscar. He'd found something that he thought might work and, at the back of the book, he'd found a hand-drawn map of a powerful magical site in the Bremin Forest. He'd just managed to copy it down when Phoebe had caught him and chased him from the shop.

Felix took a deep breath. Hopefully, in this world, Arcane Lane would be run by a sweet old lady.

He peered through the window. Bugger. No such luck.

A grumpy-looking Phoebe was sitting behind the counter, packaging crystals in little Ziploc bags.

Felix hesitated. He needed to think this through. He couldn't just walk in there and ask to look at her precious Book of Shadows. He looked around, searching for an idea.

A set of wind chimes hanging outside the shop clinked in the wind.

Felix considered them for a moment. If he could loosen them, he might buy himself enough time. He reached up and grasped the chimes closed to keep them quiet, then carefully loosened the string they were hanging from.

That should do it.

Felix entered the shop and Phoebe glanced up. 'We don't sell vampire books.'

'I don't want vampire books.'

Phoebe rolled her eyes and returned to her crystals. 'My mistake.'

Felix looked around the shop. It was just as he remembered

it. Dream-catchers hung from the ceiling. Strange statues of North American native people shared the floor with ceramic frogs, knee-high candles and crazed-looking fairies.

He ran his finger along the book titles, pretending to be interested: ALCHEMY, SPIRITUAL HEALING, SELF HELP, WICCA, DIVINATION.

Crash! Perfect timing.

Phoebe pushed her chair back with a sigh and stomped her way through the shop. She wrenched open the front door and, as soon as she did, Felix slipped behind the counter.

He parted the beaded curtain and stepped into the back room. On the walls were framed diagrams. The bookshelves were heavy with dusty books and glass jars with strange-looking specimens swirling in liquid. In the middle of the room was a large wooden desk where Phoebe kept her Book of Shadows.

Felix crept to the desk. If nothing had changed, it should be in the second drawer on the right. He pulled the drawer open and there it was. He grabbed it, stuck it up his jumper, and sneaked back into the front of the shop. To his relief, Phoebe was still outside, struggling with the collapsed wind chime. Felix hid himself behind a rack of fairy costumes. He placed the ancient-looking Book of Shadows on top of a pile of books and opened it.

Inside were pages of spells, just as he'd remembered. Spells for anything you could think of: *How to fly*; *How to speak in tongues*; *How to stop your rabbit running away.* Felix flipped through them anxiously, and then stopped. There it was: the spiral diagram. He quickly pulled out his Book of Shadows and looked at his drawing. A perfect match. His eyes lit up. He turned the page and began to read. *These symbols represent the marks of* –

'Find what you're looking for?'

Felix slammed the book shut and turned. Phoebe was standing behind him with her arms crossed.

'Ah, no. Still looking.'

Phoebe put her hand out. 'I'll have my sister's book back, thank you.'

Felix hesitated. 'It was on the shelf.'

'Don't lie to me.'

Felix tried another tack. 'I just . . . Please. I really need to check something out.'

Phoebe shook her head. 'No.'

'Please!'

'No.'

Felix reluctantly handed the book over, and Phoebe took it back to the counter. Felix followed her. He couldn't give up. He had to find out what those spirals were.

Phoebe pushed the Book of Shadows under the counter, out of sight. She looked up at Felix. 'I think we're done here.'

Felix took a deep breath. He had to take a chance. 'We . . . I mean . . . I'm being chased by something evil and I need –'

'Don't use the word "evil". It's so judgemental.'

Felix sighed. She wasn't making this easy. But he wasn't going to give up. He knew she was connected to all of this, somehow. 'OK, not evil but bad. Very bad. I think it's some sort of spirit.' He eyed her carefully.

Phoebe rolled her eyes. 'A *bad* spirit? How terrifying for you.' She gestured to the box on the counter full of crystals in bags. 'Why don't you buy a bag of protective amulets?'

Felix looked at the unpromising crystals. 'How much are they?'

'How much have you got?'

Felix shrugged. 'Nothing.'

'Thought as much.'

Felix wondered if he should take some. It would be better than having no protection. 'I could work it off, if you like. Do some shifts here for free.'

Phoebe looked horrified at the thought. 'God, no. Just take a bag. They're past their use-by date anyway.'

Felix picked a bag out of the box. 'Since when did protective amulets have use-by dates?'

'Since they came from Korea.'

The crystals looked like plastic shards. 'Will they work?'

'Depends if you have the gift, Felix.'

Felix looked up sharply. Phoebe was staring at him intently. 'How do you know my name?'

Phoebe held his gaze. 'It's on your book.'

Felix looked down to see his name on his Book of Shadows, which was poking out of his open bag. He grabbed another couple of bags of crystals just to be sure. 'Thank you, *Phoebe*.'

Felix headed for the door.

'Wait. How did you know *my* name?'

Felix smiled and let the door bang behind him. That'd make her wonder.

Felix made his way back down the steps and on to the street. He had a strange feeling. There was a noise coming from above him, a bit like he'd heard in the powerlines a few days ago. He looked up, and realised it wasn't coming from powerlines, but from the trees. It was a humming noise, and it was getting louder. He fingered the crystals in his pocket. Man, he hoped plastic crystals from Korea could protect them.

Ahead of him, standing on the corner, Felix caught sight of Ellen. She was standing by a pole, taping a flyer to it. His heart leapt. 'Hey, Ellen, er – isn't it?'

She looked up. Her eyes were red as if she'd been crying.

'How are you?' asked Felix, not sure what else to say.

'Great,' she answered sarcastically. 'First I nearly get run over by a bus on the way to school, and now Wiki's gone missing.'

Felix read the flyer.

MISSING

ONE JACK RUSSELL

ANSWERS TO THE NAME OF WIKILEAKS

'What happened to him?' asked Felix.

'I don't know. He didn't come home last night.'

'Maybe if you put some Twisties on the back porch?'

'How do you know Wiki likes Twisties?' she asked suspiciously.

'Just a guess.' Felix shrugged. 'I can help you look for him if you like.' Ellen definitely wasn't the same in this world, but maybe if they hung out together, they'd reconnect.

'If he saw you coming, he'd probably run,' said Ellen, walking away.

Felix watched her, stung. Being rejected by your best friend was not a good feeling.

'Watch out!'

Someone suddenly came flying around the corner, nearly knocking Felix to the ground.

Felix regained his balance. 'Oscar?'

Trent and Dylan appeared around the same corner in fast pursuit. They pushed past Felix and sprinted after Oscar, disappearing down a lane.

Felix sped after them. Oscar might not be his brother in this world, but he could still help him.

He found Oscar being cornered by Trent and Dylan at the end of the lane. 'Hey, leave him alone.'

Dylan and Trent ignored him. Dylan held Oscar against the brick wall while Trent went through his schoolbag.

He opened Oscar's lunch box and shoved a jam doughnut

in his mouth. 'Tell your mum we much prefer chocolate doughnuts, Oscar.'

Oscar squirmed under Dylan's hands. Trent pulled a toy spaceship out of Oscar's bag. 'Would you look at that? The weirdo has a little toy.' He placed the spaceship on the ground and hovered his foot over it.

Oscar wriggled desperately. 'Please don't. It's a Valtirian . . .'

'Leave him alone!' said Felix, more forcefully.

Trent turned and gave Felix a long once-over. 'You hear something, Dyl?'

Dylan shook his head and Trent's foot came down on the spaceship.

'That's what you get for being such a freak, *freak!*'

Felix felt the anger rising up in him. It was one thing, people calling him a freak. But his little brother?

He launched himself at Trent. 'Don't call him a freak!'

Trent and Felix hit the ground. Trent grabbed Felix's arm and twisted it with a jerk. Felix brought his knee up hard, right into Trent's groin.

Trent yelped with pain and released his grip on Felix's arm. 'Get him, Dyl!'

Dylan loosened his hold on Oscar as Trent rolled into a ball.

'Run, Oscar! Run!' yelled Felix.

Oscar sprinted away as Dylan advanced menacingly on Felix.

Felix stuck his foot out and Dylan tripped over it, landing with a thud on the cobblestones. Before Dylan could work out what had happened, Felix jumped up and sprinted down the laneway after Oscar.

Oscar was quick. When Felix finally caught up with him, he'd nearly made it all the way home.

'Wait up, Oscar,' Felix called. 'They're not coming after you.'

But Oscar didn't seem to hear him. He turned into their driveway, ran up the path to the front door, bounded up the steps and slammed the door shut just as Felix reached it.

Felix banged on the door, but there was no answer. 'Oscar?'

A muffled voice came from behind the door. 'Go away.'

'Oscar, let me in. Come on.' Felix swiped at a bee that was buzzing insistently around his head.

'Just leave me alone.'

'Come on! I just saved you.'

Oscar opened the door a crack and looked out. 'You didn't save me! You just made them hate me even more. Normally I'm number four on their hit list, but after today I'll be number two. Above Mikey Parker – and he brings a stuffed unicorn to school. So just leave, OK?' He slammed the door shut.

Felix listened to Oscar's footsteps recede. *Great.* That had worked out really well.

A bee dive-bombed his head. Felix flicked it away,

annoyed. What was with these bees?

Another one came at him, and then another.

Now half a dozen bees were circling him. Felix suddenly realised what the strange humming noise he'd heard before was. Bees.

He watched them warily. Right. He had to go into the house, whether Oscar liked it or not.

He looked at the old elm tree in the front yard. There was a branch that led directly to Oscar's bedroom window.

The last thing Felix wanted to do was climb the elm tree. He'd avoided that tree for years. But this time he had no choice. If he stayed out here he was going to get stung to death.

Felix swung his leg up on to the first branch and started to climb. The bees stayed below, circling. As Felix climbed, he tried to shut out the memory but it kept coming: he and Oscar climbing together. Felix reaching the top branch, urging Oscar to climb just a little bit higher, just a little bit more. Then the terrible sound of cracking wood, like a bone snapping in half, and Felix looking down to see Oscar – just a broken body lying on the ground far below.

He pushed the painful memory away. It didn't matter any more, right? Oscar could walk. He didn't have to feel guilty any more. Well, at least not about that.

He reached Oscar's window and looked in. Oscar was on the floor, playing with his spaceships. His bedroom was filled with models of aliens, *Star Trek* paraphernalia and comic books, all overseen by a massive skull that doubled as a light. Man, Oscar sure was a nerd in this world.

Felix banged at the window.

Oscar looked up and shook his head, annoyed.

Felix banged again harder.

Oscar ignored him.

Felix looked down and saw the bees were starting to swarm up the tree. He yelled desperately through the glass: 'If you don't let me in, I'll stay here all night and you'll be known as the guy with the freaky BFF who lives in a tree. Then you'll be number one on Trent and –'

Oscar sighed in defeat and lifted up the window sash.

Felix fell into the room, quickly slamming the window behind him.

'Only girls say BFF,' said Oscar, returning to his game.

Bees swarmed the window and batted against the glass.

'Look, we hardly know each other,' said Oscar. 'And I don't know why you want to be my friend so much. It's weird.'

Felix shrugged. 'Maybe I like you.'

Oscar looked slightly disturbed by that idea.

Felix looked around the room, searching for a more convincing line. 'Or maybe I just really love playing with Trianite motherships and attacking Centauras the Deadly.'

Oscar's eyes lit up. 'You do?'

'Sure,' said Felix. He glanced nervously at the window,

which was now almost covered in bees.

'Woah,' said Oscar. 'You must have disturbed their hive.'

Felix felt a tug of fear. This had to be another attack. He pulled the Korean crystals from his pocket and held them out towards the window. 'Behold the repelling power of the crystals.'

The bees seemed only to gather in strength.

Oscar gave him a strange look. 'What are you doing?'

Felix pocketed the crystals. What a load of junk. *Thanks for nothing, Phoebe.*

He had to get back to the shop and convince her to show him her Book of Shadows. It was their only chance. He needed real magic, not stupid crystals.

But he couldn't just leave Oscar here. What if the bees got inside?

'Listen, we have to get out of here and get help. But we can't go out the front, so we'll have to take the secret escape route.'

Oscar looked at him suspiciously. 'How do you know about the secret escape route?'

Damn, he had to be more careful. In his world, Felix and Oscar had made up a secret escape route through the laundry window and out the back of the house. In this world, Oscar must have done the same thing.

'Ah, telepathy,' said Felix, not sure how else to answer.

To his surprise, Oscar smiled. 'Woah, cool! Are you, like,

an alien with intergalactic powers?'

Felix figured that was about as good an explanation as any he could come up with. 'Yeah, something like that. Come on.'

Felix and Oscar sprinted downstairs. 'Holy crap!' said Felix, seeing that the bees, now in their thousands, had covered the lounge room window with their angry, vibrating bodies.

The boys raced into the kitchen. Oscar flung open the cupboard under the sink and grabbed two cans of insect spray. He gave one to Felix.

They ran into the laundry and jumped up on the washing trough beneath the laundry window. The bees hadn't reached the laundry yet, but their buzzing was deafening.

Felix and Oscar held their cans poised, fingers on the nozzles.

'Are you ready?' said Felix.

Oscar grinned. 'You're actually kind of cool – for an alien.'

Despite the possibility of death by a thousand beestings, Felix smiled back. 'One, two, three!' He flung open the window. '*Go!*'

felix: earth water air fire

Felix and Oscar burst through the door of Arcane Lane. Felix slammed the glass door behind them as Oscar sprayed the life out of the lone bee that had slipped in with them.

Phoebe glanced up from the counter. 'Hey, get that stuff out of here. It's full of fluorocarbons.'

'Then give me something that isn't totally useless,' said Felix, dumping the Korean crystals on to the counter.

Phoebe picked up the crystals and dropped them in the bin behind the counter. 'Could have told you that.'

Felix leant in. 'I need to see your Book of Shadows.'

'Sorry, it's adults only.'

'I need to see it. Please.'

Phoebe looked up, exasperated. 'Listen, kid, I can't –'

Felix had walked back to the front door and, in one swift movement, pulled up the venetian blinds.

Phoebe's eyes widened. Swarming against the door was a wall of bees so dense that the street was no longer visible.

'I'm guessing you haven't just disturbed their hive?'

Felix shook his head.

Phoebe dislodged herself from her chair and retrieved the Book of Shadows from under the counter. 'All right. Follow me.'

Felix and Oscar followed Phoebe into her back room. Oscar looked around in wonder as Phoebe placed the book reverently on the desk.

She was about to open it when she stopped. She gave Oscar a long, hard look. 'Who are you, exactly?'

'He's my . . .' Felix began.

'Friend,' Oscar finished the sentence for him.

Felix smiled. Friend would do, for now.

Phoebe turned back to the book. 'I wouldn't be smiling if I were you. Not if I was being chased by an army of bees.'

'It's not just the bees . . . that's the thing.' The words tumbled out of Felix. It was a relief to be able to tell someone. 'First there was this weird tornado, and last night there was this storm that left all these spiral patterns, and a hooded figure –'

Phoebe looked up sharply. 'A hooded figure? Where were you?'

Felix hesitated. Had he said too much? 'In the forest.'

'Did you see its face?' asked Phoebe. Her eyes seemed to be radiating an odd light.

Felix suddenly had a very strong feeling that maybe he shouldn't tell Phoebe everything that had happened in the past few days. He had no idea whether or not he could trust her, and revealing too much could be a big mistake. He quickly backtracked. 'No. In fact, it may not have even been a figure. The storm was really wild and everything was moving in the wind. It could have just been a tree.'

Phoebe looked at him suspiciously. 'A tree?'

'Sure.'

'There wasn't a storm last night,' said Oscar, puzzled.

'Still as a stone in Bremin last night, Felix.' Phoebe's eyes bored into him.

He looked warily at them both. 'Are you sure?'

'Which means,' said Phoebe, returning to the Book of Shadows, 'that something is targeting you in particular.' She found the page she wanted. 'Here we are. Elemental attacks.'

Felix craned his neck to see. 'What are they?'

'Earth, fire, air, water. Sound familiar?'

'No. Not really,' Felix said evasively.

'Well, they're the building blocks of the natural world. If something has disturbed them, any of the natural elements can rise up in defence.' She looked at him piercingly. 'Have you disturbed something you shouldn't have, Felix?'

'No. Of course not.' Felix looked away. Of course he had. He'd disturbed everything.

'He *is* an alien. Does that count?' offered Oscar cheerfully.

Phoebe ignored Oscar and opened a drawer. She pulled out an old battered box and placed it in front of her. 'Most

127

of the people who come in here are after scented candles and dolphin statues. No one knows anything about real magic.' She stroked the box thoughtfully. 'But if you're the victim of elemental attacks, then it stands to reason you are a threat, and to be a threat you must have magical power. Am I right?'

Felix was starting to regret coming here for help. Too many questions he couldn't answer. He was about to make his excuses and leave when he remembered what was waiting for him out the front. He didn't actually have a choice.

He shrugged. 'Maybe. I don't really know.'

Phoebe opened the clasp of the box. 'OK, then. Let's find out.' Inside the box was a round, roughly hewn talisman on a string. It was divided equally into four parts. Each part was engraved with indecipherable lettering. Phoebe scooped it out and placed it carefully on the desk. Then she lit a candle.

'This talisman belonged to my sister, Alice. It can protect against elemental attacks, but first it needs to be activated by someone with special powers.' Her black eyes drilled into Felix as she passed him the Book of Shadows, open at a spell. 'Alice was a very powerful witch. This was her book.' She nodded at the open page. 'Read it.'

Felix looked at the spell.

Phoebe filled a small bowl with water and another with dirt. She placed them on the desk as Felix began to read.

'Divinity of the elements, I summon thee. Earth . . .'

Phoebe took his hand and placed it in the bowl of dirt.

'Water . . .'

Phoebe put his hand in the water bowl.

'Air . . .' Felix blew onto the talisman.

'Fire . . .' Felix took the candle and held the flame to the talisman.

> '*Within this stone I invoke ye place,*
> *Your greatest strength, your kindest grace.*
> *And while this stone remains at hand*
> *Thou shall be safe throughout this land.*
> *Earth. Water. Air. Fire. I invoke thee.*'

Phoebe picked up the talisman and placed it around Felix's neck. 'OK, let's show those bees who's boss.'

Felix stood nervously at the front door. There were even more bees than before, if that were possible. He touched the talisman and then, taking a deep breath, flung the door open.

The bees swarmed at him – mini kamikazes intent on their mission of ultimate destruction. Felix fell back inside, yelling in pain.

Phoebe slammed the door shut. She picked up the insect spray and blasted the half-dozen bees that had got inside. She put the can down and looked at Felix. 'Well, that was disappointing.'

Felix felt the searing pain of the bee stings. 'You're telling me.'

Phoebe picked up some calendula ointment off a shelf and threw it at him. 'Try this.'

Felix sat up. He smeared the ointment on the stings. It helped a bit, but his skin was throbbing all over.

'Give me the talisman back.' Phoebe put out her hand.

Felix held it to his chest. He wasn't going to give it over that easily. It could be his only hope. 'We've only tried it once.'

'What? You want another go? Be my guest.'

Felix looked at the door. The bees seemed to be growing in size as well as in number. Maybe not.

He turned to Phoebe. 'Maybe it wasn't activated properly.'

'Well, it can only be activated by someone with magical powers, which clearly you don't have, so . . .' she reached out her hand again. 'Give it.'

Felix felt suddenly strangely possessive. He didn't want to give Phoebe the talisman. It felt like it belonged to him. He wasn't going to give it up without a fight.

He thought hard. Earth, fire, air and water were the elements needed to activate it. The same elements *he'd* needed. And Phoebe had said elemental attacks occurred if something in nature had been disturbed.

Felix looked up suddenly. 'What if the elements needed to activate the talisman come from another world?'

Oscar looked at Phoebe, his theory confirmed. 'I told you he was an alien.'

Phoebe looked confused. 'Not sure I'm following the logic.'

'To protect ourselves from the elements of this world, we need elements from our own world,' Felix continued excitedly.

Phoebe and Oscar exchanged glances. 'What?'

'Come on. We have to find the others.'

'What others?' said Oscar.

'And how are you planning on getting out of here?' said Phoebe.

Felix stopped. Good point. There was absolutely no way of getting past those bees.

'I want the talisman back, Felix,' Phoebe insisted.

Felix thought fast. 'Give me one more chance to activate it and if it doesn't work, I'll give it back to you. I promise.'

'And if it *does* work? asked Phoebe.

Felix hesitated. What did she want, exactly?

Phoebe moved towards him. 'I'll help you to get out of here on the condition that if it *does* work, you'll do something very important for me in return.'

What choice did he have? He had to get out of there and find the others. 'Sure,' Felix agreed. 'Anything.'

Phoebe smiled. 'OK, then. Follow me. My van's in the garage out the back.'

———

Phoebe's Kombi van pulled up outside the shack and Felix and Oscar jumped out. They seemed to have outrun the bees, for the moment at least.

'Thanks, Phoebe,' called Felix.

Phoebe put her head out the window. 'What? That's it?'

Explaining Oscar to the others would be hard enough, let alone explaining why he was hanging out with the creepy woman from the magic shop.

'For the activation to work I need there to be minimal interference, that's all. I'll let you know what happens.'

Phoebe narrowed her eyes. 'You remember our pact, OK? I'll be waiting.'

Felix and Oscar walked briskly towards the shack.

'So, don't mention magic to them, OK?' Felix said. 'They don't understand.'

'Are they aliens like you?' asked Oscar.

'Sure they are. From the planet Cretin.'

'So we have to find the elements, right?'

'Yep. I'll tell you what to –'

Felix heard a rising rumble, then saw a swarming cloud of black appear above the rise. 'Run!'

They ran towards the shack and, once inside, Felix slammed the door firmly behind them. Jake, Andy and Sam looked up.

'What's he doing here?' asked Jake, staring at Oscar.

'Doesn't matter right now.' Felix threw Sam and Jake the two cans of insect spray. 'Bees,' he said, pointing towards the roof, which was now vibrating with the sound of thousands of bees swarming. 'Just keep the bees away.'

The bees were finding every possible crevice in the roof and walls to get inside. Sam and Jake let fly with the cans while Andy desperately tried to plug up the holes in the walls.

'What now?' Oscar whispered to Felix.

'OK. To activate this protective talisman, I think I need to put it in contact with four elements from our world.' He looked around. 'Jake! There's a hole over here,' Felix yelled. 'We need to plug it. Throw us your shoe.'

Jake ripped off his shoe and pegged it at Felix.

Felix gouged at the dirt in the sole. He smeared it on the talisman. 'Jake. Practical, stubborn, brutish. Earth.'

Oscar's eyes lit up. 'So, these guys are the elements?'

'If they're not, we're done for,' replied Felix.

A swarm of bees burst in through a rusty patch in the wall. Sam sprayed at them madly. Andy coughed.

'Andy. Fluid thinker, kind of wet. Water.'

Felix handed Oscar a hankie to give to Andy. 'Here.'

Andy grabbed it and blew his nose hard, then handed the snotty hankie back to Felix, who rubbed it on to the talisman.

'Gross,' said Oscar, screwing up his nose.

'That leaves selfish, superficial, lives in the clouds, Sam. Air. We just have to catch his breath.'

The bees continued their assault, thudding hard against the outside walls.

'This is it. The championship quarter. Prepare for war!' yelled Jake. He screwed up his nose. 'Who let rip?'

'I hope that's not the last thing I ever smell,' groaned Andy.

'Sorry, guys. Pre-comp nerves,' apologised Sam.

Felix nudged Oscar. 'Go.'

Oscar waved the talisman behind Sam, collecting the 'air'.

As the others continued to fight, Felix slipped under some planks that were doubling as a makeshift bed.

In near darkness, Felix flicked on his lighter. He drew a circle in the dust and placed the talisman in the centre. *'Divinity of the elements, I summon thee.'* He lit the talisman.

'Earth, water, air, fire.
Within this stone I invoke ye place,
Your greatest strength, your kindest grace.
And while this stone remains at hand
Thou shall be safe throughout this land.'

The talisman released a flash of light and then slowly started to glow. A gentle golden glow that gradually grew stronger as the sounds of the bees slowly faded to silence.

Felix stared at it. It had worked! He couldn't believe it. He had activated the talisman. He may not have worked out how to get home, but he had worked out how to protect them until he could.

'D-minus for participation, freak,' said Jake as he pulled the planks off Felix.

The others all stood looking down at him.

'You coming out to collect your chicken award?' said Sam.

Felix slipped the talisman into his sleeve. He wasn't ready to reveal it to them yet. Maybe when they stopped acting like total jerks.

'It was Felix who saved you,' Oscar interjected. 'He did a magic spell.'

'Oh really, Oscar?' said Jake. 'I think you'll find that he hid under the bed.'

Oscar turned to Felix. 'Tell them, Felix.'

'That's cool. They seemed to have it under control so I left them to it.'

Oscar looked at him in disbelief. 'But . . .'

Jake, Sam and Andy walked off in disgust.

Oscar crouched down next to Felix. 'Why didn't you –'

'What did I tell you? Cretins.'

Oscar smiled. 'That was totally awesome! The spell worked.'

'Thanks. You were a big help.'

'I reckon we make a pretty good team.'

'Yeah, we do.'

Oscar shuffled his feet. 'Maybe you should come around more often. You know, if you're not too busy with your alien business and fighting off insect attacks.'

Felix smiled. Stuff the others. At least his brother was starting to like him. 'That'd be awesome.'

jake: father go figure

Jake sat by the river throwing stones into the water.

The others were driving him nuts. Andy and his insane theories – first there was amnesia, then wormholes, and now he was banging on about string theory, whatever that was. Felix hadn't washed for three days and spent all day staring at his book, reciting weird poems. Like that was going to get them home. And as for Sam – sure, he was dealing with heavy stuff, but he still managed to snore ten hours a night, preventing anyone else from getting a decent sleep.

Jake threw another rock and watched the water ripple out into bigger and bigger circles. But even worse than all that was the fact that he was stuck here with no idea what was going on, while his parents were living perfect lives without him.

His dad was no longer the guy at the local pub yelling insults at the TV. No, he was now the one telling that guy to go home. And his mum wasn't haggling with real-estate agents about late rent anymore. She was the one renting out properties and owning the best house in the street. Man, their lives were so much better without him. So where did he fit in?

He threw another stone. His parents were happy, right? He should just accept that, but man it was hard. He wanted to be part of it.

He wanted his new cop dad to shoot hoops with him and take him for rides in his car. He wanted to cook dinner with his mum and sit together watching crime dramas on TV, seeing who could pick the killer first. That's what he wanted. Not being stuck in the bush with these three –

'Hey, Jake.' It was Felix. 'Come on. It's hard-rubbish day in town.'

'So?'

'So we can get stuff. Useful stuff. For the shack.'

Jake threw another stone. Great. Now they were doing home improvements. *Yippee.*

———

Jake trailed the others as they scoured the back streets of Bremin. Andy had scored a shopping trolley and was loading it with useless junk. He had collected an old stereo complete with speakers, a microwave, and now he was trying to fit in a chicken coop. Jake sighed and kicked at some leaves. Seriously, what was the point?

'Cops. Get down,' Felix called.

Jake ducked down behind an old washing machine. A cop

car cruised slowly down the street. Jake watched it pass by. In the driver's seat, his dad surveyed the street with an eagle eye. Jake watched him pass.

Sam turned to him. 'Dude, was that your dad?'

Jake looked away. 'Yeah.'

Felix and Andy stared at him. 'Your dad's a cop?'

Jake took a deep breath. 'Yeah. And my mum's married to Bates and runs her own real-estate agency.' It was almost a relief to say it out loud. There was silence.

'Man, that seriously sucks,' said Sam.

Jake looked sideways at him. Sam seemed almost relieved that someone else's life was as screwed up as his.

'Totally mind-blowing, but it absolutely fits my theory,' said Andy, taking it in.

'Which is?' said Felix cynically.

'That we're in a parallel universe and our old world still exists. We just have to get back to it.'

'So,' said Sam slowly, 'our home still exists?'

'Of course. That's why we need to find the wormhole. So we can find our way back.'

'And how are we supposed to do that?' asked Jake.

'I'm working on it,' said Andy. He turned to Jake. 'It's extraordinary, isn't it, that in one universe, your mum's a struggling single mother and your dad's the world's biggest loser, and in another, your mum's a married businesswoman and your dad's an officer of the law.'

Jake pulled himself up to his full height, not caring who saw. 'So, what are you saying?'

'Nothing,' said Andy evasively. 'It's an observation, that's all.'

'An observation that their lives are so much better without me being born.'

'I didn't say that.'

'You didn't have to.'

'Come on,' Felix called out. 'All clear.'

'Thanks for that, nerd.'

Andy furiously tried to backpedal. 'I didn't mean it like that. Change isn't necessarily better. Cops have notorious cholesterol and hypertension issues, and in a survey I once read, real-estate agents ranked below telemarketers in trust-worthiness.'

Jake walked away from the others. He didn't want to hear it. He knew it was true. His parents' lives *were* better without him. Even Andy couldn't argue his way out of that one.

Jake stopped. A black crow was standing on the footpath, eyeing him menacingly.

'Shoo!' Jake waved a hand at it, but it refused to budge.

'Hey, Jake,' Felix called. 'Can you help me with this?'

Jake turned reluctantly back to the others.

The crow hopped along beside him. Jake kicked out at it, but it refused to leave his side. It flew up on to an old gas stove and cawed at him.

'What's with the bird?' Felix moved towards it and, almost

immediately, the bird flew up into a nearby tree.

Jake shrugged. 'Kept following me.'

'Come and help me move this bed base,' said Felix.

But Jake was staring at the old stove, the memory of an access visit with his dad flooding back to him. His dad had stood in front of a stove just like this, wearing nothing but his jocks, waving a can of baked beans at Jake.

'How are you going to cook when your gas has been cut off *again*?' Jake had asked.

But that hadn't stopped his dad, had it? He'd found a way. Jake smiled. Maybe. Just maybe . . .

'Hey, Felix. Over here,' he called.

The boys pushed the overflowing trolley into the shack. Sam and Jake heaved the old stove out and placed it by the wall.

Sam shook his head. 'Dude, I hate to tell you this, but you can't cook without . . .'

Jake wasn't listening. He made his way back outside. He'd seen it when they'd first come here. Must have been left behind when whoever used the shack had barbecues.

And there it was – dusty and rusted, but a gas bottle, nevertheless.

Jake heaved it back inside. It must have some gas in it, surely. His dad had given him a long and involved lesson in how to beat the system. Jake hadn't paid much attention at the time but he remembered the basics. Check the threads match. Always use a regulator when you connect the hose. He picked up the hose and fitted it to the back of the stove. The threads matched.

'Hey, Felix. Chuck us your lighter.'

Without looking up, Felix threw his lighter over.

Sam turned the knob and Jake flicked the lighter on.

Whoosh. The jet caught.

Jake, Sam and Andy whooped with joy. Sam clapped Jake on the back. 'You're a legend, man!'

Jake looked over at Felix, who was sitting on his sleeping bag with his book open, playing with a weird-looking necklace. 'Hey, Felix! Check it out.'

Felix barely looked up. 'Yeah, cool.'

'Don't wet your pants with excitement, will you?' Jake turned back to the others. 'Who's up for a home-cooked meal? I do a mean BLT.'

'We've got no food,' said Sam.

'So we go shopping!'

'But we've got no money,' said Andy.

'So?' Jake felt bold all of a sudden. Maybe he should make the most of being in an alternate world with no parents. 'Who's coming?'

Sam and Andy looked at each other. 'If it involves food, sure,' said Sam.

They all turned to Felix, who had his eyes shut and appeared to be chanting.

'Forget him,' said Jake.

———

As they walked into town, a small figure in a Superman outfit rode his BMX into their path and stopped.

'Is one of you called Andy?' asked Telly. Sam and Jake pointed to Andy. 'My mission was to deliver this.' He handed Andy a pink note folded into triangles.

Andy looked at it suspiciously. He put it to his nose and sniffed. 'What is that?'

'Lavender,' said Telly, looking warily at Jake.

'Chillax, would you? I've got no reason to steal your bike,' said Jake crossly. To be honest he kind of wished he did. Riding all over Bremin with false hope was a hell of a lot better than having no hope.

Andy unfolded the note. 'U plus M to the power of E equals heart symbol,' he read. 'What is M to the power of E?'

'It's *you* plus *me* equals *love*,' said Telly. 'But not as in *me*,' he added quickly.

'Who's it from?'

'That's a secret,' said Telly. He got back on his bike and rode away.

Andy turned to Jake, confused. 'I've never been admired before. Except by my parents, of course. But that's compulsory.'

'Don't sweat it, man. You're lucky someone in this universe actually likes you,' said Jake bitterly.

The boys walked down the main street of Bremin and wandered into the town's Mini Mart, where they saw Felix's dad eyeing them suspiciously.

'Not sure this is a good idea,' Sam whispered to Jake.

'Fine, then. You stay out the front and keep watch. Start singing if you need to warn us.'

'Dude, I can't sing.'

'Doesn't matter. Just go. Andy and I will do the dirty work.'

Andy looked horrified. 'Jake, I can't.'

'Aisle two. Quick, we're being watched.' Jake pushed Andy down one aisle and wandered casually down another towards the refrigerated section.

Eggs, bacon, bread. That should do it.

He picked up a carton of eggs and considered how to fit them down his pants. He could of course take them out and put them individually in his pockets but they'd probably break. He put them back. Shoplifting wasn't as easy as it looked. He moved down further and picked up a packet of bacon. OK, this was possible. He shoved the bacon down his pants.

'Ma-ry had a li-ttle lamb . . .'

Jake heard Sam singing tunelesly. He quickly pulled his jumper down and turned into the next aisle. Andy was

143

standing with his hands full of free microwave popcorn samples.

'We've got a stove, not a microwave,' Jake hissed.

'Its fleece was white as snow . . .'

'That's Sam. Come on, we've got to get out of here.'

They ducked into an aisle where they had a clear view to the front of the store. There, entering through the sliding doors, was Jake's dad. He quickly spoke to Felix's dad, who gestured towards the boys.

'And eve-rywhere that Mary went . . .' Sam's singing was more a screech than a song.

'OK,' Jake turned to Andy. 'Let's go when I say run. Ready?' Andy nodded. *'Run!'*

Jake and Andy sprinted to the front of the shop. They burst out of the doors, collected Sam, and turned left down the main street.

'Hey, get back here!' Jake's dad yelled after them.

'Don't worry. Dad's a slob. He'll never catch us,' said Jake breathlessly as they ran.

He glanced over his shoulder. Dammit. Cop Dad was fit. In fact, he was gaining on them.

'This way,' yelled Jake, veering off down an alleyway.

Sam and Andy followed him. They careered down the alleyway but ran into a dead end.

Jake turned to see his dad powering towards them.

When he got within fifty metres, he slowed down.

'Right, boys. I think we need to have a little chat, don't you?'

'I'll distract him,' Jake whispered. 'You two make a run for it.'

His dad looked them up and down. 'A gang of three shoplifters, eh? There was also a gang of boys that broke into the school last weekend. Thanks to the security cameras, we got them on tape. Know anything about that?' He moved towards them.

Jake watched him. It was kind of incredible that even his walk was different. His old dad always wore flip-flops and kind of shuffled. Cop Dad actually lifted his feet.

'I'm talking to you, kid.'

Jake kicked a bin, hard, right into his dad's path, knocking him off balance. '*Run!*' he yelled.

Taking their cue, Sam and Andy charged back up the alley, dodging Jake's dad and sprinting away.

Jake stood still. Good. Andy and Sam were safe. But what about him?

His dad stepped towards him. The bin lay between them. Jake hesitated. His instinct was to run away but something was fighting it. Maybe if he let his dad catch him, he could find out how it was possible that one person could have changed so much.

His dad quickly grabbed his arm. 'Right, you. What's your name?'

'Jake.'

'Jake who?'

Jake looked at the nametag on his dad's uniform: SNR SGT GARY RILES.

What would he say if he told him the truth?

'Just Jake.'

'Well, Just Jake, you're coming with me.'

Plop!

Jake smiled nervously as the packet of bacon he'd shoved down his pants fell on to the cobblestones.

At the police station, Jake's dad gestured to a chair for Jake to sit in and took a seat at his desk, opposite.

Jake surveyed Senior Sergeant Gary Riles's desk curiously.

'Rightio. Address?'

Jake picked up a Bremin Bandicoots mug. 'You like the Bandicoots?'

'No, mate. I'm just their number-one ticket-holder. Phone number?'

Jake shook his head.

'Parents' names?'

Jake shook his head again.

His dad put down his pen. 'I can sit here all day if I need to. So, why don't you just cut to the chase and tell me who your parents are? They're probably worried sick.'

Jake wanted to laugh, but thought better of it. 'You think so?'

'Strange as it may sound to you, parents do actually care for their kids, despite the trouble they cause.'

Yeah? thought Jake. *Even the ones they never knew they had?*

'So, how's this for a deal?' His dad continued. 'You tell me who your parents are and we'll drop the shoplifting charges.'

For an instant, Jake thought about telling his dad everything: that he was the son he and Sarah had fifteen years ago. That in another world, Gary Riles was an unemployed loser who never remembered to pick him up and take him to footy training. That he couldn't even cook baked beans without burning the pan. That he'd started six college courses and never finished any of them.

'That's a fair deal, kid.'

Jake hesitated. 'I don't know who they are anymore.' Which was actually pretty much the truth.

His dad let out a sigh. 'Well, unless you can "remember" who they are, I can't release you so . . .'

Jake smiled. 'That's fine. I'll hang with you.'

His dad was taken aback. 'Er, Roberts,' he called out.

A young constable appeared.

'Get this kid's mugshot taken and run it through missing persons.' He clicked at something on his computer.

'What are you working on?' asked Jake.

'What I'm working on is finding four vandals who broke into the school gym last Sunday and trashed it,' he said sternly.

He flipped the screen around to show Jake.

Jake's jaw dropped. There they all were – running around the gym, throwing balls and flinging rolls of toilet paper around like maniacs. He wasn't sure whether it was good or bad news but one thing was clear: they definitely existed.

'Look familiar?'

Jake shook his head. Luckily the footage was from such a wide angle that it was impossible to recognise faces. But his dad clearly knew it was them. So now what? Would they be arrested and charged? What would the police do with them if they couldn't find their parents?

His dad zoomed in on a figure sitting in the cleaning trolley. 'Remind you of anybody?'

Jake shook his head again but the resemblance to Andy was pretty obvious.

His dad turned the screen back to face him. 'I'm going to give you a bit of advice, kid. If you don't tell me the truth, there will be dire consequences.'

Jake laughed out loud. Could anything be more dire than his current situation?

'You think this is funny? Well, it's not going to be funny in ten years when you're a no-hoper with no money, no job and no future.'

What a perfect description of Dad, thought Jake. 'Yeah, Mum used to say the same thing about my dad.'

'And how did he end up?'

Jake was wondering how to answer that when Roberts reappeared.

'Sarge, Sarah Bates just called in. Apparently her dog, Pippin, has been missing since last night.'

Jake watched his dad carefully. He wondered if his dad had even dated his mum in this world and, if he had, did he still have feelings for her?

'Tell her not to worry. I'll put out an alert.'

Jake thought he saw him soften, but he could have been imagining it.

Roberts produced a camera and got Jake to stand against a blank wall. He took a number of shots from different angles. *Just like in the movies,* Jake thought. Only if this was a movie, he would escape and be reunited with his family, and that didn't look like happening any time soon.

Jake watched as Roberts and his dad had a muttered conversation. Jake felt pretty sure the missing person's search was going to come up zero. They'd have to let him go, right? It's not like he could hang around the station indefinitely.

Or maybe he could? Maybe Senior Sergeant Gary Riles would offer to look after him until his parents could be found. Maybe Jake would move in with him. Then he could get his mum to see how great his dad was now, and she'd ditch Bates and they'd all be together.

He shook his head. Dream on.

When his mugshots had been taken, Jake was escorted back to sit in Senior Sergeant Gary Riles's office.

Jake picked up a photo of his dad wearing a Bremin Bandicoots jumper and a beanie. He had his arms around a German Shepherd.

'That's Zeus. Comes to every game.'

Jake put the photo down. 'So, you don't have kids?'

'No, mate. Married to the force as they say. All I can do to look after a dog.' He looked away, seeming kind of sad. 'Anyway, don't know about you, kid, but I'm starving. Got some baked beans out back if you'd like some?'

Jake's face broke into a smile. His old dad was still in there somewhere. He knew it. 'Sure, Da – er, Sergeant.'

'Coming right up.' He stood up and, as he did, a woman opened the door to the station. She made a beeline towards him.

'Senior Sergeant Riles?' She put her hand out like a dagger. 'Thanks for the call. Janet Hawker from Child Protection Sevices. Come to collect the boy.'

Jake felt the ground opening up beneath him.

He'd been betrayed by his own dad.

felix: counting crows

Felix sat alone in the shack. He'd barely even registered the others leaving. Something to do with food. Strange how he wasn't hungry. His stomach felt permanently jittery. He imagined if he did eat something it would probably just bounce around inside him with all his other strange feelings.

He looked at the talisman lying in his hand. It looked so ordinary – just a dull, muddy, stony brown. Nothing magical about it. But when it glowed, that was something else. Knowing how powerful it was kind of terrified and excited him at the same time. The bees had disappeared instantly, so whatever came at them next wouldn't stand a chance. At least, he hoped.

Felix put the talisman carefully around his neck. He knew he should probably tell the others about it, but Andy would diss it as unscientific, and Jake and Sam were taking everything pretty hard – he couldn't imagine how they'd react to a magical talisman. He would tell them soon. But first, he had other things to work out. It was all very well, being able to protect them from the attacks – but he still didn't know *why* they were being attacked.

He opened his Book of Shadows and looked at the drawings he'd made of the spirals. The bees had distracted him from finding out what they meant. He needed to see Phoebe's sister's Book of Shadows again. He was pretty sure those patterns held a clue as to who or what was after them. If he could work that out, then maybe he could work out how to get them all home.

Home. It was a nice word – safe and warm. Only problem was when Felix thought about home, he thought about his parents' constant anxiety, Oscar's life of doctor and physio appointments, and how every day he had to live with his guilt. Guilt for encouraging Oscar to climb just that little bit further.

He'd known Oscar hadn't wanted to. He'd known Oscar was scared, but he'd still pushed him. Why? To prove he was braver? To make Oscar admire him?

Truth was, he didn't know why he'd done it. Maybe he'd just wanted to share the awesome view from the top of the elm tree. The feeling of being above everyone, away from parents and school and judgement and then –

Crack.

That sound again. The awful splintering sound that had haunted Felix for two years and three months.

That's what *home* meant to him. Having to relive that sound every single day – no, every single hour of every single day. He closed his book and paced around the shack. Living here with no food or water was nothing compared to living with that sound.

Oscar could walk, so Felix should be happy, right? But he wasn't happy. And it wasn't because any minute there might be an elemental attack. It was because he could see that Sam, Jake and Andy were miserable. They wanted to go home.

Felix had never intended this to happen. The spell was just supposed to unmake Oscar's accident, not unmake all of them. But that's what had happened. And now it was his responsibility to get them home.

Not that he knew how, yet.

But getting them home would mean he would have to go home too and that was something he wasn't sure he –

Creak.

Felix looked up. The door opened as if by magic, and a silhouetted figure stood in the doorway.

'Thought we had a deal.' The figure moved into the room. Phoebe. Damn.

'I was just on my way to see you,' Felix said weakly.

'Save me the BS. Did it work?'

Felix felt the talisman under his shirt. If he told her it worked she'd probably want it back. If he told her it didn't, she'd take it back anyway. What to say?

'I'm not sure.'

'What do you mean you're not sure? You survived the attack of the killer bees, didn't you?'

'They didn't come back. So I haven't had a chance to test it.'

It was a bad lie and Phoebe knew it. She narrowed her eyes. 'Really.'

Behind Phoebe, a crow hopped into the shack. It was just like the one Felix had seen that morning with Jake. It flicked its beady eyes around the room as if looking for something.

Behind it, another crow appeared.

Without wanting to appear obvious, Felix moved towards them. Both crows stood their ground. A third one appeared in the doorway.

When Felix had approached the crow that morning, it had flown away immediately. But these ones weren't fazed by him at all.

Phoebe watched him curiously. 'What are you doing?'

Felix pushed the crows outside with his foot and slammed the door. 'Nothing. You should just close the door behind you, that's all.'

He heard the scraping sound of a dozen or more claws landing on the roof.

'Another elemental attack, perhaps?' Phoebe stared at him intently.

Felix wasn't sure exactly why he didn't trust Phoebe

enough to tell her the truth. She'd trusted him with the talisman, hadn't she? If he told her he'd activated it, she'd be happy. All he had to do was one small favour for her in return. How hard could that be?

Felix hesitated. What if she just wanted the talisman activated for her own purposes and had no intention of letting him keep it? And if they didn't have it to protect them –

Phoebe held her hand out. 'Give it to me, Felix.'

The sound of cawing outside grew louder. Phoebe moved closer to Felix. 'I said give it to –'

The door flung open and Sam and Andy burst into the shack, slamming the door behind them. 'A bunch of crows chased us from town.' They collapsed on the floor, breathless.

Felix ran to the window and looked out. Crows were gathering around the shack, perching on every tree, every log. The ground was a moving mass of black feathers. Conscious of Phoebe's eyes on him, he quickly glanced down at the talisman. Not glowing. If this was another attack, why wasn't it protecting them? He started to mutter the spell: *Divinity of the elements, I summon thee.*'

Andy looked at him in disbelief. 'Do you really think a poem is the right response?'

'*Earth, water, air, fire.*' Felix stopped suddenly. That was it! The protective talisman didn't just need all four elements to be activated. It needed all four elements to *work*. It was just like the spell he'd cast in the forest. 'Where's Jake?'

'He got arrested,' said Sam.

'What?'

'By his dad,' said Andy.

'For shoplifting,' added Sam.

Felix looked at the dull talisman. Without Jake they'd have no hope against an attack. 'We have to get him back!'

'Yeah, well, good luck with that,' said Sam. 'His dad knows all about the gym break-in. He's got us on tape, so if any of us go near the station, we'll be arrested.'

Felix looked out the window at the steadily increasing number of crows. 'I don't know about you, but I'd rather be locked up than clawed to death by crows. And without Jake, that's pretty much our only option.'

Phoebe moved out of the shadows. 'Maybe I can help?'

Andy yelped in surprise.

'Did you just scream like a girl?' asked Sam.

'No.'

Sam turned to Phoebe. 'Who are you?'

'Never you mind. I can get you to the police station. I'll tell them I'm Jake's guardian. As long as they don't have evidence to hold him, they'll have to let him go.'

'Why would you help us?' Sam asked.

'Let's just say I'm waiting to collect on my investment,' answered Phoebe, looking pointedly at Felix.

'If they've got us on the security tape, they're not going to let us go,' said Sam.

'I can fix that,' offered Andy. 'It just needs degaussing.'

Everyone turned to him.

'De-magnetising,' Andy explained. 'You just need a magnet of equal strength to overwrite the magnetic code.'

'And where are we going to get a magnet from, doofus?' asked Sam.

Andy looked around the room at all the junk they'd collected from hard rubbish. 'I know where we'll find one. Who feels like smashing open some speakers?'

Andy, Felix, Sam and Phoebe stood behind the door of the shack. The crows were flapping against the windows like black curtains in the wind.

Andy handed out his packets of popcorn samples. 'So, we fling the kernels as hard as we can and run for the Kombi. OK?'

'OK.' Felix put his hand on the latch. 'One, two, three.'

The popcorn barely distracted the cawing birds. Andy, Felix, Sam and Phoebe raced across the grass to the Kombi pursued by a furious black cloud of claws and feathers. The boys leapt into the back, slamming the door.

Phoebe adjusted her hair in the rear-view mirror. 'I'm sensing some *déjà vu*. Bees, birds, what will it be next?' She caught Felix's eye in the mirror.

A crow landed on the windscreen and opened its beak as

wide as a screaming fan at a football match. Phoebe started the engine. 'OK, OK, we're leaving. Keep your pants on.'

'Why did you have to get her involved?' Sam whispered to Felix. 'She totally creeps me out.'

Felix sighed. 'No choice.' He looked out the window. It was true – Phoebe was backing him into a corner. She wanted that talisman working and was using Felix to do it. He wasn't sure he could trust her, but he'd just have to play along, at least until they got Jake back.

The Kombi made its way quickly through the bush and bumped on to the Bremin backstreets. Phoebe drove erratically and the boys were thrown around in the back like fish flailing in a bucket.

Phoebe screeched the Kombi to a halt outside the police station. The boys spotted Jake's dad talking to a severe-looking woman who was leading Jake towards her Prius.

Phoebe jumped out. 'I thought I told you to unstack the dishwasher,' she yelled.

Jake turned, surprised. The boys slid open the Kombi door and tumbled out.

Felix looked down at the talisman. Yes. His hunch was right. With the four of them together, the talisman began to glow – that warm, orange, comforting glow meant everything was going to be all right. He quickly hid it under his shirt.

Jake's dad moved towards Phoebe. 'What do you want, Phoebe?'

'Just here to collect my nephew.'

Jake's dad snorted. 'Really?'

'Yes, really.' Phoebe gestured to the other three. 'They're all cousins.' Noting Andy, she added, 'He's a step-cousin. Chinese brother-in-law. OK? Let's go, boys. Who's on dinner duty?'

'Not so fast.' Jake's dad moved in front of her. He eyeballed the teenagers. 'Four boys, huh? I think I've got something that might be of interest to you. Inside, *now*.'

Felix looked up as a flock of crows swooped on to the roof of the station.

'Leave it to me,' Andy whispered, tapping his pocket.

Felix nodded, but he knew this was bigger than Andy and his magnet. Way bigger. He clenched the talisman, which was glowing beneath his shirt. He hoped its magic was going to be strong enough to get them out of this one. The boys made their way into the station.

Jake's dad plonked himself in front of the computer monitor. 'Righto. I'm sure you'll all be relieved to know that the mystery of the school break-in has finally been solved.'

Felix watched as Andy pulled out the magnet he'd salvaged from the speaker. Jake's dad clicked his mouse and sat back in his chair as the security footage started to play.

On the screen, Felix could see the empty gym. He glanced at Sam and Jake's anxious faces and touched the talisman, now glowing fiercely. He could hear crows cawing outside, their wings batting against the police station doors, and their claws scratching on the roof as they tried to find a way in.

Felix started to whisper under his breath: *'Divinity of the elements, I summon thee.'*

A small surge in power – and the lights flickered. *'Earth, water, air, fire.'*

The cawing of the crows became deafening.

'Within this stone I invoke ye place,
Your greatest strength, your kindest grace.
And while this stone remains at hand
Thou shall be safe throughout this land.'

The talisman flashed brightly and then there was a sudden silence.

The video kept rolling, but the boys didn't appear onscreen.

Jake's dad sat forwards and checked that it was playing. It was. He pressed rewind and then fast-forward. Nothing. No mystery figures running amok. No Andy spinning around in the trolley. Furious, he turned to Jake. 'You saw it.'

Jake shrugged. 'I don't know what you're talking about.'

'On the tape. I showed it to you.'

Jake looked at him blankly.

Felix felt the glowing talisman through his shirt, surprised at its power. It had protected them against bees, crows and now –

Andy looked across at him, his thumbs up in victory.

Felix nodded, but he knew it wasn't a magnet that had wiped them from the tape. Somehow the talisman was protecting them from anything that might threaten their safety.

A small smile crossed his face, but it faded when he looked up. Phoebe was staring at him. Her eyes were on the talisman, pulsing and visibly glowing underneath his shirt.

sam: back to school

Sam turned on the rusty tap outside the shack. He put his face under the stream and splashed water under each armpit. If he had to go back to school, he wasn't going to go stinking like Felix.

He slid his fingers through his hair. Man, there was enough grease in there to fry chips.

The sound of a muffler exploding made Sam look up.

Phoebe's Kombi had just pulled up out the front. She leant out the window. 'Don't keep Aunty Phoebe waiting, now.'

Andy, Felix and Jake banged out of the shack and Sam jogged across the grass to join them.

'So, Felix. Tonight after school, how about I cook you dinner?' said Phoebe, as the Kombi made its faltering way through Bremin.

Felix shrugged. 'That's cool, we've got a stove now so –'

'Dude, you're knocking back a home-cooked meal?' said Sam. 'I'm in.'

'Didn't invite you,' said Phoebe, bumping on to the kerb as she negotiated a roundabout.

Sam looked out the window. Great. Their 'guardian' was rude as well as weird. He had no idea why Phoebe had helped them at the police station. It was actually kind of freaky. She didn't seem to have any interest in any of them, except Felix.

Phoebe wasn't giving up, despite Felix's complete lack of interest. 'You don't have to eat, Felix. Just come over and we'll have a *talk*.'

'OK, sure,' said Felix reluctantly.

Sam watched Bremin High approach. Secretly he was kind of relieved that Jake's dad had handed them over to Phoebe on the strict condition that she make them go to school. There were only so many days you could spend hanging around that lame shed thinking about where your next meal was going to come from.

School would be paradise compared to that. There were hot showers, girls to talk to, and maybe if he did some skate-busking he could buy something from the canteen.

He might not belong to his family anymore, but he'd always belonged at school. People looked up to him and respected him.

He checked himself out in the side mirror. Not bad.

A plastic-wrapped sandwich hit him on the back of the head. 'Stop checking your reflection, boofhead,' said Phoebe. 'I've got a shop to open.'

Sam picked up the sandwich and wrinkled his nose at its contents: a kind of green slush.

'You got a problem with alfalfa and wheatgrass mayo?' asked Phoebe.

'No, all's good.'

'Then get out.'

Sam realised the other three were already inside the gates. He stepped out of the Kombi. *OK, here goes. Watch out Bremin High, Sam the Man is back.*

He jumped on to his board and skated towards the school gates.

As Sam caught up to the others, a gaggle of girls made their way towards him. They were pointing and giggling.

'Is that really him?'

'He's so cute.'

Sam skated confidently up to Jake. 'Different universe, same Sam.'

'Dude, they're not talking about you,' said Jake.

Sam stopped his skateboard.

Ellen rushed up to Andy, accompanied by a posse of girls who were all Mia's friends. 'Can I interview you for my blog at recess?'

'You were so brave, saving Ellen,' said Raquel.

'Uh, yeah sure,' said Andy, looking at the others uncertainly.

'Saving Ellen?' said Felix. 'What are they talking about?'

'Ellen was about to get run over by the school bus and Andy jumped in front of it and saved her,' Raquel chirped.

Sam, Felix and Jake looked at Andy.

'It was nothing. I was going to tell you about it, but what with everything that's been going on . . .'

'*It was nothing*,' repeated a breathless Ellen. 'You're so modest. You saved my life.'

The girls surrounded Andy and dragged him towards the school steps. Sam, Jake and Felix watched in disbelief.

'Andy, a chick magnet?' said Jake. 'What the hell?'

Felix walked off with his head down.

Sam watched as more girls ran towards Andy. This wasn't right. This wasn't how it was supposed to go. At least Mia wasn't one of them.

Sam followed the others down the corridor towards the noticeboard, where their timetable was posted.

Great, same as their old timetable. The first period was science with Bates.

The corridors were bustling with kids but no one gave Sam a second glance as he wandered towards the science labs.

He swung open the door. Jake, Andy and Felix were already in the classroom. In fact, almost all the seats were taken. Luckily the one next to Mia was free. He grinned and made a beeline for her.

'Watch your bags, peeps, here comes the thief,' a voice called from the back of the class.

Sammy.

Sam ignored him and was about to slide into the seat beside Mia when Ellen slipped in front of him. 'There's a spare seat over there.' She pointed across the room to the only spare seat left – next to Mikey, the most unpopular kid in class.

Sam looked at Mia who was suddenly very interested in her science book.

He sat down next to Mikey, who put his hand out with a friendly smile. 'Hi, I'm Mikey.'

'Yeah, I know who you are.' Sam looked away.

'All right class, listen up,' Bates walked in and banged on the desk with a ruler. 'We have four new boys starting at Bremin High today. Stand up, boys.'

Felix, Sam, Andy and Jake all stood up.

Bates stared hard at Jake. 'What a pleasure to see you again,' he referred to his notes. 'Jake.'

Jake looked at the floor.

'Apparently, they're cousins.' Bates shook his head in disbelief. 'I'd like everyone here to make them feel welcome.'

Like that was going to happen. Sam could feel Sammy's eyes boring into the back of his head.

'All right, then. Books open at page twenty-three. We will be continuing our research into the extraction of chemical compounds from plants.'

Sam opened his book but before he could even find page twenty-three, a scrunched-up ball of paper bounced off his shoulder. He flattened it out, and saw the word 'loser' scrawled on it.

Mikey looked apologetically at Sam. 'Sorry, that was probably meant for me.'

Sam turned to see a grinning Sammy making an 'L' shape on his forehead. He screwed up the note. 'I don't think so.'

As Bates droned on about extracting iodine compounds from seaweed, Sam opened his exercise book. At least he had some paper and a pen in front of him now.

He began to draw. Drawing always made things better. You could draw your fears, your feelings, your dreams – anything that was bothering you. Sam's pen moved across the paper in fine strokes. He focused hard. Maybe he could draw his way back to his real world.

Before he knew it, the bell had rung. Sam carefully slipped his drawing into his folder and stood up. Sammy pushed past him and made a show of putting his arm around Mia as he made his way towards the door.

Sam joined Felix, Jake and Andy in the corridor. He watched Sammy saunter off down the corridor with Mia. 'What does she see in that jerk?'

Jake raised an eyebrow. 'That's pretty obvious.'

'What's that supposed to mean?'

'Well, you're kind of the same. You're both vain, both skater dudes –'

'I'm nothing like that twisted gimp!' Sam protested.

'Nah,' said Andy, thoughtfully. 'He *is* better-looking than you.'

Sam turned on him. 'What?'

Andy made a quick exit. 'Ah, I said I'd meet Ellen on the oval.'

A basketball bounced in Jake's direction. 'You coming to shoot hoops, bro?' called Trent.

'Sure,' said Jake, throwing the ball back.

Sam looked at Felix. 'You want to eat our Incredible Hulk sandwiches together?'

Felix shook his head. 'Sorry. I'm going to find Oscar,' he said, walking off.

'Whatever,' Sam said to the empty corridor.

Sam wandered out into the schoolyard. Everywhere, groups of kids were hanging out together. He sat down on an empty bench and looked around. Well, this sucked. He'd never been alone at lunchtime before. For the past year, he and Mia had met every lunchtime. Before that, he'd gone out briefly with Sally Harper – until she'd realised she preferred horses to boyfriends.

But even without girls, there had always been his skater mates – Jacko, Will, Seb and Oscar. They'd been friends since primary school, but now . . .

Sam looked over to where the skaters hung out. His friends were all there, and not one of them knew who he was. Not one of them remembered that they'd gone to each other's

birthdays for the last twelve years. That they'd slept at each
other's houses, gone on holidays together, eaten live cicadas
for a dare. Instead, there was someone else who'd done all
that with them. Smack bang in the middle of his friends was
Sammy. He'd called Sam a thief, but *he* was the real thief.
He'd stolen Sam's whole life.

Sam saw Mia walking quickly across the quad towards
Sammy.

'Hey, babe,' Sammy called to her, a little too loudly.
'Wanna come and watch us jump the bins?'

Sam stood up. He wasn't going to let that poser take
everything that belonged to him. 'Hey, Mia!' he called out.

She was halfway across the quad. Halfway between them.
She turned around. 'Yeah?'

Sam walked up to her. 'I just was wondering if we could
maybe have lunch?'

She shook her head, and spoke to him slowly like he had
some sort of difficulty understanding English. 'You know
what? I'd really appreciate you leaving me alone because, like
I already told you, I *have* a boyfriend.'

'I know that. I just thought we could maybe talk –'

'What are you? Some kind of sicko?' Sammy had come
over and stepped protectively in front of Mia. 'Who do
you think you are? You break into my house. You steal my
skateboard, and now you're after my girl. Just back off!' He
gave Sam a push.

Sam felt his blood start to boil. He pushed Sammy back, hard. 'It's my house, my skateboard and *my* girl.'

Mia rolled her eyes. 'Yeah, good one, guys. What do you think I am? Some piece of property you own?'

Sammy picked himself up. A crowd was starting to gather. 'You're a mental patient, man. They should lock you away.'

'*Fight, fight, fight,*' the crowd started to chant.

'Sam! Stop it!' Sam heard a voice yelling. But he didn't care. This loser was going down.

He launched himself at Sammy and they both fell hard on to the asphalt.

Sammy tried to fight him off but Sam was fuelled by a rage he'd never felt before. He *hated* this guy. He hated him so much he wouldn't care if he knocked him out for good.

He lifted his fist. The crowd was roaring with delight. He was going to smash his knuckles straight into Sammy's smug, self-satisfied face. That would teach him.

Sam saw a flicker of fear pass across Sammy's face. Then he felt two strong arms, pulling him away. He kicked and struggled, but the arms were too strong. He could hear the groans of the disappointed crowd as he was dragged on to the grass of the oval and dumped.

'Jeez, man, are you out of your mind?' Jake flopped down beside him. 'It's our first day. If my dad finds out about this we'll all be picked up by that woman from children's services.'

Sam looked over to where Sammy was surrounded by his

skater friends. 'You should have left me alone. I wanted to smash his skull in.'

Jake put his arm on Sam's shoulder. 'I know, man. But you've got to control it.'

'Yeah, easy for you to say.'

At that moment, Mr Bates strode across the playground towards Sammy.

'Actually, I feel the same way, man,' said Jake.

Sam followed Jake's gaze.

Jake nodded. 'You think I want that jerk anywhere near my mum? I feel sick thinking about it.'

Sam saw Sammy pointing him out to Bates.

'You'd better get out of here,' said Jake.

Sam jumped up and made a dash for the out-buildings. He didn't need Bates on his back. Sammy had probably told him some sob story about the new kid beating him up for no reason.

He slipped behind the boys' toilets. He'd head down to the trees on the school perimeter. He and Mia sometimes used to hang there.

As he approached, he saw Mia sitting by herself under the wattle tree by the fence. Seeing Sam, she immediately stood up. 'Is there a part of *leave me alone* that you don't understand?'

'Mia, I'm sorry. I didn't know you'd be here.'

'Really?' Mia looked at him for a beat. 'You know what? You and Sammy – you're exactly the same. Completely selfish.'

Sam shook his head in frustration. Why did people keep saying that? It was so far from the truth. 'I'm nothing like that dickhead.'

'So coming up to me all the time, even when I ask you not to. That's not selfish?' asked Mia, barely controlling her anger. 'Stealing, fighting with my boyfriend, embarrassing me in front of my friends, that's for *my* sake, is it?' She turned away, shaking with emotion. 'I'm not some prize to be fought over.' Then she walked away.

Sam swallowed hard. What she'd said was true. None of it had been about her. It was all about him and Sammy. Maybe he *was* just like Sammy: a selfish boofhead who cared more about being top of the heap than anything else.

'Mia! Wait.' Sam ran after her. He pulled the drawing he'd done in science out of his folder. 'I won't bother you again, I promise.' He handed her the picture. 'Here. I did this for you.'

She took it reluctantly, without looking at it.

'And you should learn to skate. I know you want to,' said Sam.

Mia looked at him curiously. 'How do you know that?'

Sam shrugged. 'Where I come from I used to go out with a girl who wanted to learn to skate. She wanted me to teach her but I never did,' he said. 'I told her it was because I was worried she'd fall. But you wanna know the real reason?'

'You were worried she'd be better than you?' challenged Mia.

172

Sam scoffed at that idea. 'No way.' But he stopped himself. That's exactly the sort of thing Sammy would say. He looked at the ground. 'The real reason was that I liked having you – er, I mean her – watching me. I liked how that made me feel.'

'Yep. Like I said. Totally selfish.'

'Guess so.' Sam smiled sadly. 'Lucky I moved here. 'Cause she was probably about to dump me.'

'Probably,' said Mia. And, despite her obvious annoyance with him, she smiled back.

Sam looked at Mia. Every part of him wanted to reach out and touch her. His hand moved slowly towards hers but then he froze.

Directly behind Mia was a massive German Shepherd. It growled and fixed its bloodshot eyes on Sam.

'Mia,' said Sam, 'I think we need to *run*!'

andy: who let the dogs in?

Andy walked across the oval with Ellen and her friends Raquel and Suzie, and a girl with blonde pigtails, who he seemed to remember had once stuck his head under the bubbler for making their team lose at mixed volleyball.

This girl was now smiling at him in a slightly deranged manner. 'So, can you tell us again how it happened?'

'No, Betty,' said Ellen. 'Wait until we sit down. I'm going to record it for the blog.' She smiled at Andy. 'I've got my own blog called *Wot the Elle*.'

Andy nodded, then noticed where the girls were planning to sit. 'Do you mind if we sit on the north-west side of the oval? The pollen from the Norfolk Pine sets off my allergies.'

The girls looked at him uncertainly, then Ellen smiled. 'Sure.'

On the other side of the oval, Ellen pulled out her phone and pressed record. 'I'm calling this "Interview with a Hero".'

Andy looked at the four girls' eager faces. It was strange,

being admired like this. He wasn't sure what to do.

'Andy?' Ellen was staring at him. 'Come on. From the beginning.'

Andy took a deep breath. *From the beginning*. Well, there was a problem right there. If he told it from the beginning then he'd have to tell her about his amnesia theory, which had been supplanted by his wormhole theory, which had been updated to a theory of lucid dreaming, although that was now well and truly disproven, given they'd been attacked by bees and birds and he'd still not woken up.

'Andy? My battery's running low.'

Andy finally opened his mouth. 'Sorry. OK. Well, I was just walking along the road, minding my own business . . .'

The girls surrounding him were silent, all seemingly transfixed.

'Then all of a sudden the ground started to rumble. I knew the bus was coming.'

Ellen nodded encouragingly. 'And then?'

'And then I saw Ellen coming towards me. She looked –'

'Yes?' said Ellen eagerly.

'Like . . . like she was listening to music and not paying enough attention to the road.'

Ellen's forehead crinkled like that wasn't quite what she'd wanted to hear, but Andy kept going regardless. He was starting to enjoy himself.

'And then I saw it,' he said. 'The bus coming, like a fiery

dragon behind her. The driver turned, and in that second I thought, *What would Bear Grylls do?*'

'What *would* he do?' asked Raquel.

'He'd risk life and limb to save the damsel.'

Betty wrinkled her nose. 'Damsel?'

'So I leapt towards her. The bus missed us by millimetres. I felt the heat of its engine as it roared past us. The world went into slow motion.' He stopped. The next bit wasn't so easy to talk about.

'And then what happened?'

'Er, that's it, really. That's all.' He couldn't talk about the fact that he'd ended up lying on top of Ellen. Just thinking about it made him nervous. His heart pounded in his chest and he started sweating.

'Nothing else happened?' asked Ellen, twirling her hair.

Andy was finding it hard to breathe. He jumped up. 'Is that the bell? I've got to go. I've got a free period.'

He scampered across the oval. Free period? What kind of dumb excuse was that?

When he reached the school building, he gave a sigh of relief. All that attention had made him nervous. And the whole thing was a great big lie, anyway. He was no hero. If anything, Ellen had saved *his* life. If she hadn't been walking along the road, he probably would have thrown himself in front of the bus.

He wiped his face with his sleeve. He felt sweaty and

disorientated. He made his way to the library. He'd be safe there. Maybe he could do some research on inappropriate perspiration? Although, he had a feeling that what he was experiencing was not something that could be researched.

He took the library steps two at a time and opened the door. Good. It was quiet. He needed to sit down, read something he understood.

He made his way over to rack 530–533. The physics section was where it always was. That was a good start. He pulled out some books on quantum mechanics and relativity. These should do it. He opened a book called *Black Holes and Time Warps*.

'I had a free period too.' Ellen came around from the other side of the rack, surprising Andy so much he dropped his pile of books.

'I didn't want to ask you in front of the others, but have you had any interesting correspondence lately?'

Andy stared at her. How had she got here so fast? 'That would presuppose the existence of a letterbox, so, no.'

'Or it could have been hand delivered?'

Of course. The note. He knew it had to be from her. Andy swallowed hard.

Ellen smiled. 'What you did was amazing. I wanted to thank you, and I couldn't find you on Facebook.'

She had such a pretty face, and he could smell that clean shampoo scent of hers again, kind of flowery and sweet.

She took a step closer, and the lights flickered on and off. Then the library was suddenly plunged into darkness.

'Must be an electrical fault. We should go and see,' said Andy.

Ellen took his hand. 'Kind of romantic. Don't you think?'

Andy did think. He thought very much. In fact, if he thought any more he might do himself some damage. He should stop thinking.

He looked at Ellen's face. Her slightly parted lips. If he moved his head towards her, their lips might meet. Would that be a good thing? It felt like it would be, but then what would happen once he got there? Would he know what to do?

Of course he would, he told himself. It would be like positive and negative forces meeting. He moved his head towards her, but froze.

A hissing, snarling sound was coming from behind Ellen.

Andy looked up and saw a dog, one that looked a lot like his own, baring its teeth. 'Terabyte?' The dog snarled at them, its hackles raised and eyes gleaming in the semi-darkness.

Ellen looked at Andy, frightened. 'What is that?'

'Um. I think it's my pet.'

'*That's* your pet?'

The dog inched across the carpet towards them. Andy's eyes had adjusted to the darkness, and he could see now that it was definitely Terabyte. But something was wrong with him. *Very* wrong.

Andy pulled Ellen towards him. 'Whatever you do, don't look him in the eye.'

They both looked away and, to Andy's surprise, Terabyte backed off. 'I saw Bear Grylls do that to a rhino once,' Andy whispered.

Terabyte growled, then leapt at them, snapping his jaws.

'*Run!*' yelled Ellen.

As they burst out of the library, Andy saw the school was in chaos. Kids ran down corridors, with wild-eyed dogs barking and chasing after them. Felix, Sam and Jake emerged from the confusion and ran towards them.

A Jack Russell ran past, snapping and growling madly.

'It's Wiki,' Ellen yelled, taking after him. 'Wiki, heel!'

'Ellen, don't!' cried Andy. He went to follow her but Felix grabbed his arm. 'Let go of me!' yelled Andy, but Felix had a vice-like grip.

He pulled a necklace with a weird glowing stone from under his shirt and started chanting. '*Divinity of the elements, I summon thee.*'

Andy tried to wrest his arm free. Felix was going to give him a massive bruise. He had to get to Ellen. It wasn't safe out there. The dog could attack her any second. 'Ellen!' he called after her.

Felix clenched Andy's arm with one hand, and held the necklace in front of him with the other.

'Earth, water, air, fire
Within this stone I invoke ye place,
Your greatest strength, your kindest grace.'

The fire alarm suddenly went off in a piercing shriek. Water started to splash down on them. Felix kept chanting, oblivious.

'And while this stone remains at hand
Thou shall be safe throughout this land.'

The stone flashed brightly. Almost immediately, the dogs stopped barking. They shook their fur, whimpered and started behaving normally. Felix let go of Andy's arm.

'Did you have to do that?' said Andy, rubbing his arm. 'I can take care of myself.'

Felix put the necklace back under his shirt, muttering, 'Actually, you can't.'

Jake turned to Felix. 'What is that thing? What did you just do?'

Felix looked at them warily. 'You won't believe me, even if I tell you.'

'Oh, come on,' said Sam. 'That thing around your neck – it stopped the dogs attacking.'

Andy scoffed. 'The dogs stopped attacking because of the fire alarm. The high frequency affects their behaviour.'

Sam and Jake ignored him. 'Felix?'

Felix reluctantly pulled the necklace out from under his shirt. 'It's a talisman, OK? Phoebe gave it to me to protect us against elemental attacks.'

'Against what?' asked Sam.

'We're being attacked by elements of nature. The storm, the bees, the crows and now, dogs. They're all part of this world. And the attacks are getting bigger each time.'

Jake inspected it. It was still faintly glowing. 'And it actually works?'

'Well, yeah. That's the third time it's saved us.'

Andy looked at it sceptically. 'Where's the battery?'

Felix gave him a dark stare. 'It doesn't have a battery. It's powered by us all being together, and the spell I chant.'

Andy rolled his eyes. How could Felix believe such nonsense? 'Oh, come on! The bees were driven away by insect spray, I erased the security tape with a magnet, and the dogs were stopped by the fire alarm.'

The other three looked at him, unconvinced.

'What?' said Andy. 'It's obvious.'

'Not everything can be explained rationally,' said Felix.

'Really? You name anything and I'll explain it to you.'

'Us. Here. Now,' piped up Sam.

Andy hesitated. That was a good point. 'Well, I'm working on that.'

Sam turned to Felix. 'If witchy lady has powerful stuff

like that, then she might know other spells. Spells that could get us home.'

'Maybe.'

'What do you mean *maybe*? What you just did then, that was . . .'

'Magic,' Felix finished.

'Oh, come on!' said Andy.

'No, he's right,' said Jake. 'Magic makes no sense – just like us being here makes no sense. So maybe magic can get us home.' He looked hopeful.

'Does she know what happened to us?' asked Sam.

Felix shook his head. 'No. Just that we're being attacked.'

'Maybe we should ask for her help?' Sam pressed.

'There's this Book of Shadows.'

'Book of what?'

'It's a book where witches keep all their powerful spells. I'm pretty sure the clue to what's attacking us is in there.'

'Then we need to get it,' said Jake firmly.

'I've been trying,' said Felix. 'But she keeps it in her back room.'

'Well, let's break in and get it,' said Sam.

'And the train to Hogwarts leaves in thirty minutes,' Andy scoffed. He felt something brush against his leg and looked down to see Terabyte, pawing at him. 'Hey, he remembers me.' Andy leant down and ruffled his dog's fur.

'OK, fine,' hissed Felix. 'If you don't believe me, you can

just hang out with your dog and your girlfriend. But don't expect me to save you if there's another attack.'

'Ellen's not my girl—'

'Hey, Andy,' called Ellen, walking down the corridor towards him with Wikileaks in her arms.

'Hey, Ellen,' said Andy, turning red.

'You want to go and do some "study" in the library?' Ellen smiled sweetly.

Andy felt the sweat start to pour off him. He was pretty sure she didn't actually want to study.

Felix looked at him darkly. 'Answer your girlfriend, Andy.'

'Sure,' Andy said to Ellen, wiping the sweat from his forehead. He wasn't going to listen to any of Felix's nonsense.

He'd taken one step in the direction of the library when he saw Viv round a corner at the other end of the corridor. Her hair was dyed purple and her school uniform looked like it had been slashed with a knife. She saw Andy and raced towards him.

'Oh my God. Get your hands off my dog, stalker,' she yelled. 'First you're after me and now you're after my dog.'

'That's so wrong,' Andy protested, taking a worried sideways glance at Ellen. 'I'm not after you!'

'I found you in my bedroom,' shrieked Viv. 'And then you hang around our restaurant. You're a total weirdo.' She grabbed Terabyte and stormed down the corridor. 'Just keep away from me,' she called over her shoulder.

Ellen's face dropped. 'Actually, I just remembered I've got band practice.'

'But you don't play an instrument and you're tone deaf,' said Felix.

She glared at him and walked away.

Andy looked at Felix. Was he actually smiling?

felix: a bona fide hell-bent-on-murder demon

Felix watched Ellen walk off. He felt a stab of pleasure that she was upset with Andy. At least now he wouldn't have to watch them making eyes at each other. Ellen and Andy? Man, he'd love to go back to his reality just to see Ellen's face when he told her she'd fallen for that nerd.

He sighed. He missed the real Ellen horribly. Yeah, it was great that Oscar could walk. But losing your best friend? That hurt.

The corridor was starting to fill up with kids again. Felix made sure the talisman was hidden away under his shirt. He wanted to get out of there – he didn't want the whole of Bremin High questioning him. Andy was bad enough.

'Come on, let's go.'

'We can't just leave,' said Andy. 'You need a permission slip if you're leaving before three-thirty.'

'Well, go and ask your parents then,' Felix snapped. 'See how that goes.'

Andy looked hurt, but Felix didn't care – Andy was getting on his nerves, and not just because of Ellen. The whole *science can prove everything* line made Felix want to yell, *It can't! It can't prove this, because science didn't make this happen – magic did!* But then he'd have to explain how he knew that, and he wasn't ready to do that yet. Not until he'd worked out how to change it.

Jake gave him a shove. 'Come on, dude. Let's go nick this Book of Spirits thing.'

'Shadows,' Felix corrected him.

'I don't care what it's called, so long as it gets us home,' said Sam.

The boys made their way down the corridor. The school was still in chaos. The sprinklers had been turned off but there were puddles of water all over the floor and kids everywhere. It was the perfect time to slip away unnoticed.

They were walking past the staffroom when Bates appeared at the door.

'Boys! Hang on!' He came out, clutching a few sheets of paper. 'You all OK?' A poncy little poodle trotted at his heels.

'Fine,' said Andy, then turned pointedly to Felix. 'Although my arm is rather bruised.'

Felix gave him a death stare. Man, if they didn't all have to stay together, he would happily leave Andy in a locked dumpster.

'Doesn't sound like anything to worry about,' said Bates.

'But I don't know what's brought all these dogs here. Never seen dogs behave like that.'

He picked up the poodle. 'We've been looking for Pips for days, and then I find her here at school with a pack of wild dogs! Not sure what got into her. She's normally so good-natured. My wife is going to be over the moon to see her.'

Felix noticed Jake clenching and unclenching his fists as the poodle licked Bates's nose.

'Thanks, Mr Bates. We're all good,' Felix stepped in. 'Just got to do some study before our next period.'

'Good. Oh, and before I forget, I need you to get these forms filled out before tomorrow.'

'OK, thanks, Mr Bates,' said Felix brightly, taking the forms.

The boys waited till Bates had disappeared back into the staffroom, then stuffed the forms in their bags and made their way towards the front door.

This was their chance. They had to get to Arcane Lane, distract Phoebe and get the Book of Shadows. How they were going to do that, Felix wasn't sure. He'd been avoiding Phoebe since the day before. To be honest, he was kind of terrified about the deal he'd made with her.

―――――

The boys made their way out the main entrance. Felix noticed the quad was covered in muddy paw prints. Everywhere he looked were paw prints, big and small. They ran over and around each other. Felix stared at them – they looked strangely familiar. There was a pattern, a logic.

Jake nudged him. 'Felix, look over there.'

Felix looked up. Standing amongst the ring of cypress trees at the edge of the oval was Phoebe. She was staring intently at the quad. She pulled a book out of her bag and studied it. She looked back at the paw prints.

'That's the Book of Shadows,' said Felix.

'What's she doing with it?'

'I don't know.' Felix pushed the others back out of sight, behind a pillar. What *was* Phoebe doing at the school? Some sort of spell?

He felt his skin go cold. Maybe it had been Phoebe who was attacking them all along. She had been in the forest the day they'd gone missing. The bees had come to her shop. She'd been at the shack when the crows came – and now she was here when the dogs attacked. Surely it was too much of a coincidence.

He watched her carefully. She had made her way to the quad and was bending down to scrape at a muddy paw print. Weird.

'So we just go and ask her for her book, right?' said Sam, eager to get on with it.

'It's not that simple,' said Felix.

'Sure it is,' said Sam.

'It's not,' snapped Felix. 'I've tried that already.' He watched as Phoebe placed some mud in a vial, then snapped the book shut and headed towards the school gate. She hadn't seen them. That was good. 'We need to follow her. See what she's up to.'

'I thought you said she was helping us,' said Jake.

'I'm not so sure,' muttered Felix. 'Come on.'

Phoebe turned left at the gate. The boys quickly crossed the quad and followed her. Felix looked back and his stomach leapt. With a bit of distance, the paw prints formed very clear patterns. The same spiral patterns he'd seen outside the shack after the storm. The spirals twisted and turned, and led towards the front of the school – towards them. Whatever was after them, it was getting stronger.

'Felix, come on. She's just turned down Dickens Street,' called Jake.

Felix turned and jogged to catch up to the others. Phoebe was out of sight. They turned down Dickens Street and saw her disappearing around the corner into Elm Grove. That was Felix's street. Was she going to his house? Was she planning an attack there against Oscar or his parents? He quickened his pace.

Phoebe disappeared up the driveway of number eleven. Felix's house.

'Quick, up here!' Felix led the others into Ellen's driveway and they crept along the fence line. They squatted beside some broken planks in the fence and Felix peered through into his garden.

'It would be a hell of a lot simpler to just ask her for the book,' grumbled Sam.

'Shh,' said Felix.

Phoebe was standing under the elm tree. She had the book open again and was studying the bark carefully. She put it back in her bag and got out a small metal file. She scraped at the bark and placed the shavings in another glass vial.

'She's collecting ingredients,' whispered Felix.

'What for? Bark pie?' said Sam.

Satisfied, Phoebe headed back down the driveway.

Felix hesitated. What to do? They should really follow her and see what she was going to do next. But what had she done to the tree? If she was casting some spell on his family, he needed to know about it. Without consulting the others, he leapt over Ellen's fence into his front yard.

At the elm tree, Felix froze. There, on the bark, was the same pattern again. Spirals twirled up the bark of the tree towards Oscar's window. They looked like they had been etched into the bark.

The bees! thought Felix. That mark was made by the bees. But why would Phoebe be interested in that? It didn't make any sense.

He heard the sound of a car and turned to see a green Volvo coming up the drive. Bugger. It was his mum.

She parked and stepped out of the car.

'Hello, Fergus. Oscar's not home from school yet.' She sneezed violently, then looked puzzled. 'Shouldn't you be at school too?'

'Er, yeah.' Felix thought fast. 'But I had a free period so I thought I'd come and hang here until Oscar gets home.'

It was a lame excuse but his mum didn't question it. She just seemed happy that Oscar had a friend. She pulled a tissue out of her handbag and blew her nose.

'You can come and wait for him inside if you'd like. I'll make you some afternoon tea.' She sneezed again, and her eyes started watering. 'Sorry, it's my hayfever playing up again.'

Felix was tempted. Really tempted. He couldn't remember the last time he'd had his mum's full attention. And he'd give anything to eat her home-cooked food. But he caught sight of the other three, staring at him from behind Ellen's fence. 'Ah, that's cool. Actually, I've got some homework to do so maybe I'll come back later.'

A flicker of disappointment crossed his mum's face. 'No problem. I'll tell Oscie you came around. I'm sure he'll be sorry he missed you.'

Felix watched her go inside. It was kind of strange that despite being in a wheelchair, Oscar was a whole lot more popular at home than he was in this world.

He made his way back to the others.

'Dude, you could have invited us all in. I'm starving,' said Sam.

'Got no time. We've got to find Phoebe.' He looked around. 'Where's Andy?'

'I think he's writing Ellen a love note.' Jake laughed.

Andy was slipping a note under Ellen's front door. He caught Felix's eye and suddenly became very interested in doing up his shoe.

Felix felt a surge of anger. Here he was, doing everything he could to get them home, and Andy was poncing around like a love-struck idiot. 'Come on,' he said tightly. 'We have to find Phoebe.' He stormed off down Ellen's drive.

Andy jogged up beside him. 'I was just trying to explain that my feelings for Viv are and will only ever be brotherly –'

'Save it for someone who cares,' Felix hissed. There was no sign of Phoebe on the street. 'We'll go to Arcane Lane. Wait for her there.'

The boys made their way through town and up the back steps to Arcane Lane. The sign on the front door said OPEN.

Felix cupped his hands to the glass and saw Phoebe sitting behind the counter with the vials and the Book of Shadows open in front of her. If she was trying to harm them, they'd probably walked right into a trap.

But he had the talisman, didn't he? He knew it worked. And if they were all together and Phoebe attacked, they'd be protected, right?

He took a deep breath and flung open the door.

Phoebe glanced up from the glass vials. 'Oh, so you actually decided to keep your word this time,' she said, nonchalantly.

Felix was taken aback. 'Um, yeah.'

Phoebe put down the vials and looked past Felix to the others. 'You didn't have to bring the boy band.'

'Actually, I did,' said Felix boldly. 'If something is threatening us, we need to stay together or the talisman doesn't work.'

Phoebe raised an eyebrow. 'Is something attacking you now?'

'Well, no. Not right now. But I've reason to believe that you are behind the attacks.'

Phoebe laughed out loud. '*I'm* behind the attacks?'

'Well, we saw you,' said Felix, feeling less certain. 'At the school and at my house.'

'So, tell me,' said Phoebe. 'Is the talisman glowing right now?'

Felix pulled it out from under his shirt. It just looked like a dull brown stone.

'So, what were you doing then?' he asked, annoyed at his own oversight.

Phoebe turned the Book of Shadows towards him. It was open at the page Felix had seen earlier, showing the spiral patterns that perfectly matched the ones left behind after the attacks.

'This is the demonology section,' Phoebe said darkly.

'Demonology?' said Andy. 'Oh, this gets better and better.'

Phoebe fixed him with a glare. 'I've been trying to work out what's been attacking you, and I think I've found the answer. You boys have a demon after you. A bona fide, hell-bent-on-murder demon.'

Sam's eyes nearly popped out of his head. 'What?'

Felix moved towards the book and started to read. 'So,' he said finally, 'these elemental attacks. They're all the same demon coming at us, but in different forms? What kind of demon is it?'

Jake looked dismayed. 'There's more than one kind of demon?'

'This here,' said Phoebe, pointing at the spiral, 'is the signature of a restoring demon.'

Felix read the passage aloud. 'Created to restore the natural order after a magical disturbance.'

'What's a magical disturbance?' asked Sam.

'I'm thinking that's . . . *you*?' said Phoebe. 'You boys got something to tell me?'

Everyone's eyes turned to Felix. He took a deep breath. If Phoebe really was trying to help them, there was no harm in telling her the truth. Well, at least some of it.

'Um, well . . .' But where could he even start?

Luckily, Sam jumped in. 'There was this school excursion, right? And we got lost in the forest, and when we found our way back to Bremin, nobody remembered us anymore. So we need you to help us get back to our real world because, let me tell you, this world totally sucks.'

Phoebe's eyes lit up. 'I thought as much. So you've completely disappeared from your own world?'

'I guess,' said Felix.

Phoebe picked up from the counter a framed photograph of a young woman. She took a deep breath. 'This is my sister, Alice. Ten years ago she disappeared. The police searched for months, but they never found a trace.'

'There must be people searching for us like that in our world,' said Sam.

Phoebe nodded. 'I'd say so.'

'What do you think happened to her – to Alice?' asked Felix tentatively. He wasn't sure he wanted to hear the answer.

Phoebe looked at him intently. 'Magic, Felix. Alice was a witch and she cast a powerful spell, but something went wrong. Of course, when I told the police that, they thought I was crazy.'

Felix looked away. He knew more about powerful spells going wrong than he wanted to admit.

'Which brings me to our deal, Felix.'

'I'm – I'm not sure how I can help you,' he faltered.

'OK then, I'll have the talisman back.'

Felix was backed into a corner and he knew it. There was no way he could give Phoebe back the talisman. This restoring demon was going to keep coming at them and the talisman was the only thing protecting them. They needed it until he could work out how to get them home.

'Do you know what spell she cast?' asked Felix.

Phoebe shook her head. 'That's what I need you for.'

'But if you've been trying to work it out for ten years, what chance have I got?'

'You know what the difference between you and me is, Felix?'

Felix looked at her. Plenty of things were coming to mind.

'You can do magic, and I . . .' She looked away.

'You can't?' asked Felix. He suddenly realised why he was so important to her.

'I've studied magic all my life, but I've never had any ability. Alice was the witch in the family. The only real witch I'd ever met. Till you.'

The other boys stared at Felix.

'Dude, you're a witch?' asked Jake.

Felix tried to brush it aside. 'Well, I've read some books, been to some websites. But that's what goths do.'

'You made Alice's talisman work,' said Phoebe. 'Only a true witch can harness the power of the elemental talisman.'

'So, if he helps you, can you get us home?' asked Sam, eager to get back to the matter at hand.

'If he helps me find Alice, she can get you home.'

'OK, it's a deal,' said Sam.

'Wait,' said Felix. 'How am I supposed to find Alice and bring her home, when I can't even get us home?'

'You find the spell she used. Cast again, in the same way, in the same place, the spell will be reversed,' said Phoebe simply.

Felix took that in. Was that really all he had to do? If it was that simple he should be able to get them all home.

'Felix?'

'Sure. I'll give it a try.'

'I'm counting on you. And in the meantime, be careful. The demon is building strength. It will take some time to regroup after today's attack. But when it comes back, it will be stronger than ever.'

Felix shuddered. The demon had turned every dog in Bremin on them. He'd rather not think about what it could do next.

The boys made their way along the bush track towards the shack. Felix hung back from the others. He needed time to think. If Phoebe was right about how to reverse a spell, he felt pretty confident he could get them home. He owed it to the others, but it sure was going to be hard to leave this world where his brother could walk and his mum wanted to feed him afternoon tea.

When they got back to the shack, Jake stood in the gloom holding out the piece of paper Bates had given them. 'Guys.'

'What?'

'Check this out.'

The others gathered around him.

'Permission slip for excursion to the Bremin Ranges,' read Andy.

The boys stared at each other.

'It's the same excursion,' whispered Sam.

'It must have been postponed in this world,' said Andy.

Felix stared at the slip. The same excursion, to the same place. The fates had spoken. The others were looking at him.

'Do you think you can bring Alice home?' asked Sam.

Felix smiled. 'I can do better than that. I think I can get *us* home.'

jake: we're going on a wormhole hunt

Jake sat by the window of the shack. Outside, the sun was rising. The whole world was bathed in a soft, hopeful light. Jake leant his head against the window. He'd hardly slept all night. In his hand was the excursion form. He remembered how his mum had signed it on the fly, rushing as usual to get out of the house. She'd finished her last shift the night before and was starting a new one at eight that morning. She'd given him a kiss and told him to enjoy himself before rushing out the back door to avoid Real Estate Phil.

The sun rose higher in the sky. Jake could almost see the shadows of the trees shortening as he watched. The day was coming fast and he wasn't sure how he felt about it. Did he really want his mum to go back to living a life of drudgery, just because she'd made a decision to have him at eighteen?

'It doesn't work like that.'

Jake looked up. Andy was watching him from his bed.

'Huh?'

'In parallel universes, both realities exist simultaneously. It's not one or the other.'

Jake stared at him. 'How did you know what I was thinking?'

Andy shrugged. 'Lucky guess.'

Jake looked away. 'I was just thinking, you know – that if today is our chance to go back, then I'm not sure –'

'I know,' said Andy. 'I sort of feel the same.'

'Really? I thought you were desperate for your *nai nai*'s cooking and your dad's three hours of extracurricular homework.'

Andy looked thoughtful. 'Well, if I had to break down how I feel about being here, I sixty to seventy per cent hate it; but am seventeen per cent . . . overstimulated, mainly because a girl likes me – or did like me. And it's thirteen to twenty-three per cent kinda fun.'

Jake smiled. Had he been in the bush too long, or was Andy starting to actually make sense?

Sam sat up, rubbing his eyes. 'My brothers hate me here and my parents replaced me. So I one hundred and ten per cent want to go home.'

They all looked at Felix who was snoring peacefully, one hand firmly grasping the talisman.

'What about him?' asked Jake.

'He actually seems pretty happy here,' said Andy. 'His brother can walk. His family are always inviting him over.'

Jake watched Felix's chest rise and fall. Of all of them, Felix seemed to have the best deal.

Felix must have felt their eyes on him, because he woke up. 'What are you looking at?'

'Come on, dude. You said it,' said Sam, giving him a shove. 'We're going home today.'

'Well, I'm not sure it's quite that simple.'

'Sure it is,' said Sam. 'We just retrace our steps.'

'And find the wormhole,' added Andy.

'Exactly,' said Sam. 'Wait. What wormhole?'

'The one that transported us here.'

The others looked at Andy uncertainly.

'In this world, the excursion was delayed. So the wormhole was probably delayed as well. We just need to find it again.'

Felix rolled his eyes. 'And you think *magic* is a long shot.'

Andy ignored him. 'Repeat the same actions to get the same result. That's the basis of the scientific method.'

Jake looked at him. That did actually make sense. And if his mum could exist in multiple worlds, then he would at least like to be in the world where she knew who the hell he was.

'Magic. Science. I'll believe in anything if it gets us home,' said Sam.

Felix picked up his bag. 'OK, then. We've got a bus to catch.'

Jake was staring at the permission form. 'Guys, wait. We need Phoebe to sign the slip.'

Without blinking an eye, Felix pulled a pen out of his bag and scrawled *Phoebe Hartley* across the dotted line of all four permission slips.

'That's f-forgery,' stuttered Andy.

'Take me to the cops, then,' said Felix, giving him his darkest stare and heading towards the door.

'What's up with him?'

Jake shook his head. 'Dude, you stole his girl. He's hardly going to be your best friend.' He saw the shocked look on Andy's face. 'Come on, let's go hunt some wormholes.'

The boys walked towards Bremin High. Outside, a bus was idling.

Jake looked up at the sky. A few dark clouds were threatening an otherwise cloud-free sky. Exactly like last time.

Out of nowhere, a football came flying towards him. On instinct, Jake reached up and caught it. There was a burst of applause as Trent and Dylan cheered him.

'Wasn't meant for you, dude, but pro mark,' said Trent, clapping him on the back.

Jake turned to see who it was meant for and saw Felix scowling. Oh yeah. He'd forgotten about that. He passed the ball back to Trent.

'You know we need another halfback on the footy team?' said Trent as he handballed it to Dylan.

Jake grinned. 'Sure, that sounds awesome.'

'You're in.'

A black BMW pulled over next to the bus and Bates hopped out of the passenger side, wearing a freshly ironed mauve V-neck jumper.

Jake's smile faded as his mum got out of the driver's side. Together, she and Bates opened the boot and started unloading a pile of orienteering markers. Jake watched their easy conversation. The pile unloaded, Bates turned and gave her a kiss on the mouth.

Jake turned away.

'That's totally gross,' said Sam, who was standing next to him.

'Told you,' said Jake. He pulled the excursion form out of his pocket.

Right. Any doubts he'd had about leaving this world were gone. He was on the next bus out of here.

'Take your seats, ladies and gents. Nature waits for no one.' Bates was at the door of the bus collecting permission forms.

Jake slammed his form into Bates's hand. He boarded the bus and slid into a seat next to Sam.

'Next stop, home.' Sam grinned. His enthusiasm was infectious.

'Yep, next stop,' Jake agreed.

The bus revved its engine and started to move. Jake looked out the window. *Goodbye, weird alternate-world Bremin, and hello, real world.*

A soft, pink sparkly toy flew over Jake's head and landed with a thump in the aisle. There were loud jeers from the back of the bus. Jake turned to see Trent, Dylan and the rest of their gang pulling Mikey out of his seat.

'Aw, poor bubby's lost his little toy,' said Trent.

'Don't worry, he can suck his little thumbie instead.' Dylan shoved Mikey's thumb hard up towards his face.

'*Trent. Dylan.* In your seats *now*,' yelled Bates.

Trent and Dylan high-fived each other and collapsed into the back seat. Jake watched them. Were they really once his best friends? He looked at the unicorn lying in the aisle. Its glass eye stared at him resentfully. He hesitated for a moment, then leant over and picked it up.

'Oh, good one, Jakey, chuck it here,' yelled Dylan.

Jake turned and walked slowly down the aisle. Trent was cheering him on.

'In your seat, Jake,' called Bates.

But Jake kept walking. He walked all the way down the aisle and handed the unicorn to Mikey.

Trent and Dylan's jaws dropped wide open.

Jake walked all the way back down to his seat and sat down.

Felix gave him a little smile, but Jake knew what that smile meant. He didn't need Felix to acknowledge his past self was a total jerk. It was bad enough realising it himself.

Bates was midway through his explanation of the excursion. 'On arrival you will be assigned into groups of four. This exercise is about team-building and learning to work collaboratively with your peers.'

Andy leant across the aisle to Jake and whispered, 'See? The pattern is repeating.'

After what seemed like an eternity, the bus pulled into the Bremin Ranges car park and everyone spilled out. Just like last time, Bates laid out maps and worksheets on a picnic table.

Ellen came over to Andy, who was standing next to Jake.

'Andy, I got your note,' she said.

'You did? Did it make sense?'

Ellen shook her head. 'None at all.' She leant towards him. 'But it was kind of sweet.'

Andy suddenly reached for her hand. 'Well, just in case I don't come back, I wanted to . . .' He leant in and kissed her on the cheek.

Jake noticed Felix becoming very interested in his shoes.

'OK, people,' Bates called into his megaphone. 'Form groups of four as I read out your names.' He was looking down at a piece of paper. 'Mike, Sam, Tammy and Trent.'

Sam looked at the others. 'That's not right.'

'Andy, Myles, Hugo and Dylan.'

'None of us are together,' Andy whispered. 'It should be the same as last time. Everything else is.'

'Can't you do a spell or something?' Sam urged Felix.

'It doesn't work like that,' said Felix. He'd gone even paler than usual.

Jake thought fast. If none of them were together, there was really only one option.

'Jake, Sammy, Oscar and Mia,' called Bates.

The other students were moving into their groups but none of the boys had moved.

'Come on, boys,' said Bates. 'The other year tens won't bite.'

'*Run!*' yelled Jake, and the four of them sprinted off down the forest path.

'Hey, get back here,' Bates yelled angrily through his megaphone. 'You're on report, the lot of you.'

Jake didn't care. Stuff Bates and his stupid rules. He led the way. He remembered the path as clearly as if they were here the day before.

He'd cared so much about winning the stupid exercise, and all for what? So he could beat that meat-head Trent? He ran faster. He could hear the footsteps of the others slapping behind him. It felt good to run, like he was running from his past self and all the dumb things he'd cared so much about.

He rounded a corner and stopped, breathless. The others caught up to him.

'That was awesome,' panted Sam. 'Did you see the look

on Bates's face?'

Felix looked around. 'I know where we are. This is the spot where Jake emptied out Andy's backpack.'

Jake sighed. God, did he really need another reminder of what a tool he'd been? 'OK. I get it. I was a bonehead.'

'Well, not to recognise the value of Nai Nai's poncho was pretty remiss, given the circumstances,' said Andy.

Jake couldn't help smiling. He got down on one knee. 'I would hereby like to apologise to you, Andy, and to you, Felix, for being a total jerk.' He stood up. 'There. Happy?'

Andy grinned. 'We've all changed. I was a nerd, but no longer.' The sky suddenly darkened, and Andy looked up. 'A sudden storm. Just like last time. A confluence of repeating events.'

Jake, Sam and Felix looked at each other.

'Yep, definitely no longer a nerd.' Jake laughed.

Felix started moving them down the path. 'Come on. We need to find the shortcut we took.'

The sky was steadily getting darker and a slow rumble was starting to build. Jake stopped and looked around nervously. The rumble didn't sound like thunder; it sounded like it was coming from inside the earth. What was it Phoebe had called the four of them? *A magical disturbance*? The earth rumbled again, angrily.

Feeling spooked, Jake jogged to catch up to the others.

Felix was leading them straight into the bush. 'This is where we left the path.'

Jake pushed through branches and scrub until he emerged behind the others in a familiar clearing.

'This is it,' said Felix.

'Where we fell over the cliff,' said Sam.

'And I lost the map,' said Felix.

'Whoa. It really is steep,' said Andy, peering over the edge.

The earth rumbled again, so violently this time that the ground shook like there was something beneath it, trying to get out.

They looked at each other nervously.

Jake noticed the pulsing light underneath Felix's shirt. 'Felix, the talisman's glowing.'

'I know,' said Felix. 'The demon's got its strength back.'

Jake felt a tug of fear. What was it going to hurl at them this time? What came after dogs? Bulls? Lions?

'We have to stay together,' said Felix firmly. He held out his hands. 'Come on, we need to go down.'

Jake looked at Felix's outstretched hand. He'd come a long way, admitting he'd been a jerk, but he wasn't quite ready to hold another guy's hand. 'No way, dude.'

At that moment, a massive roar came from the earth, shaking the ground beneath their feet, and Jake grabbed hold of Felix's hand. He stretched his other hand out to Andy and

Sam, and before they knew it, all four boys had jumped off the cliff. They slid fast and furiously down the side of the ravine, landing with four consecutive thuds.

Jake looked around. Just like last time, there was an eerie stillness. No breeze. No sound. He looked at the others. Their faces still registered the shock of the landing.

Felix took out the talisman. It wasn't glowing anymore.

'Batteries must have fallen out on the way down,' said Andy.

Felix put it back under his shirt, annoyed. 'You believe in wormholes and every hare-brained scientific theory ever invented, but not magic.'

'Actually, quantum physics can be proven.'

'Well, what if magic is just science that hasn't been proven yet?'

Jake looked at Andy. How was he going to answer that one? But Andy said nothing.

Felix stood up. 'Come on, we need to find the clearing where we made the sp– er, the fire.'

'I thought we were looking for wormholes,' said Sam.

'Yeah, well, good luck with that,' said Felix, heading off.

'What does a wormhole look like exactly?' asked Jake.

'A geometric tunnel that cuts through space and time.'

Jake looked around. 'Nah. Can't see one of those.'

'Well, you might not necessarily see it before it swallows you.'

'Come on,' called Felix. 'We need to stick together.'

When they caught up to Felix, he was standing in a small clearing. Hanging from the trees nearby were the strange-looking objects they'd seen last time. Felix was fingering one thoughtfully. He looked at the others. 'It doesn't make sense, but these were hanging in our old world, and they're here in this world too.'

'So, someone's been doing art-and-craft lessons in both worlds,' said Andy, looking dismissively at the woven ornaments.

Felix ignored him. 'I think it's got something to do with Phoebe's sister. This might be the place she disappeared.'

'Then all you have to do is reverse her spell and she'll come back, right?' said Jake, hopefully.

'Do you know the spell?' asked Sam.

Felix looked away evasively. 'I could try.'

'Well then, stuff wormholes. Do the spell,' said Sam.

Felix shut his eyes and began to chant softly.

'Water, fire, earth and air,
Elements that we all share.'

The sky opened with a crack and lightning blinded them. Almost immediately, a torrent of rain poured down.

'Get away from the trees!' yelled Andy.

Jake could just make out the stone ledge they'd sheltered under before. He made a run for it across the clearing.

Lightning split the sky apart. Jake ran faster. He couldn't see the others.

Then suddenly, he was falling. The whole world turned black as he fell through the earth. *This*, he thought, *is what being swallowed by a wormhole must feel like.*

sam: not out of the woods yet

Through the drenching rain, Sam could just make out Felix holding the talisman and yelling at the top of his lungs.

> *'Water wash our sins away,*
> *Earth guide us to a place.*
> *Wind brings with it fear,*
> *Flames of fire we must face.'*

Those words. Sam was sure he'd heard them before. But where? The driving rain hit hard at his skin. He made his way towards Felix. If magic was going to get them home, then Sam sure as hell wanted to be there when it happened.

> *'Walk upon this earth again,*
> *Walk upon this —'*

He'd almost got to Felix when he felt something catch

around his ankle and before he knew what was happening, he felt himself falling. Everything turned black around him, and he landed with a jarring thump.

'Owww,' said a voice.

Sam felt around in the dark. Legs. Arms. A head.

'Stop feeling me up,' said the voice.

'Jake?'

'Sam?'

'Where are we?'

'I think we might have found Andy's wormhole,' Jake whispered.

Sam felt around. They were inside some sort of mesh net. Sam put his hand through one of the holes in the mesh. He touched dirt. 'Are wormholes made of dirt?'

'Dunno.'

Sam looked up. There was a patch of grey sky, concealed by what looked like branches. 'It looks like an army trench. Maybe we've travelled to World War Two or something.'

Jake sat himself up. 'Yeah, good one. Just what we need.'

'Shh,' said Sam. 'I can hear voices.'

Jake and Sam listened carefully. From above, they could hear Felix and Andy and another voice, deep and rough.

'Who's that?' asked Jake.

'Probably an army general or something. Keep quiet,' whispered Sam.

But Jake ignored him. 'Help!' he yelled. 'Get us out of here.'

A pale light trickled in as the branches above them were moved, causing a cascade of water to land on them. A wild-looking face peered down from above.

'Roland?'

'Interesting. Very interesting,' Roland said, pulling more branches away to reveal the anxious faces of Felix and Andy at the mouth of the hole.

The rain seemed to have stopped.

Sam called up to them. 'Are we home? Did it work?'

Roland stood looking down at them, his hunting stick in one hand. 'Not quite the desired outcome,' he said thoughtfully, 'but a success nevertheless.'

'So, we're home?' said Sam hopefully.

'This is my wild-beast trap. Nothing's ever sprung it before, so good to know it's working. You never know what you'll find out here, boys.' Roland shrugged. 'Be prepared, I always say.'

Sam called up to Felix. 'Felix? Did it work? The spell you were –'

Roland reached his arm down to help Sam out. 'Guess you boys will be wanting a lift into town again.'

Again. Sam felt the sting of that word. So, they *weren't* home. If they were, Roland wouldn't have a clue who they were. Nothing had worked. No wormhole. No spell. His stomach heaved. He stared at Roland and realised how much he'd been hoping this excursion would reverse everything.

But now, their last hope was dashed.

He reluctantly grabbed hold of Roland's grimy out-stretched hand and let himself be pulled up into the light. Roland heaved Jake up after him.

Sam collapsed on the side of the hole – filthy, muddy and depressed.

'All right, boys, follow me to the car and I'll give you a ride home,' Roland said, turning back towards the bush.

Sam felt like laughing out loud. *Home*? He had no home.

Below him, the ground started to shudder. As if to mock him, it rumbled like a laugh waiting to burst out of a belly. Sam turned to the others and saw Felix grasping at his neck.

'The talisman,' said Felix. 'It must have fallen off.'

The ground around them began shaking more violently.

Sam watched Roland carefully. He looked strangely frozen. Then his body started moving in weird, robotic gestures. His neck jerked, and he looked at the boys, his eyes as dead as stones.

'We have to find the talisman,' yelled Felix above the deafening shaking of the earth. 'It's the demon. It's taking human form.'

Sam jumped to his feet. He began scrambling through the undergrowth, searching frantically for the talisman.

Roland took jerky movements towards Felix. His eyes started radiating a creepy red light. A deep, guttural roar exploded from his mouth.

Sam grabbed Andy. 'Come on. Look! We have to find it.'

'Like a necklace is going to save us,' Andy said scornfully.

Sam couldn't believe it. The time to question magic was not when a *demon* was about to attack. He grabbed Andy hard.

'Ow!' cried Andy. 'You don't have to resort to physical violence.'

'Look. Now!' ordered Sam.

Felix had skirted around behind Roland. He was terrifying, but his movements were slow. It took him a moment or two to work out where Felix had gone. He finally turned, lifted his hunting stick above his head and took a swipe at Felix, nearly knocking him off his feet. Felix quickly ducked and slipped away from him, and again Roland took a moment to work out where he'd gone.

'Let's find the talisman while Felix is distracting him,' Sam hissed to Jake and Andy.

The three of them scrabbled around in the scrub. The undergrowth was wet and Sam came up with nothing more than handfuls of damp leaves.

Roland opened his mouth and let out another furious roar. His eyes were gleaming like embers. He seemed to be gaining in strength.

'Find the talisman!' yelled Felix. He ran swiftly across Roland's path, trying to disorient him. But Roland's reflexes were improving. He reached out a hand to grab Felix and missed him by millimetres.

'Jake, we've got to stop him or he'll kill Felix,' Sam yelled. He turned back to Andy. 'You keep looking.'

As if only noticing them for the first time, Roland turned towards Sam and Jake. He flung his hunting stick to the ground and lumbered towards them.

Jake and Sam glanced at each other nervously. Roland bent down and put both arms around a massive log. Sam knew there was no way a human could lift that. But clearly this wasn't a human, because Roland lifted the log as if it were nothing more than a chopstick. He hurled it at Jake and Sam. They flung themselves out of its path and the log smashed against a nearby tree. Roland rushed towards them, roaring with a primal force that came straight from the earth and out through him.

'Surround him!' Sam yelled.

Jake nodded. 'One, two, *three*!'

They hurled themselves at either side of Roland. He batted them away as if they were annoying insects. Sam landed hard against a boulder. A sharp pain went up his right leg. He felt up and down his shin. Man, he hoped he hadn't broken something.

Roland had diverted his attention back to Felix and was gaining on him fast. Felix ducked away, but Roland was too quick. He grabbed him with both arms. Felix tried to struggle, but Roland was too strong. It looked like Roland was about to squeeze the air out of him when Andy yelled out, 'I've found it!'

Sam jumped to his feet. The pain in his leg shot into his thigh but he barely noticed it. 'Hold it out, Andy!' he yelled.

Roland turned towards the talisman. He dropped a stunned Felix to the ground and started towards Andy, like a moth to a flame.

Sam ran to Felix and pulled him to his feet. He was deathly pale and struggling to breathe. 'You have to say the spell.'

Felix coughed. Sam turned to see Andy holding out the fiercely glowing talisman towards Roland. He shook Felix hard. 'Come on. Say it!'

Felix gasped for breath, and started to chant. *'Divinity of the elements, I summon thee.'*

Roland moved closer to Andy.

Felix coughed and wheezed. *'Earth, water, air, fire.'*

'Come on, Felix,' Sam yelled desperately.

'Within this stone I invoke ye place,.
Your greatest strength, your kindest grace.'

Felix was getting his breath back. His voice was slowly gaining in strength.

Andy bravely brandished the talisman. Roland was only a few steps away.

'And while this stone remains at hand,
Thou shall be safe throughout this land.'

The talisman suddenly flashed brightly and Roland stopped short.

Sam watched, amazed, as the red light slowly faded from his eyes. His hands dropped to his sides and he shook his head like a swimmer trying to get water out of his ear. His shoulders slumped into their normal position. He looked curiously at Andy who was staring at him, holding out the talisman, with an expression of utter terror.

'What's the matter, matey? You look like you've seen a ghost.'

Sam let go of his grip on Felix, who fell to his knees.

Roland picked up his hunting stick. 'OK, what are we doing? Am I taking you boys back to town or what?'

Sam was speechless. Roland had no idea what had just happened.

Roland looked at Felix, who was deathly pale. 'What happened to him?'

'*You* happened to him,' said Sam. 'You went totally psycho and tried to kill us.'

Roland burst into a loud belly laugh. 'Oh, that's a good one. Sure there are dangerous things out here, but I'm not one of them.' He pulled a twig out of his hair and looked at it curiously.

No one knew how to respond.

'All right,' said Roland. 'Think I'll leave you boys to it, and go feed the Henriettas. Drop by the camp if you want a lift into Bremin.' He trudged off through the bushes, whistling cheerily.

The boys looked at each other. Man, they had been *this close* to total cactus. Andy hadn't even moved. He was still holding the talisman out. His arm slowly fell to his side and he looked sheepishly at Felix. 'OK, magic totally exists.'

Felix rolled his eyes. 'Finally.'

'Did it have to take us nearly getting killed for you to work that out?' said Jake, helping Felix to his feet.

'We have to get out of here,' said Felix. 'If the demon can possess people, it's getting seriously strong.'

Sam couldn't believe what he was hearing. 'Wait a minute. We came here to get home.'

'Sam,' said Felix. 'I tried, OK? It didn't work. We need to find another way.'

Sam shook his head. He wasn't going to let them give up. They were here. They had the talisman to protect them. They *had* to keep trying. 'No way. We have to retrace our steps.'

'We did that, dude,' said Jake, looking around. 'And it nearly killed us.'

'We haven't finished,' said Sam. He looked around for firewood. 'We have to make a fire like last time.' He picked up some damp twigs. 'Come on! We have to retrace our steps, which means we have to stay all night. Then tomorrow we'll know if it worked.'

No one moved.

'It's probably not too late to get the bus back,' said Andy, handing Felix the talisman.

What a traitor. Sam turned on him. '*You* were the one who said this would work. That we would find the wormhole if we repeated everything exactly as it was last time.'

Andy looked thoughtful. 'Yeah, but that was before I believed in magic. I have to say, that's a total game-changer.'

Sam wanted to scream in frustration. What was wrong with them? Was he the only one who actually wanted to go home? He grabbed some more firewood and headed towards the stone ledge.

Felix called after him. 'Sam, come on. We need to go back. Talk to Phoebe.'

Sam turned on him, furious. 'OK, fine. You go. I'm staying here.'

Felix sighed. 'You can't stay on your own out here. You just saw what happened. If we're not together –'

A loud cracking sound suddenly came from the bushes to their right.

Jake turned sharply. 'What was that?'

It sounded like a creature scrambling through the undergrowth towards them.

Sam moved back towards the others. 'It's the demon

again. Quick, do the spell.'

'*Divinity of the elements . . .*' began Felix.

Just as they realised the talisman wasn't glowing, the branches of a wattle pushed apart and a furious Bates stood there.

'What the *hell* do you think you're doing?'

The boys looked at each other.

'Demon slaying?' offered Andy.

Bates ignored him. 'I have exhausted students waiting on a bus, while you boys do what?' He looked at Sam's armful of twigs. 'Set up camp?'

'We got lost,' said Felix.

'Well maybe if you'd taken a map and stayed in your allocated groups that wouldn't have happened.' Bates could barely contain his anger. 'Come on. Follow me.'

'That's fine. We're happy to stay here,' said Sam.

Bates turned on him sharply. 'Like that's going to happen.'

'It has before,' muttered Sam.

'Follow me. *Now*,' ordered Bates.

Felix, Andy and Jake set off after Bates; his mauve jumper leading the way through the bush.

Sam hesitated. Should he stay here? Give it a try? He thought about Roland's devil eyes and superhuman strength. He'd have no hope against that on his own. He threw down his handful of wet twigs. Somehow being this close to getting home made *not* getting there so much worse.

The others were almost out of sight when he reluctantly set off after them. He trudged miserably through wet bracken. He could see Andy walking ahead of him.

'Sam.'

'Yeah, what?' said Sam crossly.

Andy turned. 'I didn't say anything.'

Sam watched as Andy kept walking. He disappeared around a bend.

'Sam.'

The voice sounded close.

'Yes?' said Sam hesitantly.

'They don't understand what you're going through . . . but I do.'

Sam looked around. The voice seemed to be coming from all around. The earth, the trees, the sky all seemed to be vibrating with its sound.

'I can help you, Sam.'

Sam stood perfectly still.

'If you'll let me.'

Sam felt his breathing settle. The voice was reassuring.

He looked around. But there was no one there. Just a gentle breeze drifting through the branches of the gum trees.

Sam shook his head. He was imagining things. He turned to catch up the others. The voice came again – a little more insistent.

'Will you let me help you, Sam?'

felix: the unmaking of ...

'So maybe the closest explanation to what happened to us is the intersection between science and magic. The interlinking point where the two systems collide.'

Felix had been trying to ignore Andy from the moment they'd got back on the bus. But even now, as they walked along the bush track, he wouldn't let it go. Like a born-again believer, Andy wanted to quiz Felix on every aspect of magic. It was driving Felix completely nuts, to the point where he almost wished Andy still didn't believe in magic. At least then Felix didn't have to deal with constant questions about how magic worked and how close the cause-and-effect system was to science.

'Yeah, maybe,' said Felix, trying to give Andy the hint to shut up. He had other things bothering him, like why the reversing spell hadn't worked. Maybe Sam was right. They hadn't exactly retraced their steps.

Jake put his hand on his arm. 'Felix, look.'

Felix had been so wrapped up in his own thoughts that he hadn't realised they'd reached the shack. Pulled up out the front was a police car.

'It's my dad,' said Jake.

The boys dropped to the ground and watched as Jake's dad paced around the perimeter. Another policeman exited the shack.

'No sign of them, sarge. But they're definitely staying here.'

Jake's dad looked out into the bush. His eyes passed by where the four boys were hiding in the grass. Felix held his breath.

'OK, then. Let's search around this area. They won't be far.'

'We have to get out of here, *now*,' Felix whispered urgently.

The boys raced back down the bush path. The sun was setting and the birds were chirping into the dusk before settling down for the night.

'Where are we going?' panted Andy.

'It's not like we've got many options,' said Felix as they reached the bitumen road.

'Oh no,' groaned Sam. 'Not *Phoebe's*.'

Felix turned on him sharply. 'You got a better plan?'

───────

By the time they'd reached Arcane Lane, the street lights were on and the birdsong had been replaced by the slow hum of traffic as commuters made their way home.

A CLOSED sign hung on the door. Ignoring it, Felix banged on the glass. No response.

'She's gone home, dude,' said Sam.

'She lives out the back,' said Felix. 'She'll be here. She's just screening.' He banged again, louder.

'You sure know a lot about her,' said Sam.

Felix ignored him. A light had been switched on. Footsteps were coming towards the door.

There was the sound of three different bolts being drawn and then Phoebe's cranky face appeared at the door. 'Can't you boys read?' She pointed at the sign. 'C–L–O–'

'Can we come in?' asked Felix.

'Have you found out anything?'

Felix shrugged. 'Maybe.'

Phoebe's eyes narrowed. 'What's *maybe* mean? You either have or you haven't.'

Felix heard a car pull into the car park. He looked anxiously over his shoulder. It wouldn't be long before the police would start looking for them in town. Why they were after them he didn't know, and he most certainly didn't want to find out. 'We need your help.'

Phoebe held his gaze. 'And I need yours. And where has that got me?'

'Just let us in. Please.'

Phoebe sighed and opened the door just wide enough for

226

the boys to slip through. She led them into her back room. 'All right. What's going on?'

'We went on this school excursion,' Andy blurted out.

'It was the same one we went on in our world and we thought we could retrace our steps and find our way home,' added Jake.

Phoebe looked at Felix darkly. 'So, you thought you could ignore our deal and find your own way home.'

'Don't worry. It was an epic fail on all fronts,' muttered Sam, who had slumped into Phoebe's armchair.

'Yeah, we got attacked by a demon in human form,' said Andy eagerly. 'But then I defeated it.'

'With magic,' added Felix.

'Yeah, with magic,' said Andy. 'It was totally cool. I just held the talisman out like –'

'So, the demon can now take on human form,' Phoebe interrupted. 'That's not good.'

'I know,' said Felix.

'That means it's getting strong. And it will keep getting stronger until it destroys you.'

'That's if my dad doesn't get us first,' said Jake.

Phoebe looked at him. 'Your dad's after you?'

'The police found our shack. We can't go back there. That's why we're here,' said Felix.

Phoebe took a moment to work out what Felix was saying. Her eyes widened. 'No.'

'We don't have any other options,' said Felix.

'You can't stay here. Four stinky boys in this tiny room? No one would come out alive.'

'Please, Phoebe.' Felix looked around the room. It was warm and dry. The couches had plump cushions, and there was a soft-looking rug on the floor.

'Absolutely no way.'

Felix reached into his bag and pulled out one of the strange hanging objects he'd found in the forest.

Phoebe looked stunned. 'Where did you get that?'

'It's Alice's, isn't it?'

Phoebe nodded, and sat down next to Felix. 'She made them for conjurations. But where did you –?'

'In the Bremin Ranges,' answered Felix.

'But the police looked there. And so did I.'

'It's a hidden path.'

'You had to fall off a cliff to get there. Literally,' added Andy.

'There was another sign of Alice as well,' Felix said slowly.

Phoebe looked up, excited. 'What?'

'If I tell you, will you let us stay?'

Phoebe knew she was backed into a corner. She sighed and rolled her eyes. 'I don't do maternal and I don't do breakfast.'

'That's fine by us,' said Felix.

'All right, then. So long as you use deodorant and there's *no snooping*.'

'We don't have deo–' began Andy.

Phoebe threw a crystal at him. 'Try that. There's a spare mattress and linen in that cupboard. Shower's through there.' She gestured to a door leading into a small corridor.

Andy, Jake and Sam got up. They were filthy and exhausted, not to mention starving.

'Phoebe,' started Jake. 'I was wondering –'

'Yes, kitchen's out there too. There's some sprouted bread and miso spread in the fridge.'

The boys exchanged glances. Jake shrugged. 'Beggars can't be choosers.'

Phoebe leant in. 'So?' she whispered to Felix. 'What else did you find?'

'Near where the conjurations were hanging was an altar.' Felix hadn't told the others this, but the wire that Sam and Jake had tripped on had pulled aside a bush, revealing a stone altar.

Phoebe's eyes lit up. 'Where she cast her spell?'

'Probably.'

'So, it was at the same place you got lost in your world?'

Felix nodded.

'I knew there was a connection between you,' said Phoebe triumphantly. 'So, now we just need to work out what spell she cast.'

Felix had a pretty good idea what that might be. On the altar were carved the four elemental symbols. 'Was there something, anything, that happened to Alice that she might have . . . you know . . . wanted to change?'

Phoebe's face darkened. 'Why do you ask that?'

'I'm just trying to work out why she would want to cast such a powerful spell.'

Phoebe looked around. Jake and Sam had disappeared and Andy was setting up his bed.

She turned back to Felix, suddenly vulnerable. Felix had got so used to grumpy Phoebe that seeing her like this was unnerving.

'Fifteen years ago, my parents, our parents, died in a house fire. Alice and I were at a party and when we came home . . .'

Felix shifted his feet. Dealing with emotion was not his strong point. In his old world, earphones and a closed bedroom door were his natural defence against it. 'I'm sorry,' he said awkwardly.

'They said it was an electrical fault,' continued Phoebe. 'But Alice never believed it. Our dad was a loan manager at the local bank and when the drought hit, a lot of farms went under. People were angry with the banks.'

'So, Alice thought it was deliberate.'

'She was a teenager. You know — erratic, emotionally unstable,' said Phoebe, sounding more like her old self.

'Yeah,' said Felix playing along. 'That's us.'

'Anyway, she talked a lot about finding a way to change the past.'

'To unmake it,' murmured Felix. His instinct was right. He and Alice had a hell of a lot in common.

'What did you say?'

'Nothing,' said Felix. 'Can I look at her Book of Shadows?'

Phoebe got up and took the Book of Shadows out of the desk drawer. She handed it to Felix. 'It's not to leave this room, OK?'

'OK,' said Felix, taking the heavy book.

Phoebe stood there for a beat. 'And Felix?'

He looked up.

'Thanks.'

Felix nodded. He could see how much Phoebe wanted her sister back. Ten years was a long time to not see your sister, and he, of all people, knew what it felt like to lose your only sibling.

Something landed in his lap.

He picked it up. It was the deodorant crystal. The others had come back.

'Don't hold back, bro,' said Jake, grinning.

Phoebe stood up. 'I'll leave you to it.' She looked intently at Felix. 'Good luck.'

Felix smiled uncertainly. He wasn't sure that luck was what he needed, exactly.

While the others got under the blankets and slowly began to fall asleep, Felix took Alice's Book of Shadows to Phoebe's desk. He sat down and carefully began to turn the pages.

There were chapters on wealth, fertility, love, and curses. Each section had a number of handwritten spells, mostly accompanied by ornate drawings of ingredients or complex patterns. Felix skimmed through them, he already knew what he was looking for. He turned a page and there it was: AN UNMAKING SPELL. The day he'd sneaked into Phoebe's back room, he'd copied the same spell down. He'd wanted to unmake Oscar's accident, and in this world, Alice had used the same spell to unmake the fire her parents had died in.

He read the last two lines of the spell, which he'd changed for his purposes. They were different from his, but with the same intent.

'Douse the flames so we may be.
Douse the flames so we may be.'

Felix carefully shut the book. Phoebe was right: he and Alice were connected. They'd both disappeared from their own worlds trying to unmake something. So what world was Alice in? He shuddered at the thought that they might be away from their world for ten years. How could he do that to the others? No, he had to get them home.

He thought about Phoebe's promise that if he got Alice back, she would get them home. He wasn't sure about that. Surely, if Alice wanted to come home, she could reverse her own spell. She knew the spell she'd used and where she'd cast it. Maybe Alice didn't *want* to come back from wherever she'd gone. And if someone forced her back, she wasn't going to be happy.

Felix shook his head. The real problem was that he wasn't even convinced reversing a spell worked. They were all still here, so clearly repeating the same spell in the same place wasn't enough to reverse it.

He thought back to the moment when he'd cast it. Maybe it hadn't worked because Jake and Sam had fallen right at the moment when it was being cast? Or perhaps it was because he hadn't wanted to say those final words. Maybe to make a spell work you had to actually *want* it to work.

Felix put the Book of Shadows away in the desk drawer. He looked over at the others. Sam and Jake had scored the couches and Sam was snoring, as usual. Andy was fast asleep on the floor. Maybe it was better for everyone if he didn't let on to Phoebe that he'd found Alice's spell. What he needed to focus on was getting *them* home.

Felix grabbed a blanket from the cupboard and lay down next to Andy. He thought it would be hard to get to sleep, but the room was warm and he was exhausted. In an instant, he was asleep.

He dreamt of a house. A lovely wooden house on the outskirts of a forest. He walked in the door of the house and found a party inside. Alice was sitting at the head of a dinner table. On either side of her were her mum, dad and Phoebe.

Everyone was laughing. Celebrating. They lifted their glasses in a toast. Felix sat down at the table and Alice turned to him. She began applauding him. Alice's mum was smiling at him with tears in her eyes. Felix didn't know what he'd done but he was glad. Suddenly they all burst into song.

'Water, fire, earth and air,
Elements that we all share.'

Felix joined in and Alice leant over and kissed him on the cheek. Felix turned his head to see that it was no longer Alice, and they were no longer sitting at a table. It was Ellen and they were in his back garden and she was smiling at him. 'I've missed you,' she said.

'I've missed you too,' said Felix.

Ellen bent her head towards his and just when their lips were about to touch, Felix had an odd feeling he was being watched.

He woke with a start, to see a figure leaning right over him. 'Sam?'

Sam shrunk back from him, and shook his head as if to wake himself up.

'Were you trying to kiss me?' asked Felix.

'In your dreams, dude,' said Sam. His voice sounded thick and deep.

'Well, what the hell were you doing?'

'Chillax, would you? I was looking for the toilet.'

Sam stood up and made his way clumsily towards the corridor.

Felix rolled over. He wanted to get back inside his dream. It was probably the closest he was ever going to get to –

Suddenly he felt something warm against his chest. He reached his hand under his shirt and pulled out the talisman. It was glowing.

sam: dating the demon

Sam rolled over on the couch. He pulled a blanket over his head to block out the sound of something banging. Probably Pete had forgotten his key again and was coming back late from a party. Too bad. Sam wasn't getting up. The banging got louder. Sam screwed his eyes tight. He was so comfy there was no way he was . . .

Hang on. He was comfortable? And he had a pillow? No wonder he couldn't get up. He'd been sleeping on the hard floor of a draughty shack for over a week. Right now he felt so cosy he never wanted to move.

Jake nudged him. 'Sam, get up. It's my dad.'

Sam suddenly remembered where he was. Crazy witch lady's youth hostel. Dinner had been thick black sludge on cardboard. He sat up and rubbed his eyes. The banging had stopped and Sam could hear voices coming from the shop.

The four boys crept towards the beaded curtain and peered through. Jake's dad was standing amid the unicorns and tarot cards, arguing with Phoebe.

'Surely you know where your nephews are.'

Phoebe was making herself very busy, dusting a row of deranged-looking fairies. 'Well, they're probably running around, throwing things. Isn't that what teenage boys do?'

'Actually, teenage boys should be at school. I thought such a devoted guardian would know that.'

The boys looked at each other. *Uh-oh.*

Phoebe cleared her throat. 'Well, of course. That's exactly where they are.'

'No, they're not. I already checked.'

Jake's dad had picked up a love potion. 'Does this stuff actually work?' he said.

'Come on. We've got to get out of here,' Felix whispered.

'Where are we going to go?'

'School. If he's already checked there, it's the safest place.'

'What do you want them for anyway?' Phoebe was asking Jake's dad, who was sniffing the love potion.

'Trespassing.'

'Crap,' whispered Jake. 'He's going to get us for breaking into the shack.'

'Come on,' urged Felix. 'Out the back.'

The boys slipped into the lane behind Phoebe's shop and made their way through town towards Bremin High. Sam brought up the rear. He hadn't really forgiven the others for not making it through in the forest. Maybe the real reason they hadn't tried harder was because they didn't actually *want* to go home. In this world, Felix's brother could walk, Jake's parents were way better off, and Andy – well, his reason came rushing up just as they'd reached Bremin High.

'Hey, Andy,' said Ellen. 'Do you want to study in the library at lunch?'

Andy blushed. 'Sure. Sounds . . . ah . . . educational.'

Jake groaned.

'Great, I'll meet you there.' Ellen headed off as the end-of-recess bell started ringing.

Andy looked after her, smitten. Yep, Andy had a crush – and that was enough to make everything else unimportant. Sam knew exactly what that felt like.

'Felix, you know Ellen better than anyone,' said Andy. 'If I were to maybe ask her out, where d'you think she'd –'

'You know what my advice to you is?' Felix's face was dark. 'Give up. 'Cause underneath that terrible dress sense is a really cool girl.'

Andy looked confused as Felix stalked off towards the main building. 'What did I say?'

Jake shook his head. 'Dude, do you really not get it?' He turned to Sam. 'He might be a maths genius but he's as thick as . . . Sam?'

Sam only vaguely heard what Jake was saying. On the other side of the quad, under the break-up tree, were Sammy and Mia.

'Catch you guys later,' Sam said as he made his way across the quad.

Finally, Sam thought, *something good is happening.*

He sat down on a bench where he could watch Mia and Sammy out of the corner of his eye. Mia seemed to be doing all the talking. Sammy put his head in his hands. Mia said some final words and walked away, leaving Sammy devastated.

Sam sprung to his feet. He knew Mia would see the light eventually. He jogged after her. 'Hey, Mia. How's it going?'

Mia turned. Her eyes were red-rimmed like she'd been crying. 'Oh. You.'

'I couldn't help noticing –'

'What?' said Mia. 'That we broke up? Well, congratulations. Are you happy now?'

This stopped Sam in his tracks. 'No, of course not. I just wanted to say if you needed someone to talk to, you know, I'd be happy to –'

'It didn't take you long, did it?' said Mia.

'What?'

'To pounce on me.'

Sam suddenly felt lost for words.

'Do you really think that just because I broke up with Sammy, I want to be with you?'

'No, I –'

'Do you know what I really want?'

Sam thought about that. He wasn't sure he did. 'No.'

'To be alone. OK?'

'Sure. No problem,' Sam mumbled. He let Mia walk away. He could have kicked himself. Would he never learn?

———

Sam made his way up the stairs and into the science lab. The others had already taken their seats and Bates was giving a lecture about the importance of rules and attendance. Bates eyeballed Sam as he slipped into an empty seat.

'Another example of a student willing to flout the rules.'

'Sorry, sir,' Sam muttered.

'Are you also sorry you ignored the excursion protocol? Are you sorry you caused a brawl in the playground? Are you sorry you and your "cousins" are continually late and under-prepared for class?'

Sam's eyes flickered towards Jake, Felix and Andy, who were keeping their heads down. 'Yes, sir.'

'And what's that supposed to mean?'

'It won't happen again, sir.'

Bates turned to the others. 'It better not. Or the four of you will be spending every Saturday cleaning graffiti off desks. Now, open your books. Today we're looking at the life cycle of the dust mite.'

Sam sighed and opened his book. Even being arrested by Jake's dad looked good compared with being stuck in an airless room with Bates and his dust mites.

As Bates turned to write on the whiteboard, the door swung open and Mia walked in. She walked straight towards Sam and sat down in the empty seat next to his. He looked at her, taken aback.

She reached into her bag and pulled out the drawing he'd done of her. It was a perfect likeness. 'You're really good.'

Sam's heart swelled. 'Yeah, well, my subject wasn't too bad,' he said, smiling.

Mia smiled back and put her hand over his. She felt cold, which was strange. Mia always had the warmest hands.

She squeezed his hand gently and before Sam knew what was happening, he began to draw. He glanced at Mia. She was paying attention to the board as if the seven stages of a dust mite's life were the most interesting thing in the world.

He looked back at his notepad and, to his shock, saw that his hand was drawing the talisman. He watched it move quickly across the page. It was the weirdest feeling – like his hand was moving completely independently of his mind. It drew a perfect replica of the talisman, complete with details Sam hadn't even seen.

'What's happening?' he whispered to Mia.

Her head twitched toward him like she was a puppet on a string. 'It is keeping you here.' Her voice was deep and raspy. 'Destroy it and you will return to where you belong.'

Sam looked into her eyes. What she was saying made a strange kind of sense. 'I can't.'

'Then you will never go home,' said Mia, turning to look straight ahead again.

Sam followed her gaze. On the whiteboard, Bates's letters and words started to crawl over each other. Wriggling like a bunch of ants, they slowly formed the words: DESTROY IT.

Mia squeezed his hand again, and smiled. Sam stared at the words. DESTROY IT.

Slowly, Sam turned around to look at Felix, who was sitting a few rows back. The talisman, as always, was hanging around his neck – and Sam saw that it was steadily glowing.

Mia was right. The talisman wasn't protecting them, it was getting in the way! If the demon wanted them to go home, why were they fighting it? Because he was right: the others weren't interested in going home. They wanted to stay here. *They* were the ones stopping Sam from getting home. Why hadn't he realised that before? All he had to do was destroy the talisman and he could go home.

Sam felt an overwhelming urge to leap across the desks and grab it off Felix. He stood up suddenly, just as the lunch bell rang.

Mia stood up with a jerk, next to him. 'Follow them.'

Felix was making his way out the door. Sam pushed through the other students, and saw Felix and Andy at the end of the corridor, heading towards the library. He set off after them. He had to get that talisman.

Sam swung open the library door and looked around. Felix and Andy were sitting at the computers. Sam moved stealthily towards them. Andy was scrolling through internet searches on magic. Sam watched, wondering what the best tactic might be.

'If science and magic are both governed by cause and effect . . .' Andy was saying.

Felix seemed too intent on his own research to be paying him much attention.

'Then what's the cause?' asked Andy. 'Why us?'

'Probably just random,' Felix said casually.

'But that doesn't make sense.'

Sam edged closer, his eyes on the talisman. He moved towards it, mesmerised.

Felix looked up, startled. 'Sam, can you stop sneaking up on me? It's freaking me out.'

Sam could almost feel the talisman. It was calling him to take it. He slid into the seat next to Felix and was reaching his hand towards Felix's neck when Ellen appeared next to them.

'You want to go and check out the physics section?' she asked Andy.

'Sure,' he said, tripping over his chair in his eagerness to get up.

'I hope the lights don't go out again like last time,' Ellen said coyly as they walked off.

'Excuse me while I throw up,' said Felix, banging at the

keys on the computer.

Sam kept his eye on the talisman around Felix's neck. 'This is the only way,' he murmured. 'One day you'll thank me for it.' He lunged for the talisman.

But Felix was too quick. He grabbed Sam's hand and they struggled.

'Give it to me,' said Sam.

Felix pulled the talisman away from Sam. 'Why are you being such a psycho?' He turned to escape, but Mia had appeared on the other side of him. 'Mia? What's going . . . ?'

She directed her gaze at Sam, her eyes turning a deep red. Her head twitched like a bird's. 'You can succeed,' she said in a strange, deep voice. 'Destroy the talisman and go back home, where you belong.'

'Oh, Jesus. No, no, no. Not Mia.' Felix got to his feet.

Sam jumped up, seizing his chance. He grabbed the talisman and pulled the cord as hard as he could. The cord snapped and Sam hurtled out the door with the talisman in his hand.

'Sam! Wait! No!' Felix yelled.

Sam sprinted down the corridor. He heard Andy and Felix yelling as they chased after him, but he didn't care. He had the talisman and he was going to get rid of it. *Destroy it*, Mia had said, so he couldn't just throw it in a lake. He had to physically destroy it. He slid down the stair rail and burst out of the school's main entrance.

Jake was crossing the quad. 'Hey man, what's the rush?'

Sam ignored him. The auto workshop. That's where he'd go.

He reached the roller door and, yanking it up, slipped inside. He looked around.

The workshop was dark and chaotic. Tools lined the walls and cars crowded the floor, their bonnets up, ready for repair.

Sam dropped the talisman on to a bench. He wrenched a hammer off the wall, testing its weight in his hand. That should do it.

He looked down at the talisman, feeling anger flood through him. It was keeping him here. It had taken everything from him. He raised the hammer above his head. He was going to smash it to pieces and finally, *finally*, he'd get to go home.

'Sam. *No!*'

Jake, Felix and Andy had slipped under the roller door.

'Sam. Stop. The talisman is protecting us.'

Sam raised the hammer higher. 'It's not. It's keeping us here. Mia told me.'

He heard Felix yelling but he didn't care. He brought the hammer down as hard as he could. Right into the centre of the talisman.

Smash!

The hammer bounced off it. Sam stared at it in disbelief. It was completely unscathed. Damn! He'd have to hit it harder. He lifted the hammer again but before he could drop it, the talisman began to shake. The air suddenly filled with an intense high-pitched sound that rang in his ears, like the whine of a thousand mosquitoes. The talisman shook harder and then split into four even pieces.

The hammer fell to the ground as Sam clutched his hands to his ears. He stared down at the four broken pieces of talisman in front of him. The ringing sound dissipated.

'Poor boys. All alone,' said that familiar deep, raspy voice.

Sam looked up. Mia was standing by the roller door. Her eyes were still blood red and she was holding a metal chain.

Oh God. Sam reeled back. He suddenly felt like he'd got control of his mind and body back. He stared at Mia. What had he done? She was possessed – and he hadn't even realised. He picked up the pieces of talisman.

'Is your little toy broken, Sam?'

Felix turned just as Mia swung the chain at him.

'Felix!' Sam yelled. 'Run!'

Mia advanced towards them, her walk as jolting as her head movements.

'Quick! Behind the cars,' Sam shouted to the others. They dropped to their haunches and scurried to the back of the workshop. 'She's the demon,' whispered Sam.

'Like, you just worked that out?' said Felix scornfully.

Sam bit his lip. *What an idiot!*

'We have to confuse her,' said Felix. 'It's like with Roland. She'll be slow at first.'

They crouched behind a car, watching as Mia turned in

circles, swinging her chain. Felix was right: she couldn't work out where they'd gone.

Sam looked at the four broken pieces of talisman in his hand. 'Can it be fixed?'

'Unlikely,' muttered Felix.

Hearing their voices, Mia started to weave her way between the cars towards them.

'Felix, I'm sorry,' whispered Sam. 'She was controlling me somehow.'

Felix picked up a spanner and threw it as hard as he could across the workshop. It landed with a clatter and Mia turned sharply. She headed towards the noise.

'Come on,' Felix whispered. 'We haven't got long to outsmart her.' He led them quietly around the back of cars towards the roller door.

Just as they reached it, Mia saw them.

Sam spotted a fire extinguisher on the wall. He thought fast. He'd got them into this – he was going to get them out of it. 'You guys go. I'll deal with her.'

Mia was moving fast towards them.

'Go. *Go!*' Sam shoved them towards the roller door. He grabbed the fire extinguisher.

Felix looked back, unsure, as Andy and Jake slipped under the door.

'Felix, trust me. Go.'

Mia moved quickly, with her eyes fixed on Felix. The

chain swung from her hand, clanking menacingly on the concrete floor.

Sam waited until she was an arm's length away, then let rip with the fire extinguisher. A cloud of white mist covered her just as Felix, taking no more chances, slipped under the roller door.

Sam breathed a sigh of relief. OK, the others were safe. Now it was just him and Mia.

The foam cleared, and Mia turned her red glare on Sam. 'Order must be restored,' she rasped as she moved towards him.

'Mia, it's me, Sam. I know this isn't you. There is something else in control,' Sam tried desperately.

Mia let the chain fall to her side.

'You can beat this thing, Mia. Don't be afraid.' He took a small step forwards. 'Fight it, Mia. I know you can.'

Sam thought he saw a flash of recognition, but then Mia lifted the chain and swung it hard towards him. He ducked, but only just in time. He remembered what had happened with Roland – the way he'd seemed to grow in strength. He had to get out of there.

He blasted Mia again with the fire extinguisher, knocking her off balance, and covering her with a mist. Disorientated, she thrashed wildly around her. Sam bolted under the roller door and pulled the door closed.

The others were waiting for him on the other side.

From inside he could hear Mia recovering. She started to bang against the door, roaring furiously.

'Quick,' said Felix. 'Give me the pieces.' Sam handed him the four broken bits of talisman. Felix quickly put them back together and held them out. '*Divinity of the elements . . .*'

They all looked at the talisman. Nothing. Not even the hint of a glow.

Mia's roar became deafening and the roller door started shaking.

'She's getting stronger,' said Jake.

'And now we have absolutely no protection,' Felix said, looking pointedly at Sam.

Sam stared at the broken talisman. *Oh God.* What had he *done*?

'We have to get out of here!' yelled Jake.

'But – what about Mia?' Sam gaped.

'Your demon girlfriend in there?'

'She's getting stronger. If we stay, she'll break out of there and rip us to pieces,' said Jake urgently.

'You guys go. I want to make sure she's OK.'

Felix shrugged as he backed away. 'It's your funeral,' he said.

Sam felt terrible. He'd just destroyed the one thing that could protect them. And now his girlfriend was a demon who wanted to kill him way more than she wanted to date him.

jake: happy mother's day

'All right, you lot. If you're staying here, you can damn well earn your keep.' A feather duster flew across the shop and landed at Jake's feet.

'You can mop,' Phoebe told Andy. Then she turned to Sam and Felix. 'And you two can clean the windows.' She handed them a bucket and sponges and then disappeared into the back room.

'Do you really think this is the time to be concerned with cleanliness?' muttered Andy as he picked up the mop.

'Yeah, like being clean is going to stop the demon coming after us,' agreed Felix.

Andy sloshed some water onto the floor. 'Maybe the smell of Pine O Cleen will scare it away.'

'Worth a try, given we've got no other protection,' said Felix, glaring darkly at Sam.

Sam looked away, shame-faced.

Jake put his hand on Sam's shoulder. 'Give him a break.

He actually saved us from the demon.'

'Yeah, well, I wouldn't have had to if I hadn't been such an idiot,' Sam admitted.

'Shh,' said Felix.

Phoebe came out the back room, struggling with a cheesy-looking sign that read MAKE YOUR MOTHER SMILE THIS MOTHER'S DAY.

Jake watched her bang out of the front door and set the sign up outside the shop. He turned to the others. 'Is today Mother's Day?'

Sam slugged some water onto the window. 'Who cares? It's not like we've got mothers.'

The door jingled as Phoebe came back inside. 'Working hard, I see.'

Jake picked up his feather duster. He started to dust an array of ceramic frogs dressed in aprons and overalls. His duster moved past them towards a collection of glass dolphins. He looked at them. His mum loved dolphins. She always talked about going to Monkey Mia one day and swimming with them. *Far more intelligent than humans*, she'd always said.

Jake picked up one of the dolphins. It gleamed a glassy blue in the sunlight, like the ocean on a perfect sunny day. His mum would love that. She could add it to her collection.

Jake looked around. Phoebe was busy arranging heart-shaped boxes on the counter. Would she even miss it? He quickly slipped the dolphin into his pocket.

'On Mother's Day, my dad always made me and my brother make a card.' Felix sidled up next to Jake, making him jump. 'And then Oscar would give it to her and she'd cry. Oh, happy days.'

Jake wasn't sure how to respond. For him, Mother's Day was always happy. Pancakes for breakfast. Picnic in the park. An early movie. He felt the dolphin twisting in his pocket like it wanted to escape.

Felix moved closer. He opened his hand to show Jake the broken pieces of the talisman. 'I found some glue in the back room. If you hold the pieces, I can glue it back together.'

Jake looked at him, unconvinced. 'You really think that will work?'

Felix shrugged. 'Worth a go. At the very least it'll keep Phoebe off our backs. If she sees it's broken, she's going to totally freak.'

Felix pulled Jake behind a shelf and lay the pieces of talisman on a book. He carefully slotted the pieces together and pulled out the glue.

'Wait,' said Jake. It didn't look right. He moved the pieces into a different order and they still fitted perfectly. They looked at each other.

Sam stuck his head around the side of the shelf and Andy walked over with a mop in his hand. They gathered around the talisman.

'Which way does it go?' asked Jake.

Sam grinned. 'OK, so the demon is weird, violent and super bad, but it just may have helped us out.' He pulled a crumpled piece of paper out of his pocket and lay it down next to the talisman. 'Demon Mia made me draw it.'

Felix quickly rearranged the pieces to match the drawing. 'Bingo.' He grabbed the glue and started to stick the pieces together.

'Oh, how I love the smell of acetate in the morning.'

The boys looked up. Phoebe stood behind them with her arms folded.

'What exactly are you doing to my talisman?'

'Ah.' Felix looked around wildly for an answer.

Jake jumped in. 'Sam's girlfriend was possessed by the demon and she controlled him and made him destroy the talisman.'

'What?' Phoebe's jaw clenched. 'Have you any idea how precious that was?'

'It's not destroyed,' said Felix, quickly gluing the rest of it together. 'See. As good as new.'

Phoebe picked it up carefully. She gave Sam a filthy look. 'I always knew you were a total bonehead.'

'Can I have it back?' asked Felix.

'Not much point, is there?' said Phoebe. 'It's hardly going to work after being smashed to pieces.'

Felix looked carefully at the talisman. 'It might just need reactivating.'

Phoebe considered this. 'Maybe. But we'll have to wait until there's another threat.'

'So, we won't know whether it works until the demon comes at us again?' asked Andy.

'Yep,' said Phoebe. 'That's about right. And this demon is becoming pretty smart if it's learnt to target the weakest link.'

Sam had gone a deep shade of red.

Jake felt bad for him. 'Sam's not the weakest link. He just didn't realise his girlfriend was possessed.'

Phoebe snorted. 'Typically observant teenage male.' She turned to Sam. 'And where's your girlfriend now? Maybe if she's still possessed we can use her to try and reactivate it.'

Sam shook his head. 'She's fine now. I waited outside the workshop. After Felix and the others left, she suddenly returned to normal.'

Phoebe frowned. 'Interesting. Once the centre of disturbance had moved on.'

'What does that mean?' asked Jake.

'It means,' answered Andy, 'that the demon is only interested in Felix, for some reason.'

'That's just one of your crazy theories,' said Felix quickly.

'Actually,' Andy countered, 'it's an observable fact.'

Felix avoided Andy's eyes.

'In the forest, Roland was really only after you,' continued Andy, 'and Demon Mia seemed more interested in destroying you than any of us.'

Felix quickly turned to Phoebe, changing the subject. 'It does seem to be taking longer to recover after each attack.'

Phoebe nodded. 'The more evolved the demon is, the more energy it expels and the time between attacks lengthens. However . . .'

Jake felt the dolphin twist in his pocket. That was all he needed to hear. He dropped the duster and headed for the door.

'Jake, where do you think you're going? You have to stay together,' he heard Phoebe calling. But he didn't care. He wouldn't be long and by the sound of it, this might be his only chance.

He bolted out on to the street. He knew what he was doing was crazy. There was really no point, but he couldn't explain it. He just had to try. After all, today was their special day.

He jogged through town. In the main street, there was a large crowd of people gathered near a banner that read BREMIN MOTHER'S DAY CLASSIC FUN RUN. There were women everywhere, laughing good-naturedly, stretching in the sunshine and looking like they were ready to race. It looked like most of the town was there, but Jake was pretty sure his mum wouldn't be – she hated running.

Jake dodged past the marquees and the crowds. The dolphin jiggled up and down in his pocket. It was probably happy to be released from Phoebe's stuffy shop. Eventually he turned into his mum's street and slowed down. If she was there, he didn't want to turn up, puffing and red in the face.

As he approached her house, he noticed a figure up a ladder. Great. Bates was probably doing home maintenance. He moved closer and, to his relief, saw that the figure was his mum.

She was balancing precariously on the top rung of the ladder, pushing leaves out of the guttering with the end of a broomstick. She leant a bit too far and the ladder began to tip.

Jake quickly jogged up the driveway and grabbed the end of the ladder.

His mum looked down, surprised. 'Oh, thanks. That was close.'

Jake smiled. 'No worries.'

She looked at him for a beat. 'What are you doing here again?'

Jake felt his throat catch. How was he supposed to answer that without sounding like a crazy stalker? He thought fast. 'I just, ah . . . wanted to apologise to Bates, er – Mr Bates. For what happened in the forest.'

'Oh, that's sweet of you. He's actually not home right now, but I'll tell him you dropped by.'

Jake felt a wave of relief. *Thank God*. The thought of having to actually apologise to Bates made him feel ill.

His mum had turned back to the guttering. 'I have to say, this is my least favourite chore.'

'Yeah, horrible job for someone who's afraid of heights,'

agreed Jake, without thinking.

'How do *you* know I'm afraid of heights?'

'Ah, just a lucky guess.' He had to stop doing that. 'Hey, why don't you come down and I'll do the rest?'

She smiled. 'You're a nice kid. Your mum's lucky to have such a considerate son.'

Jake looked away. What was he supposed to say to that?

His mum made her way down the ladder. When she reached the ground, she stopped and put her hand to her head.

'Are you OK?' asked Jake, concerned. She'd gone very pale.

'I thought I'd got over this bug, but it just keeps coming back.'

Jake guided her to a bench.

She smiled at him. 'I'll be fine. You go ahead.'

Jake moved away and climbed up the ladder. He didn't like his mum feeling unwell all the time. He was used to her soldiering on, no matter what. For as long as he could remember, she'd never taken a day off work.

He dug the broom handle along the guttering and a cluster of rotting leaves fell onto the driveway with a wet *thwack*.

'So, what do you like at school? What's your best subject?'

He looked down at his mum. She seemed a bit better.

'Um . . . football?'

She laughed. 'I'm a huge Bandicoots fan.'

'I know. I mean, everyone here is, aren't they?' He bit his tongue. If he wasn't careful, she'd think he was nuts.

'Not everyone,' she was saying. 'Brian hates football.'

Yeah, thought Jake. *Of course he does, the schmuck.* More wet leaves splattered on to the driveway.

'Really?' he said politely. 'So who do you go to the games with?'

His mum laughed. 'Gosh. I don't go to the games.'

Jake looked at her in disbelief. 'But you always went . . .' Dammit! He'd done it again.

'That's true, I used to.' She looked up. 'Wait. How did you know that?'

Jake quickly changed the subject. 'OK. Job's all done.' He headed down the ladder. As he got closer to his mum, she grimaced and her hand flew to her head.

'Damn this thing. Wait here. I'll just get something for it and then I'll make you some lunch – as payment. How's a BLT sound?'

Jake grinned. 'That's my favourite.'

His mum smiled back. 'Mine too.' She got up off the chair and made her way unsteadily to the front door.

Jake watched her disappear inside. He felt a wave of happiness. She liked him. She may not have a clue who he was, but they'd at least had a chat and she seemed happy to hang out with him.

He put his hand in his pocket and felt the smooth glass of

the dolphin. He wanted so badly to give it to her. But would she find that weird? Maybe he should just leave it somewhere for her to find. He looked at the open front door. Yes. That's what he'd do.

Jake tentatively walked through the front door. There was no sign of his mum. He looked around the lounge room. He couldn't believe his eyes. Not a thing from their place was there. The couches were a soft leather, the carpet white and plush. Perfectly placed cushions were scattered around and a massive flat-screen TV took up a whole corner. Jake stared in disbelief. Where was the colourful chaos of his home? The crocheted rugs, the mantelpiece full of photo frames, the beanbag that always left a trail of tiny white balls?

He took the dolphin out of his pocket and looked at it. It didn't seem right to put it here. This room didn't belong to his mum. It didn't have any of her warmth.

He heard a crashing sound come from the kitchen. He quickly stuffed the dolphin back in his pocket. 'Mum?' There was no answer. 'Mrs Bates?' He hated the sound of those words. Still no answer.

Jake made his way across the white expanse of carpet towards the kitchen. He opened the door and found her collapsed on the floor. He ran to her and turned her over. She was unconscious. Jake grabbed her wrist. He could feel her faint pulse but then he noticed that where he'd touched her, a bright red rash had appeared. He pulled his hands away and stared in horror as the rash rose up her arm. 'Mum? Wake up! Mum?'

The front door banged loudly. 'Sarah? Are you home?'

Jake looked up in alarm. It was Bates. How was he going to explain why he was –

'What the hell have you done to my wife?' Bates stood in the kitchen doorway, his jaw hanging open.

'Nothing,' said Jake. 'She came in to get some tablets and then she collapsed. I'll call an ambulance.'

Bates turned on him. 'You'll get out of my house this instant. You have no right being here.'

Jake didn't move. He couldn't just leave her.

'Go. Now. Before I call the police,' bellowed Bates as he knelt down beside her.

Jake hesitated for a moment, and then ran. He raced through the main street of Bremin. If Bates called an ambulance then they'd take his mum to the hospital. That's where he'd go. He had to make sure she was OK.

The sound of sirens stopped him. Ahead of him in the main street, two ambulances skidded to a halt near the square.

A crowd was gathered around the fun-run banner. Four paramedics jumped out and ran towards the first-aid tent.

Jake watched as the crowd parted to reveal three women looking ill and distressed. Felix, Andy and Sam were all in the crowd nearby. What were they doing here? And then, with a jolt, he realised: the three women were their mums.

He pushed his way through the crowd to the other boys.

'It's our mums,' said Andy. 'They collapsed as soon as we started talking to them.'

'Mine too,' said Jake.

The boys watched, concerned, as their mums were loaded into the back of the ambulances.

'Try now, Felix,' came a voice. They turned to see Phoebe standing behind them, holding the talisman.

'Are you following us?' said Felix.

'You think I'm going to let you out on your own with a demon after you? I'm your guardian after all,' she said sternly. She handed him the talisman. 'Go on. Try.'

Felix began to chant. '*Divinity of the elements, I summon thee.*'

The talisman didn't glow.

'*Earth, water, air, fire . . .*' Felix kept chanting, but nothing happened. He stopped. 'There's no point. This thing is totally dead.'

They all turned to look at Sam.

'Guys, I'm sorry. What else can I say?'

'Unless,' said Phoebe thoughtfully, 'this is not a demon attack.'

Jake watched the ambulances take off, their lights flashing and sirens blaring down the street. Demon or no demon, what did it matter? He had to get to his mum. 'I'm going to the hospital.'

'Wait,' said Phoebe, putting her hand up. 'Is this the first time your mums have responded to you like this?'

The boys looked at each other.

'Actually, mine always sneezes when she sees me,' said Felix.

'And mine complained of a stomach ache when I first saw her,' said Andy.

'Mine collapsed and had that same weird rash when I was at the house,' said Sam.

Jake nodded. Since they'd been here, every time he'd talked to his mum, she'd complained of a headache.

'It's like our mothers are allergic to us,' said Andy miserably.

Phoebe nodded. 'That could be right.'

Jake felt the air rush out of him. It was *him* making his mum sick. He was the problem.

'So, if we stay away from them, they'll be all right?' said Felix hopefully.

'Might be the safest option,' said Phoebe.

Andy suddenly looked up. 'Wait a minute. If our mothers are allergic to us, it's because we shouldn't be here. We're like foreign bodies to them.'

'Yes,' said Phoebe carefully.

'So, to cure them, they need to be inoculated against the virus. Which is . . . us. And then they'll be OK.'

Phoebe looked at him through narrowed eyes. 'You're

262

actually smarter than you look.' She turned to the others. 'Andy's right. An inoculation could be the answer.'

'And how are we supposed to do that?' asked Jake impatiently. 'We're not doctors.'

'A magic inoculation, of course.' Phoebe's eyes lit up. 'We need something – an object – that each of your mothers would have had in both worlds. If you can find that, I'll look for a spell for Felix to cast.'

'But the talisman doesn't –' began Felix.

'Don't need it,' said Phoebe. 'This is not about the demon. Go on. I'll meet you at the hospital.'

Jake hesitated. 'But my mum's life is completely different here. She doesn't live in the same house or have any of the same stuff.'

'There must be something. You just have to find it. Go on,' ordered Phoebe. '*Go.*'

———

Jake jogged back to his mum's house. All that talk about inoculation had his head spinning. He wasn't convinced that Andy or Phoebe knew what they were talking about, but if there was a chance it would make his mum better, he had to give it a go.

When he reached the house, it looked like no one was there. *Phew!* He sneaked around the back looking for an open window. Bates was probably the sort of guy who had alarms everywhere. To Jake's relief, the kitchen window had been left open wide enough for him to slide through.

He landed on the floor and looked around. The kitchen, like the rest of the house, was in perfect order. There was nothing here that his mum would have had in their world. Maybe he should try the bedroom. He made his way up the carpeted stairs. This house was way too big for just two people.

At the top of the stairs was a double bedroom. Jake tried to avoid looking at the king-sized bed. He couldn't bear the thought of his mum and Bates sleeping together. Instead, he looked at the bedside table. Here there was nothing except an alarm clock and a light. He touched the dolphin in his pocket. Should he leave it here? But what if Bates found it first?

He looked around. How was he supposed to find something that his mum had in both worlds? This world was completely different. He opened the wardrobe and looked through her clothes. They were all fancy and designer-made. No T-shirts and trackpants anywhere. He sighed and was about to close the door when he saw a small red box tucked away in the back of the wardrobe, behind the shoes. He knelt down and pulled it out. Very carefully, he lifted the lid. Inside was a collection of his mum's most personal things. Jake pulled out a photo of his mum and dad as teenagers, their arms around each other. He looked at the other items in the box. A pressed corsage. Some letters and more photos, and then, right at the bottom, he found a Bremin Bandicoots pin. So, his parents *had* been together in this world!

Jake picked up the pin. This was it. In his old world, his mum wore this pin to every game. He quickly pocketed it and was about to put the box back when he heard a footfall on the stairs.

Someone was coming.

andy: a chinese bear grylls

Andy stood outside Lily Lau's Chinese Restaurant. He hadn't dared go back since the meat-cleaver incident, but now his mum was in danger he had no choice. But how, he wondered, was he going to get past Nai Nai? She guarded the place like a pit bull.

Andy considered his options carefully. Should he go in the front door of the restaurant, and sneak around to the back stairs? Or should he go through the kitchen at the back, and get to the stairs that way? Either way was risky. But he knew if he was going to find anything personal of his mum's, he had to get upstairs to the living area. He saw a figure moving around in the restaurant. It was Nai Nai, setting the tables for the lunch crowd. OK, decision made. He was going in through the kitchen.

Andy sneaked around the side of the building and into the alleyway. The back door to the kitchen was open. The large plastic fly strips moved gently in the breeze. Staying down low, he crept towards the door, parted the strips quietly and slipped inside.

Inside the kitchen, Andy was hit hard by an intense rush of homesickness. It was the smell. Why was that? Why was the olfactory memory so potent? Another question for his dad, if he ever saw him again.

If he ever did get home, would he miss Ellen's smell? She had a fresh, sweet smell that was so alien, and yet so appealing. He shook the thought away. *Focus, Andy. Your mum needs you.*

He crept silently past the piles of bamboo steamers, the oiled woks, the boxes of freshly delivered herbs and vegetables. He could see the stairs. He was almost there.

So long as Viv wasn't upstairs, he was home free.

'Aiiiieeeeee!'

Something whizzed past his head and lodged itself in the wall. Not a meat cleaver this time, but a fairly vicious-looking pair of kitchen scissors.

Andy turned and smiled weakly. 'Hi, Nai Nai.'

'You again. What you doing here? Viv not interested in crazy stalker boys.'

Andy sighed. 'I'm not interested in Viv, OK?'

He looked at Nai Nai for a beat, and something occurred to him: maybe, just maybe, Nai Nai might actually believe the truth.

He hesitated. Nai Nai picked up a skewer for roasting duck. OK, well, it was either the truth or face death by kitchen implement. He took a deep breath.

'Nai Nai. My name is Andrew Qiao Li Lau. I'm your grandson.'

Nai Nai advanced on him. 'What you talking about, you crazy boy?'

'I'm not crazy. Viv is my sister and Michael and Nicole are my mum and dad.'

Nai Nai threw down the skewer, picked up a wooden spoon and started to beat him with it. 'Stop it. You talk rubbish.'

Andy put up both hands to protect himself. He had to convince her or he'd never come out alive, and nothing would help his mum. 'I know Dad likes to sit in the shed and do experiments with mass and time. I know Mum's favourite food is spaghetti bolognaise but she's too frightened to tell you. And Nai Nai, I know you need glasses but you don't want anyone to know, so you hide them in the third drawer of your dressing table. And there's lots more that I know. Because this is my family . . . and I'm your grandson.'

Nai Nai gasped and dropped the spoon she was holding. 'Ai-yaieee,' she said under her breath. 'A ghost!' She reached for Andy's arm and pinched it hard, making him yelp.

'*Gu Hun Ye Gui!*' she whispered. 'The ghost of the son they never had. The grandson she never gave me.'

'That doesn't even make sense.' Andy rubbed his arm. 'Listen, Nai Nai. Mum is very sick and I need your help to

268

make her better.'

'Aiya, that girl. Always something wrong with her.'

Andy knew there wasn't a lot of love lost between Nai Nai and his mum, but now wasn't the time. 'Nai Nai. Please.'

Nai Nai sighed. 'OK. What she need? Chinese herbs?'

Andy hesitated. How was he going to explain the whole idea of a magic inoculation spell to someone who thought he was a ghost? He shook his head. Too hard.

'Mum's in hospital and she needs me to bring her something that'll make her happy. Something she loves.'

'Why she send you, ghost boy?'

Andy didn't know how to answer that. Maybe the truth would work? 'She didn't. She doesn't know me. But I'm her son and I want her to get better. Please, Nai Nai.'

She frowned. 'OK. Wait here.' She disappeared up the stairs and came back down a few minutes later, carrying a photo frame.

Andy looked at it, delighted. Perfect! He remembered this photo. It always took pride of place by his mum's bed. It was of old Foo Ling, his mum's dad, standing somewhere in the wilds of Russia, holding up a pair of antlers.

Nai Nai thrust the photo at Andy. 'Stupid man. Killed by bear in Siberia. Should have been an accountant.'

Andy took the photo. He'd always loved his mum's stories about Foo Ling. He'd been an adventurer in the sixties – footloose and fearless. A Chinese Bear Grylls.

'Thanks, Nai Nai.'

She leant in and gave him a kiss on the cheek. 'No problem, ghost boy. I always wanted grandson. Come visit me again.'

Andy raced out of the restaurant and made his way as fast as he could towards the hospital.

Andy saw Phoebe, Sam and Felix through the front doors of the hospital, waiting in the foyer. The doors slid open and he rushed in.

'They've taken your mothers up to the first floor,' Phoebe explained. 'For the spell to work, we have to be as close as possible to them.'

Felix was pacing. 'Where's Jake? We can't do anything without him.'

'We can't just walk into the ward and start chanting,' said Sam. 'The hospital will call the police.'

'I know that, doofus,' snarled Phoebe. 'I'm working on a plan.'

The doors slid open and Jake appeared. He was so puffed he could barely breathe. He bent over double.

'What happened to you?' asked Phoebe.

'A neighbour called the police,' he said, trying to catch his breath. 'And my dad caught me in the house and chased me.'

Phoebe rolled her eyes. 'Well, that's just great. Now he'll

have you on burglary charges. Like we haven't got enough problems.'

'Where's my mum?' asked Jake.

'They're all upstairs,' said Phoebe. 'Come on. We've got to move fast.'

The boys followed Phoebe as she strode towards the lifts.

Andy looked down at the photo of Foo Ling. 'Come on, Foo,' he whispered. 'You can save the day.'

The lift pinged open at the first floor and they got out.

A doctor with a clipboard was standing outside the ward, talking earnestly to a nurse. 'I don't understand it,' Andy overheard him say. 'It's like their immune systems have gone completely berserk.'

The boys looked at each other. Seemed like they were right.

'Stay here,' Phoebe hissed, then followed a hospital orderly down the corridor.

Andy looked through the glass door into the ward. He could see his mum lying in bed. She was hooked up to a drip and her face was as white as a sheet. His dad sat next to her, holding her hand. He looked sick with worry.

Phoebe came back with the orderly, smiling triumphantly. 'This is Dave. He's going to let us into the broom cupboard.'

Dave slipped his key into the lock and the broom cupboard door creaked open.

'Inside. Quick,' ordered Phoebe. She tossed her hair and smiled flirtatiously at the orderly. 'Thanks, Dave.'

Phoebe slammed the door shut, but there was still enough light that Andy could see her glowering at them. 'Yes, yes. I know what you're thinking. But surprise, surprise, Phoebe did once go to high school and have dates, and Dave just happened to be one of them. Now shut your mouths and let's get on with business.'

Phoebe pushed aside a mop bucket to clear some space on the floor. 'Now, one by one, place your item on the floor and explain why it connects you and your mum. Think of each item as a bridge connecting the two worlds together. You first, Andy.'

Andy carefully laid the photo of Foo Ling on the ground. 'This is my grandfather, my mum's dad. He was an adventurer in the sixties and travelled the world. My mum used to tell me stories about how he strangled boa constrictors and ate barbecued moths. But then later she'd cry, because he was killed by a bear when she was a child and she never really got to know him.'

Phoebe nodded. 'Sam?'

Sam laid down a paintbrush. 'This is my mum's favourite paintbrush. She taught me to paint with it and she told me that whenever I'm feeling sad, I can paint my feelings into something else.'

Felix laid down a small garden trowel. 'When my brother had his accident, my mum couldn't sleep, couldn't work, everything changed. The only time I ever saw her smile was when she was in the garden. It was the only time she seemed to forget . . .' Felix faltered.

Phoebe quickly jumped in. 'And you, Jake?'

Jake laid down the Bremin Bandicoots pin. 'My mum got this brooch from my dad, on their first date. They went to the footy and the Bandicoots won. My dad's a loser in our world, but this is evidence, I guess, that they loved each other once.' He stepped back.

'OK,' said Phoebe. 'Everybody hold hands, and Felix will recite the spell I gave him.'

'Actually,' Felix said, avoiding Phoebe's eyes, 'I've created another one. It's a combination of a restoration spell and . . .'

Phoebe's eyes darkened. 'Fine. Whatever. You're the witch.'

Andy watched as Felix got out his black book and studied it. 'I thought that was your diary.'

Felix was always so cagey about that book. Never letting anyone near it. A few times, Andy had tried to look at it over Felix's shoulder and he'd snapped it shut immediately.

'It is.' Felix sounded defensive. 'I just sometimes write other stuff in here.'

'Like spells?' asked Andy.

Felix silenced him with a glare. 'We need to focus. Everybody think about their mothers and the object you brought in. The memory has to be from our world and it has to be happy.'

Andy shut his eyes. He thought about his mum sitting on

the end of his bed, laughing as she told the story of Foo Ling being chased out of the water by a crocodile. He had told her you must always run in a zigzag to confuse a crocodile.

Felix started chanting.

'Water, fire, earth and air,
The power to heal we all do share . . .'

Andy opened his eyes. Outside he could hear a loud rumbling sound like distant thunder. He looked at the others. Their eyes were tightly closed as they concentrated on their memories.

Felix kept chanting.

'Inside our mothers, place this spell.
A son was born and by his hand
Your safety, health and happiness stand,
So wake and know that all is well.
So wake and know that all is well.'

There was a loud crack of lightning, and then a deafening rumble of thunder overhead. Felix let go of the other boys' hands. They all looked at each other.

'Come on,' said Jake, opening the door a crack. 'Let's see if it worked.'

The boys tumbled out of the broom cupboard and ran to

the glass door of the ward. A smile spread across Andy's face as he saw his mum sitting upright. The colour had returned to her cheeks.

He looked across at the other mums. Jake's mum's eyes were open and the doctors were scurrying around her in disbelief.

Sam's mum was looking at her arms in wonder. Her rash had completely disappeared.

Felix's mum was drinking a glass of water and reaching for a magazine.

Andy turned to Felix. 'You did it!'

Sam clapped Felix on the back. 'Awesome, dude.'

Felix smiled.

Jake was staring at his mum thoughtfully. 'That spell you did. Does that mean that our mums will remember us now?'

'I don't know how it works, exactly,' said Felix. 'But the memory works like a vaccine. It places the memory of us in them, so they have a negative reaction to us in real life.'

Phoebe looked knowingly at Felix. 'Well played, Felix.'

By the time the boys left the hospital, dusk had fallen and the streets of Bremin were covered in long grey shadows. Jake and Sam walked ahead, a spring in their steps. Andy watched as Phoebe walked beside Felix, urgently whispering something into his ear. Felix was nodding in agreement.

It was curious. Ever since Andy had started to believe in this whole magic thing, something had bothered him: magic ran along the same principles as science. Cause and effect. You do something and there is a consequence.

The problem was that *they* were the consequence, the *magical disturbance* as Phoebe had put it. But what was the cause? Things didn't just happen randomly. There was always a reason.

Andy noticed how protectively Felix held the bag containing his black book. If Felix could cast a spell as powerful as the one he cast today, then what else was he capable of?

That night, Andy put the photo of Foo Ling by his bed. He kept his eyes on Foo while he waited patiently for the others to fall asleep. Old Foo was a Chinese Bear Grylls, bravely going into new worlds, just like Andy. But Foo knew why he was in those new worlds and how he'd got there. And unless you knew *that*, there was no way you could find your way home again. That was the difference between him and Foo.

Sam fell asleep first, then Jake. And finally, Felix's breathing deepened and he rolled on to his side.

As quietly as he could, Andy crept towards Felix's bag. He reached in and pulled out his black book.

He took it to Phoebe's desk and turned on the lamp. No one stirred. Carefully, Andy began to turn the pages. The first few made no sense to him. Lots of drawings of dark-looking creatures. Notes about odd plants. Random verses. But then – there it was: THE UNMAKING SPELL. Next to it was a photograph of Oscar before his accident. Oscar walking.

Andy started to read: *To make this spell, all four elements are required.*

EARTH, AIR and WATER had been written as headings and under each element a number of names had been written and scrubbed out. Andy stared at his name written in bold letters under WATER.

ANDY LAU: PISCES. WET, FLUID THINKER. He kept reading.

Water, fire, earth and air
Elements that we all share.

That was the song Felix had played around the campfire.

Water wash our sins away
Earth guide us to a place.
Wind brings with it fear
Flames of fire we must face.
Walk upon this earth again
Walk upon this earth –

Andy read over the words in disbelief.

Felix had cast the spell that had got them here.

Felix was the cause.

And all this time, he'd been lying to them.

felix: the fifth element

Three pairs of eyes stared accusingly at Felix. He looked away. What could he say?

'I'm sorry,' he muttered, looking at the floor.

Sam banged his fist hard into the wall. 'You're sorry?' he shouted. 'That's it?'

'I didn't mean for this to happen.' Felix heard the words coming out of his mouth. They sounded as weak as he felt.

He'd known all along that eventually they'd find out. In fact, now that it had happened, it was almost a relief. All Andy's prying questions about why the demon would target him, and his insistence that an effect must always have a cause. A maths genius wasn't going to take long to put two and two together.

'I was trying to unmake Oscar's accident, that's all. I didn't realise that the spell would unmake all of us as well.'

'But you used us,' said Andy. He held Felix's Book of Shadows open at the unmaking spell. Sam and Jake crowded around him to look.

Jake grabbed the book and read out loud. '*Jake Riles: Capricorn. Practical, stubborn, brutish. Earth.*' He handed it to Sam.

'*Sam Conte: Gemini. Selfish, superficial, lives in the clouds. Air.*' Sam flung the book to the ground in disgust.

'I needed the four elements to make the spell work,' said Felix quietly. 'That's all that was meant to happen. We were all supposed to go home after the excursion and nothing would have changed, except Oscar would be able to walk again.'

'So, us getting lost in the forest,' Jake spat. 'That was all arranged by you?'

Felix nodded. 'I knew I had to do the spell at a certain place for it to work. I had a magic map I got from Alice's Book of Shadows and I had to get you all to that particular place.'

'But how did you know we'd be in the same group? Bates organised that,' said Andy.

'I knew the codes to the staffroom, so I changed the groups on his computer. He never realised.'

There was silence as the others processed this.

'Man, you sure put a lot of work into ruining our lives,' said Sam eventually.

Felix felt terrible. 'I'm sorry, Sam. I've been doing everything I can to get us home.'

'You should have told us the truth,' said Jake, clenching his fists in anger. 'All this time, we had no idea what was going on. And you *knew*.'

'I'm sorry.' Felix felt the taste of failure in those two words. But what else could he say? Nothing would make them forgive him. And why should they?

'Repeat the same actions to get the same result,' muttered Andy.

'What are you talking about?' said Jake.

'That's what we have to do. That's the key to getting home.'

'I've tried that,' said Felix. 'In the forest. I did the spell again, but it didn't work.'

'I knew I'd heard those words somewhere,' said Sam.

Andy frowned. 'Then something must have been different.'

'I've had enough of this,' said Jake, standing up. 'He betrayed us once. You really think he's going to get us home? It's all lies.'

'I'm with Jake,' said Sam.

'Guys, please just give me a chance. I'm sure we can work –'

'Give me your phone,' Andy suddenly jumped to his feet.

'Why?' said Felix. 'It's completely dead.'

'Because in scientific methodology, there can be no variables.'

'I've spent weeks with him, and he still makes absolutely no sense,' Sam muttered to Jake.

Andy ignored them. 'When we were in the forest you played us some extremely melodic music. That was the spell, right?'

'But his sense of humour has definitely improved,' Jake replied to Sam.

Felix nodded.

'So for everything to be exactly the same, I think we need to play the spell on your phone.'

Felix pulled his phone out of his bag. Maybe Andy was right. Why hadn't he thought of that?

Andy walked over to Phoebe's desk and plugged the phone into her charger. He turned back to the others. 'OK, so we go back to the forest with the phone, and we try again.'

Felix shook his head. 'If the talisman doesn't work, we'll never survive another demon –'

A loud banging on the shop's front door stopped Felix mid-sentence.

'Great,' said Jake. 'That's probably my dad with the burglary charges.'

Phoebe appeared at the doorway, still in her dressing gown. 'Do you want the good news or the bad news?'

'Ah, the good news?'

'The demon's at the door.'

The boys jumped to their feet. 'That's good news?'

'Sure,' said Phoebe. 'So now we can try and activate the talisman.'

'And the bad news?' asked Sam.

Phoebe looked at him like he was a moron. 'The demon's at the door, of course.'

Felix ducked through the beaded curtain into the shop. The others followed close behind him.

The shadow of a fist reached up and banged at the door again.

'How does she know it's the demon?' whispered Andy.

Felix put his fingers to his lips and crept towards the front window. From there, he could see outside. A figure stood at the door. It raised its fist to bang again. Suddenly its head twitched jerkily to the right and it stared straight at Felix.

'Bates,' whispered Felix. 'Quick. Out the back.'

'Why does Bates being the demon not surprise me?' said Jake, as they quickly made their way into the back room.

Phoebe had arranged bowls of water and earth on her desk and was lighting a candle. 'Felix, come on, quick. We need to reactivate the talisman. We can use these to evoke each of the elements.'

'Good idea.' Felix pulled the talisman out from under his shirt.

The banging came again, louder this time.

'Do the spell, Felix,' ordered Phoebe.

Felix turned to the others. 'When I say your element, you need to put it on the talisman,' he said, indicating the water, earth and fire that Phoebe had placed on the desk.

He put the talisman on the desk and began to chant.

'*Divinity of the elements, I summon thee. Earth . . .*' He nodded to Jake, who placed his hand in the bowl of dirt and sprinkled some over the talisman. '*Water . . .*' Andy put his hand in the water bowl and did the same. '*Air . . .*' Sam looked at him, unsure what to do.

'Blow on it, airhead,' said Phoebe urgently.

'*Fire.*' Felix took the candle and held the flame to the talisman.

> '*Within this stone I invoke ye place,*
> *Your greatest strength, your kindest grace.*
> *And while this stone remains at hand*
> *Thou shall be safe throughout this land.*'

Felix stared at the talisman, willing it to glow. But there was nothing. Not even the faintest gleam.

'He's stopped banging. Does that mean it worked?' asked Jake hopefully.

Phoebe shook her head. 'He's just working out another way to get at you. If the talisman doesn't glow, it's not offering protection.'

'Maybe it's the glue,' said Andy, turning the talisman over and inspecting it. 'The cyanoacrylate could have interfered with the magic.'

Phoebe shook her head. 'The talisman is only a vessel for magical energy, so theoretically, you should be able to repair it.'

Sam gasped. 'You could have told me that yesterday.'

Phoebe's lips lifted at the corners in a wry smile. 'Why would I do that?'

'So why isn't it working?' said Felix impatiently. Bates was outside and it was only a matter of time before he smashed the glass and got in.

'I don't know,' said Phoebe. 'Something must be different between now and when you activated it the first time.'

Felix thought hard. What was different? Bees? The shack? He'd been under a bed when he did the spell.

'I don't –' He stopped. Of course! 'My brother. Oscar. Oscar was there.'

'That nerdy guy with the buckteeth is your brother?' said Phoebe.

'He's not that nerdy,' said Felix. 'Well, maybe just a little.'

'Could he have anything to do with why you're here?' asked Phoebe.

Felix hesitated.

'Tell her,' said Jake.

'I'm not sure –'

'Oscar's the whole reason we're here,' Sam jumped in. 'He had an accident in our world and Felix was trying to unmake it, and he was pretty crap at magic so he unmade all of us as well.'

Phoebe narrowed her eyes at Felix. 'Were you planning on telling me this?'

Felix avoided her gaze. 'Sure. I just –'

'You did an unmaking spell and disappeared from your own world? Kind of significant information, don't you think?'

There was another loud, urgent banging on the front door.

'Come on,' said Andy, drawing their attention back to the talisman. 'How do we make this thing work?'

'OK,' said Phoebe, squaring her shoulders. 'According to pagan lore, there are four worldly elements: earth, wind, fire and water. Then a fifth element. Spirit. If Oscar is the reason why the spell was cast, then he's the connection between your world and our world. Oscar's the fifth element. Find him and the talisman will work.'

'Phoebe!' yelled a voice from the front of the shop. 'Open this door immediately.'

'It's Dad,' Jake whispered.

'Well, at least he's not a demon.' Phoebe gave Felix a piercing stare, then walked towards the beaded curtain.

He'd let her down. He knew it. He'd let everyone down.

The boys listened as Phoebe opened the door and spoke to the police.

'We should go out the back way,' said Felix. 'Find Oscar. Make this thing work.'

The beaded curtain suddenly parted and Senior Sergeant Riles and Constable Roberts stood there.

'Right. You boys are coming with me,' said Jake's dad.

'On what charges?' Phoebe pushed her way past them.

'How about vagrancy, trespassing, burglary, impersonation – gosh, and that's just the start. Come on, boys.'

'Don't forget wilful damage to school property,' said a deep voice from behind the Senior Sergeant.

Bates.

Felix felt a cold rush of air. He'd followed them in.

'What are you doing here, Brian?' asked Jake's dad.

'Door was open,' Bates's voice rasped horribly.

'You should get some lozenges for that throat, mate.' Jake's dad nodded to Roberts. 'Let's go, constable.'

Jake's dad grabbed Sam and Jake by the arms, and Roberts reached for Andy.

Phoebe tried to get in front of them. 'You can't just take them. I'm their guardian.'

'Really?' said Jake's dad, as he dragged the boys through the shop. 'Show me the papers.'

'They're, ah . . . in the mail,' stammered Phoebe.

Roberts opened the front door and pulled Andy towards the car. Jake's dad followed with Jake and Sam. Felix watched helplessly as they were shoved into the back seat.

Jake's dad walked towards Felix.

'Only three seatbelts in the back, Sarge,' said Roberts. 'It wouldn't be legal.'

'I'll bring Felix in,' said Bates.

'Thanks, Brian, but I think I can handle this,' said Jake's dad.

Bates's head twitched as he turned to stare at him. 'As well as you've handled everything else, Gary?'

Jake's dad looked like he was about to explode. He turned to Phoebe. 'Make yourself useful and follow us in with Felix, would you?' He jumped into the driver's seat and reversed with a screech.

'Come on,' Phoebe urged Felix.

But Bates's hand had jerked out and grabbed him. 'Come with me, Felix.'

Felix tried to fend him off, but Bates's hand gripped him like a clamp.

Phoebe wasted no time. She moved towards Bates and kicked him as hard as she could in the shins.

He staggered back and shook his head, disorientated.

'Go!' Phoebe said urgently. 'Find Oscar and get to the police station. You need all five of you to activate the talisman.'

'I can't leave you with him!'

'Don't worry, he's not after me. Go!'

Felix hesitated. Bates was regaining his balance. He started to move stiffly towards Felix.

'*Run!*' yelled Phoebe, giving him a push.

Felix turned and bolted. He ran as fast as he could through Bremin. Phoebe was right. He had to find Oscar. Chances were he would be at home. At least that would be the obvious place to try. He took a shortcut down a lane and sprinted across the cobblestones.

He stopped dead.

Standing at the other end of the lane was Bates. How had he got there so fast? It wasn't possible.

Bates's red eyes drilled into him. A roar exploded from him – the sort of roar Felix had heard coming from Roland, and then Mia.

Felix sprinted back towards the main street, but he knew he couldn't outpace Bates. He quickly dropped to the ground and slipped under a parked car.

Lying on his belly, he saw Bates's shoes crunch past on the gravel. The shoes stopped, and then turned. Was he confused? The demon sure wasn't that smart. Not at first, anyway.

Sure enough, Bates's shoes disappeared up the street. Breathing a sigh of relief, Felix was about to slip back out from under the car when another pair of shoes came into view. A familiar pair of red-and-green runners.

'Oscar!' Felix hissed.

The shoes stopped. Their owner was clearly trying to work out where the voice was coming from.

'Down here!'

Oscar's face suddenly appeared next to his. 'Cool. Aliens live under cars. Makes sense.'

'Listen. Oscar. Can you see Mr Bates?'

'Yeah, he's outside the supermarket.'

'OK, pretend you're doing up your shoe.'

'Why?'

'Just do it, OK?'

Oscar started to untie and retie his shoe.

'Listen carefully. I need you to help me with a spell. A very important spell. Mr Bates is possessed by a demon and he wants to kill me.'

Oscar turned away.

'Oscar? Did you hear me?'

'Hi, Mr Bates,' said Oscar weakly. He stood up, out of Felix's sight.

Felix rolled his eyes. *Oh, crap.*

'How are you, Oscar?' came Bates's thick voice.

'Oh, ah, pretty good . . .'

Felix hesitated, hating the decision, but knowing there was only one option. He quickly rolled out from under the car. '*Run!*' he yelled to Oscar.

The two of them hurtled down the street.

Bates took a moment to process what had happened and then, in jerky, robotic movements, set off after them.

Felix and Oscar bolted through town. 'We have to get to the police station,' panted Felix.

'But that's back there,' said Oscar.

'I know, but we have to confuse Bates. We'll go down to the bridge and then cross back the other way. Demons have a terrible sense of direction. You have to disorient them.'

'Cool,' panted Oscar. 'I've never been chased by a demon before.'

As they belted down the road to the river, Felix heard the

sound of a car behind them.

He glanced around to see a black SUV bearing down on them. *Oh God.* Bates had a car. They were cactus.

'This way!' Felix called desperately, leading Oscar off the road.

The SUV screamed to a halt and Bates jumped out.

'Run!' yelled Felix, urging Oscar on. He glanced back to see Oscar trip on a tree stump and land hard on the ground.

'Oscar, get up. Come on!' yelled Felix.

Oscar staggered to his feet, but Bates was gaining on him.

Felix ran back towards Oscar. He stared Bates down. 'Don't you dare touch my brother.'

'I'm . . . your brother?' Oscar asked in surprise.

'Yeah. Where I come from, you're my brother.'

Oscar grinned. 'Wow. I've always wanted a bro–'

'Oscar, watch out!'

Bates had put his hand up to strike him, but he stopped suddenly in midair and his hand jerked back to his side.

Felix breathed a sigh of relief. 'It's OK. He's still too weak. Come on, run!'

But Oscar didn't move.

Felix stared at him.

Oscar's eyes were completely vacant. He took one jerky step towards Felix.

Felix felt a scream rising from deep within him, but before he could release it, everything turned black.

jake: farewell bremin

'Enough with the nonsense, kid. You want me to call up Child Protection Services again?' Jake's dad threatened. 'I can get the lot of you sent away in a second. All I have to do is make the call.'

Jake glanced towards the front door of the police station. What was taking Phoebe and Felix so long? They should have been directly behind them. It's not like they would have stopped off for a burger with Demon Bates.

Sure, Felix had totally screwed them over, but that didn't mean he deserved to be mauled to death by their science teacher. Besides, selfishly, Jake didn't think they stood much chance of getting home without Felix. If he'd done the spell to get them here, then they needed him to do the spell to get them home.

His dad cleared his throat. 'I'm waiting.'

Sam leant forwards. 'OK. Here's the thing,' he tried, earnestly. 'We're from another world – exactly like this one.

Except here, we don't exist.'

Jake's dad stifled a laugh and lifted one of his legs off the ground. 'You want to pull this one as well?'

'We need to go and look for Felix. He should be here by now,' said Jake.

Constable Roberts was trying to process what Sam had just said. 'If you don't exist, how come we can see you sitting in front of us?'

'Yes, we're physically present. But you don't know who we are. No one here does,' explained Andy.

'So, *who . . . are . . . you*?' asked Jake's dad. He lengthened each word as if he was talking to someone with a mental impairment.

Time was running out. Jake figured Bates would've caught Felix for sure, by now. 'If we tell you the truth, will you go and look for Felix?'

'Sure. If you're capable of that,' said his dad.

Jake took a deep breath. 'OK. My name is Jake Riles and, in my world, I'm your son.'

His dad laughed out loud. 'You are seriously unhinged, kid. I don't have a son.'

'Maybe not in this world. But in my world, you and your ex-girlfriend Sarah had a child together when you were teenagers. That child is me.'

His dad shook his head in frustration. 'You know what? This is clearly a mental-health issue.' He turned to Roberts.

'Call Child Protection Services.'

But just then, the phone rang at the reception desk and Roberts got up to answer it.

Jake leant forwards. He had to get through to his dad. It was their only chance.

'In your world, you didn't have the baby. It wasn't the right time. But in my world you did, and . . .' Jake swallowed hard. 'It changed everything.'

Jake saw something flicker in his dad's eyes. He could see that he was calculating dates in his head.

'That's not possible.'

'It is, because it happened,' said Jake. 'I know, deep down, you know me.'

His dad looked at him carefully. Jake thought he saw something shift in him.

'You have to trust me, Dad.'

His dad took a deep breath. 'Roberts, ring Phoebe,' he called out gruffly, 'find out what's holding her up.'

Jake smiled. 'Thanks, Dad.'

He shuffled some paperwork on his desk. 'Don't push it, kid.'

Roberts put down the phone and walked back into the office. 'Sorry, Sarge. What did you say? That was a call from Mrs Lau, reporting a man chasing two teenagers down the street.'

'Two teenagers?' whispered Sam.

'Must be Oscar and Felix,' said Jake. 'If Felix found him, they'll be looking for us.'

Andy jumped out of his seat. 'Sergeant Riles, I think it's time we informed you that Mr Bates is possessed by a demon and wants to kill Felix.'

'Oh, for God's sake. What next?'

'Sarge,' said Roberts. 'I think we should go and check it out. She was quite upset.'

Jake's dad reached for his hat. 'Fine. I'll go and talk to her. You stay with this lot and get Phoebe and Bates on the phone. Find out where they are.'

Andy was about to protest, but Jake shook his head at him. They'd have more chance of escaping with his dad gone.

'Good luck, Dad,' he called out as his dad reached the door.

'Thanks, son.'

Jake smiled as his dad realised what he'd said and almost walked into the glass door.

Jake watched Roberts, who was back in reception looking for Phoebe's number on his computer. Jake quietly leant over and picked up his dad's desk phone. He pressed the reception button and then slipped under the desk with the receiver.

Andy gave him the thumbs up as Roberts picked up.

'Bremin Police Station. How can I be of assistance?'

Jake put on a croaky old-lady voice. 'Help me. I've been mugged.'

'Where are you, ma'am?' asked Roberts.

'Just behind the police station. Please come quickly.' Jake quietly hung up the receiver.

'Ma'am? Ma'am?' Roberts yelled into the phone. He hung up and looked around uncertainly at the boys. 'You boys stay here. I won't be long.' He grabbed his hat and made his way quickly towards the back entrance of the station.

'Let's go,' Jake whispered, as soon as Roberts was out of sight.

The boys sped out the door and down the steps of the police station. Further up the main street, Jake could see his dad by the supermarket talking to Mrs Lau. They couldn't go that way.

'How are we supposed to find them?' asked Sam.

Jake hesitated. Good question. They could be anywhere.

'We need a car,' said Sam. 'Then we can look fast.'

The boys looked at each other. There was only one place to go. Phoebe's.

———

They raced up the steps towards Arcane Lane. Phoebe was out the front, collapsed against the shop window. Mia and Ellen were crouched next to her.

'Mia,' said Sam. 'What're you doing here?'

'We were walking past on our way to school and we found her like this.'

Phoebe put one hand on the wall and one on Ellen's shoulder as she gradually pulled herself to her feet.

Andy dashed around her and into the shop.

'Where's Felix?' Phoebe asked in a faint voice.

'What happened to you?' asked Jake.

Phoebe was deathly pale and she was struggling to hold herself upright. 'The demon was after Felix. I tried to hold it back but it overpowered me.'

Mia's eyes widened. 'The demon?'

'Oh, for God's sake,' muttered Phoebe. 'This from the girl who was possessed.'

'What's she talking about?' Mia asked Sam.

Sam looked uncomfortable. 'Er, it's a long story.'

'Let's go,' said Phoebe. 'We have to find Felix before Bates does.'

'Did you say Bates?' asked Ellen.

'Yes. The demon has possessed Bates,' explained Phoebe, as if that was the most natural thing in the world.

'Um, I don't know what's going on,' said Mia slowly. 'But we saw Mr Bates running just now, and Felix and Ellen's neighbour were running ahead of him.'

'He was chasing them, you fool. Demons don't go jogging,' snapped Phoebe.

'You don't have to be rude,' said Sam, looking at Mia's hurt face.

'It's OK,' said Jake. 'My dad's after Bates. A call came

through to the station.'

Phoebe let go of the wall. The colour was coming back to her face. 'The police don't stand a chance. The demon is becoming more and more powerful. We need to find them so Felix can reactivate the talisman.'

Andy burst out of the shop, Felix's phone in his hand.

Ellen held up her hand. 'Can we just back up a second? Our science teacher is a demon and he's chasing Felix and my freaky next-door neighbour. Sorry, but WTF?'

'Tell us what's going on,' said Mia.

'Er, there's not a lot of time,' said Sam.

Andy pulled Sam aside. 'We might not get another chance to tell them.'

Sam nodded. 'OK, I guess it's time to 'fess up.' They turned back to the girls. 'So, it all started with this excursion into the forest . . .'

'Jake,' said a voice.

Jake turned to see his mum standing at the top of the stairs, smiling at him. He moved away from the others. 'Hey.'

'Gary told me you were staying here with your aunty.'

'Yeah. Well, for the time being.' He looked down, and noticed something glistening in his mum's hands. The glass dolphin was twisting and turning between her fingers.

'When I was in the hospital, someone put this next to my bed.'

Jake looked at her.

'It was you, wasn't it?'

Jake nodded.

'How did you know I love dolphins?'

'Lucky guess.'

'You know an awful lot about me,' she said softly. She looked at him carefully. 'Who are you, Jake?'

Jake opened his mouth to lie. But then it hit him: what did it matter? Either the demon was going to kill them all, or they were going home. Whatever happened, he didn't need to pretend anymore.

'This sounds crazy, but . . .' He took a deep breath. 'Imagine a world where you and Gary had that baby.'

'How did you know about that?' she gasped.

Jake struggled to find the right words. 'It's just . . . if that baby had been a boy, imagine what he'd be like now.'

Her breath caught in her throat. 'He'd be a fifteen-year-old boy. Just like you.'

Jake held her gaze and nodded slowly.

Emotion flooded his mum's face. 'I don't understand.'

'Come on, you lot,' Phoebe yelled across the car park. 'We've got a demon to find.'

Jake gestured towards the Kombi. 'I've got to . . .'

His mum brushed a tear from the corner of her eye. 'Of course. You go and do what you need to do. I just wanted to say thank you.' She smiled sadly as she reached out and squeezed his hand. 'See you, Jakey.'

Jake smiled. 'See you, Mum.'

Jake ran across the car park to the Kombi. Phoebe was behind the wheel, and Sam was in the front seat with the window down so he could talk to Mia. Jake slid the door open and jumped in the back seat.

Andy was still standing with Ellen. She clasped a ruby necklace around his neck. 'To give to the other Ellen when you see her.' She leant forwards and kissed him on the lips.

Andy's face flushed a deeper red than the necklace.

'Most boys are such morons,' said Ellen. 'And when I finally fall for one, he turns out to be from another dimension. Typical!'

'Come on, lover boy, this demon isn't going to fight itself,' yelled Phoebe.

Andy jumped into the back next to Jake.

Sam had reached out and was grasping Mia's hand. 'When I get home, I'm going to be the most awesome boyfriend to you.'

She wrinkled her brow. 'Except it won't be me. You and me have never even had a date.'

Phoebe started to reverse and Sam was forced to let go of Mia's hand.

'Goodbye, parallel-universe boyfriend,' called Mia.

Jake looked out the window of Phoebe's Kombi as the streets of Bremin sped by. There was no sign of Felix or Oscar anywhere.

'Where exactly are we going?' asked Sam.

'Demons are creatures of habit,' said Phoebe grimly. 'If it's got Felix and Oscar, it will take them to the forest. The site where its power will be strongest.'

Jake looked over at Andy. He'd pulled Felix's phone out of his pocket and was searching through his recordings.

This is it, thought Jake. *We're going to go home. Or die trying.*

felix: the final battle

Felix lay perfectly still in the back seat of the SUV. His arms had been belted to his sides so he couldn't move even if he wanted to. Through the scratchy hessian bag that had been put over his head, he could just make out Bates and Oscar in the front seats. Bates had put on a CD and he and Oscar were banging their heads in time to the doof-doof music. *Great*, thought Felix. *Demons with crap taste in music.*

He felt the smooth glide of the bitumen road give way with a jolt to a dirt road. So, they were taking him to the forest. He should have guessed that. If they got him as far away as possible from the others, they could do what they wanted with him. And whatever that was, he was pretty sure it would be bloody, and possibly fatal.

He manoeuvred the hessian bag towards his mouth and started to chew on it. If he made a hole, maybe he could somehow open the back door with his teeth and roll out. Anything was better than death by demonic sacrifice.

He stopped with the hessian between his teeth, thinking he'd heard something in the distance. It sounded like a police siren. He listened carefully. The music was still blasting but, yes – it *was* a police siren, and it was getting louder. Maybe it was Jake's dad coming with the others to rescue him? He started to chew on the bag again. If he made a hole he could at least see what was going on.

He felt the car speed up. Damn. Bates was going to try and outrun the police.

The siren got louder. It was coming fast.

Felix yanked hard at the hessian with his front teeth and heard it rip. Yes, he'd done it! He'd made a hole.

He moved the sack with his head, so his eye was over the hole. He had a clear view of Bates now. He'd stopped banging his head to the music and was focused intently on the road. Felix caught a glimpse of the speedometer: 160 kilometres an hour. Man, the cops were never going to catch him.

In the distance, he could hear a voice yelling through a megaphone, calling for Bates to pull over. In response, the speedometer climbed to 170 kilometres per hour. Felix was thrown around in the back as the SUV bumped crazily along the dirt road. He wriggled around until he could put his eye to the hole again. This time he could see Oscar. He was staring ahead with a spaced-out demonic grin on his face.

Felix listened. He couldn't hear the siren or the mega-phone anymore. He felt a wave of despair. No one was going to rescue him. It was all over.

Bates suddenly slammed on the brakes, sending Felix up into the air for a moment, before he crashed back on the car floor with an thump. The car stopped.

Felix heard the sound of the megaphone again. This time it was close. Really close.

'Step out of the vehicle with your hands in the air.'

Felix felt a surge of relief. It *was* Jake's dad. He must have driven down the fire track and come up in front of them.

'Sergeant Riles!' Felix called out at the top of his voice. 'It's me. Felix. Help!' He wriggled as hard as he could, kicking his legs in the air. 'Help me!'

A fist reached back and thumped him hard in the chest. He felt his chest constrict, winded.

As he struggled for breath, he heard the whine of the window going down and Sergeant Riles asking Bates why he hadn't stopped when ordered to.

'We didn't feel like it,' chorused Bates and Oscar.

'All right. Out of the car. Now,' commanded Jake's dad.

Felix struggled to sit up. 'Help me!' he called out weakly.

Oscar's fist flew back and whacked him again, but Felix was ready for it and kicked him off.

'HELP!' he yelped as loud as he could.

'What's that?' said Sergeant Riles.

'Just a bag of flesh,' Felix heard Bates say.

The back door was flung open and a pair of hands pulled

Felix out of the car on to the road. The belt was unbuckled and Felix felt the sack being pulled over his head.

Jake's dad stared down at him in astonishment. 'What on earth?' He turned to Bates. 'I'll have you on kidnapping charges, Brian.'

Bates's head twitched towards Jake's dad, and he smiled.

Sergeant Riles seemed transfixed for a moment.

From the ground, Felix watched in horror as the sergeant's head jerked convulsively and then his whole body shuddered like it was receiving an electric shock. When Sergeant Riles turned back to Felix, his eyes gleamed a dull red.

Oh God, no. Felix jumped to his feet. He staggered away as Sergeant Riles advanced on him.

Bates and Oscar stepped out of the car, slamming their doors in unison. All three moved towards him. Their movements were slow, but there was no doubt about their intention. 'Destroy him,' they rasped demonically.

Felix sprinted off the road, straight into the bush. Disorient them. He knew that much. He bashed through the scrub. He had no idea where he was going. The talisman was useless, so his only hope was to get as far away as possible.

Once he was a fair way from the road, he stopped for breath. He listened carefully. He couldn't hear them coming. OK, that was good.

He leant against a tree, waiting for his breathing to settle. A hand clamped onto his shoulder. Felix felt his blood turn cold. A deep voice was in his ear. 'Can't I get a moment's peace in this forest?'

He turned. 'Roland?'

Roland grinned at him. 'There'll be no animals left out here to hunt with all the noise you boys make.'

Felix turned to him urgently. 'Listen, Roland. There's a demon after me. Actually, three of them. And I need your help.'

Roland put his hand up. 'Steady on. A demon?'

The words gushed out of Felix. 'Look, I did a spell to make my brother walk again and I used my friends to do it, and we all ended up here where we don't exist, and now the restoring demon wants me dead.'

'Right.' Roland considered this for a moment. 'Well, fair enough. I've heard stranger stories than that at the Bremin pub.' He put his face close to Felix's. 'How can I help?'

'You need to find the others. Bring them here so we can defeat the restoring demon.'

Roland wrinkled his brow. 'Sounds like the others might be just as upset with you as this demon is.'

Felix looked at him, taken aback. 'What?'

'Well, you used them for your own ends. What did they get out of it?'

Felix slumped back against the tree. Roland was right. Why would the others help him? They hated him. He'd ruined their lives. Maybe it was better if he just let the demon get him. Get it over with.

He moved away from the tree and put both his arms out wide. 'Here I am,' he yelled at the top of his voice. 'Come and get me.'

Roland clamped his hand across Felix's mouth. 'Are you completely insane?'

Felix pushed him away. 'I deserve to die, don't I? You said it. Everything that's happened is because of me. Oscar falling. This. Maybe if the demon gets me, everything will go back to normal.'

Roland shook his head. 'Enough with the theatrics, kid. What you *owe* your friends is to get them home. Do you know how to do that?'

Felix looked at him. He did know that. At least, he thought he did. He nodded.

'Good. Then I'll go find them.'

'No, you won't.'

Felix and Roland turned sharply.

Bates was standing behind them, flanked by Oscar and Sergeant Riles. Coiled in Bates's hand was a long piece of rope.

Felix turned to Roland. 'You've got to go. Quick, before they possess you.'

Roland snorted. 'I'm not frightened by this lot.' He gestured to Oscar. 'Look at this one. He's just a kid.'

Oscar erupted with a guttural roar. The branches of the gum trees shivered, and leaves and twigs fell like hail all around them.

'All right, I'm gone.' Roland quickly disappeared into the bush as the possessed Bates, Sergeant Riles and Oscar turned their full attention to Felix.

'You have no hope,' they rasped together.

Felix tried desperately to catch Oscar's eye. 'Fight it, Oscie. Come on. This isn't you.'

Oscar roared again with such power that it felt like the earth was rumbling with him.

'We will destroy you,' chorused the demons. Bates had closed in on him. He grabbed Felix by both arms.

Felix let himself be dragged through the forest. There was no point fighting. He was no match for three demons. He looked down at the talisman. Nothing. *Come on, Roland! Come on, Sam, Jake and Andy! If you get here, I'll get you home, I promise.*

Thump!

Felix was thrown against something hard. He looked behind him. It was Alice's altar. So they were here. Back where it all began. And somehow, the demons knew about this altar.

Bates uncoiled the rope and he and Sergeant Riles started walking around Felix in opposite directions, tying him as tight as possible to the altar's stone head. As they walked they began chanting:

'Soon the disturbance will be over.
Soon order will be restored.'

Felix watched Oscar placing stones around the base of the altar. He was creating the same spiral pattern that Felix had seen at every demonic attack.

'Oscar, stop,' Felix pleaded. But there was no response. He looked down at the talisman. Nothing. Not even a glimmer.

As if on cue, Bates reached over and pulled the cord from Felix's neck. He flung the talisman into the bushes as the chant continued:

'All our troubles will be over,
All our troubles will be gone.'

Felix looked over to where Bates had flung the talisman. He could just make it out, lying on a pile of leaves.

A crack of lightning broke open the sky, and the wind began to blow a gale. Despite the ropes binding him, gusts of wind buffeted Felix about.

Bates and Sergeant Riles had finished tying him, and were now helping Oscar complete the spiral pattern. As they worked they kept chanting in low voices:

'Restore the order,
Restore the order,
Restore the order
So you can reign.'

Oscar placed the last stone at Felix's feet and, looking down, Felix realised the pattern was like a spiralling arrow – pointing directly at him.

The wind was building and Felix could hear a high-pitched humming coming from above him.

He craned his neck to see a perfectly formed twister spinning across the treetops towards him. It was just like the one that had first chased them in the forest, but this time, Felix couldn't run. He thrashed against the ropes binding him but he couldn't free his arms. Bates, Sergeant Riles and Oscar had their faces raised to the sky and chanted urgently as the twister grew in force, spinning towards them.

Felix looked around desperately, and a glimmer on the ground caught his eye. The talisman! The others were close.

Felix started to chant as loudly as he could: *'Water, fire, earth and air . . .'*

The talisman glowed brighter.

'Elements that we all share . . .'

As he kept chanting, Oscar suddenly stumbled and fell to the ground.

'Oscar,' Felix yelled over the howling wind, 'fight it!'

Oscar staggered to his feet and looked around, completely bewildered. 'Felix?'

'Come on, Oscar. Fight it,' yelled Felix.

Oscar looked around in shock. 'What's happening?'

'Get me the talisman,' screamed Felix.

Oscar scrambled towards the talisman just as Jake, Sam, Andy, Phoebe and Roland burst out of the bushes.

They struggled to get to Felix. The wind was gusting around him with such strength it was as if a helicopter was about to land. Leaves and twigs were flung about in the air.

Roland raised his hunting stick high and sprang towards Bates, but Bates stared him down. Almost instantly, Roland's hunting stick fell to the ground and he began to shake uncontrollably.

Sam reached Felix and pulled urgently at the knots, trying to loosen them. He freed one of Felix's hands.

'They've swapped Oscar for Roland,' yelled Felix.

Oscar had almost reached the talisman but he was struggling to stand in the force of the wind.

Jake ran to help. He grabbed the talisman and flung it towards Felix.

Felix snatched the talisman with his free hand. He held it out towards Bates, Roland and Riles. It was glowing fiercely now.

'Water wash our sins away,
Earth guide us to a place.'

Roland, Bates and Riles backed down, confused. The twister stopped swirling and the breeze stilled as Felix kept chanting.

'Wind brings with it fear
Flames of fire we must face.'

It was working. The demons were weakening.

But then the three demons' heads jerked up, and they rose to their full height with a surprising new strength. They opened their mouths in unison and a fearsome, deep cry seemed to come up through the earth. It shook their bodies and blasted out of their mouths. Three pairs of red eyes beamed down on the boys as they started to advance.

'Come on!' Jake yelled as he, Andy and Sam threw themselves at the demons. But they were flicked away like irritating mosquitoes.

The demons turned their sights on Felix, their true focus. The ropes still binding him fell away of their own accord, like snakes slithering.

Felix jumped off the altar and held the talisman high, but its power seemed to be waning.

He looked up into the twister, which was spinning furiously in the sky above him. There was something in its vortex – an image was forming there. What was it? A face?

Felix's legs gave way beneath him and he felt himself being dragged across the ground. The talisman fell from his grasp. The wind had such force that he couldn't fight it. The twister started to descend. He was going to be sucked into it – he could feel it.

He kept chanting at the top of his voice, but the demons were no longer affected. They stood, watching his body being dragged across the ground like a rag doll, their red eyes gleaming with satisfaction.

A hand grabbed Felix's leg, and he looked up to see Andy gripping on to his ankle as hard as he could. In his other hand he held Felix's phone. He pointed it towards Bates.

Through the roaring wind, Felix could just make out his song – the song that had got them in so much trouble. The song that could get them home.

It was the unmaking spell. *Cast again, in the same way, in the same place, and the spell would be reversed.*

Bates, Sergeant Riles and Roland put their hands over their ears and shook their heads. The song was affecting their power.

'Turn it up,' Felix yelled to Andy as he felt himself starting to slide towards the twister again. 'Everybody, sing!'

He could faintly hear Sam, Jake, Phoebe and Andy joining in.

'Water, fire, earth and air,
Elements that we all share.'

The song seemed so small in the face of the roaring wind. But it was powerful.

The demons suddenly fell to the ground. And they were

no longer roaring, but screaming – bloodcurdling screams of indescribable pain. Felix looked up at the twister. It was frozen in the sky. The face inside it was clear now. Felix knew that face. He'd seen it before. He looked towards Phoebe in astonishment.

'Alice!' yelled Phoebe.

Felix scrambled to his feet. He turned to Phoebe.

Tears were streaming down her face. 'It's Alice,' she cried. 'She's the demon.'

Alice writhed in fury as the twister started to spin inward on itself.

Andy picked up the talisman as Felix bellowed the last lines: *'Water wash our sins away . . .'*

Sam, Jake and Andy surrounded him and together they yelled to the earth, to the wind, to the lightning and the rain:

'Earth guide us to place.
Wind brings with it fear,
Flames of fire we must face.'

The sky broke apart with an almighty crack, and everything turned to white.

we're home, freak

The soft melodic sound of bellbirds rang through the forest. The boys looked around the clearing; golden sunlight was filtering in through the trees around them. The sky was a perfect, still blue. There was no sign of the storm or the twister or their demonic attackers.

'Where's Phoebe?' asked Sam.

'Where's Oscar?' said Felix.

Andy picked up the talisman that was lying on the ground between them. 'More importantly, where are we?'

The boys looked at each other, daring to hope that maybe – just maybe . . .

Felix jumped to his feet. He could hear something in the bush. He gestured for the others to be quiet.

The sound of branches being pushed aside and the soft murmur of voices came drifting their way. Trying to be as quiet as possible, the boys crept through the forest towards the sounds. Jake grabbed the biggest stick he could find, prepared for anything.

Felix led the way. He stopped and put his hand up. The others crowded around him. Through the dense branches, they could just make out Mr Bates and Jake's dad. 'They're looking for us,' he whispered. 'Everyone grab a weapon.'

Jake pushed aside a branch. 'Wait a minute.' He grinned so widely it threatened to split his face in two. 'It's Loser Dad!'

The others looked again. Sure enough, Jake's dad wasn't dressed in a police uniform. He was wearing trackpants and a T-shirt with holes in it, and had flip-flops on his feet.

'Who wears flip-flops in the bush?' muttered Andy.

'Loser Dad does!' yelled Jake. He jumped around on the spot. 'We're home. You did it, Felix. You legend!'

Felix stared at him. Had it worked? Was it possible?

Jake crashed through the bush towards his dad, whose face lit up in delight as he enveloped him in a hug.

'I never thought I'd be so glad to see you,' said Jake.

Tears welled in his dad's eyes. 'Oh son, we've been so worried.'

Bates blew his whistle as hard as he could. 'They're here,' he called. 'They're found.' His voice echoed through the forest. There were more shouts and the sound of feet crashing through the undergrowth.

Felix turned to Sam and Andy. 'I'm so sorry. For everything I put you through.'

Sam clapped him on the back. 'It's OK. We're home, freak.'

Felix smiled. 'Guess after what I've done to you, you can call me freak.'

Sam grinned. 'Oh, that's just the start.'

Felix turned to Andy. 'You know, without you remembering the phone we would never have made it home.'

'I told you, it's all about the confluence between science and magic.'

'You did great, brainiac,' said Sam.

Andy grinned sheepishly. 'Man hug?'

Jake came leaping back towards them, and the four boys clapped each other on the back and hugged with joy.

They'd done it. They were home.

'Andy!' yelled a voice.

Andy broke away and ran towards his dad, who grabbed him like he never wanted to let him go. 'We knew all along the Australian bush was no place for you.'

Andy tried to free himself from his dad's hug so he could breathe. 'It wasn't so bad, Dad. Really.'

'Never again,' his dad said firmly. 'Your *nai nai* will put you under house arrest.'

Sam's dad came stumbling through the forest.

Sam ran to him and his dad grabbed him in a headlock.

'I knew you'd be OK. I kept telling them, "Sam knows the forest. He'll be fine!"'

'But Dad, it wasn't the forest that was the problem. We've been in a parallel universe where we –'

'Sam,' warned Felix, eyeing him steadily. 'We just got lost, that's all.'

'Felix?'

Felix turned. His dad was standing in front of him.

He looked older than Felix remembered. His shoulders were stooped and the lines on his face were deeper. 'Oh, son.' His voice broke. 'We thought you'd . . .' He stopped himself, the emotion threatening to overwhelm him.

'I'm OK, Dad,' said Felix quietly. 'We couldn't find our way home. That's all.'

His dad's hands shook as he grabbed a hold of him. 'You know we love you, Felix. We really do.'

Felix swallowed hard. It was years since he'd heard those words. 'How's Oscar?'

His dad wiped his sleeve across his eyes. 'Lost without you, mate. We all were.'

———

Jake's mum plonked down next to him on the picnic rug. She tousled his hair. 'Have I mentioned how unbelievably happy I am to have you home?'

Jake grinned. 'Only about 3,568 times.'

His mum laughed. 'And I'm not stopping there.' She put a plastic plate in front of him. On it was a perfect BLT.

'Do you know how often I dreamed about this?' As he took a bite, Jake felt a wave of pure happiness.

They were sitting on their scraggly front lawn in front of their falling-down house, and Jake wouldn't have swapped it for anywhere else in the world. It was no palace, but it was home, and it was just as he remembered. Nothing had changed, except the way he felt about it. He couldn't imagine ever wanting anything other than what he had right now.

His mum was chatting away as she poured them drinks. 'He's actually a lovely man and he felt absolutely terrible about what happened.'

Jake turned to her. 'Who?'

'Brian Bates,' said his mum. 'He dropped around a few times while you were missing. Actually, we were thinking of taking you to the Bandicoots match on Saturday.' Her lips kept moving but Jake couldn't hear the words anymore.

Bates? Bates had been seeing his mum? His fists clenched and he slowly counted to ten in his head, trying to stay calm.

'Oops, I forgot the mayo. Won't be a sec.' She stood up and headed towards the house.

As she walked away, Jake looked down at his plate. His BLT was shaking. In fact, his whole plate was shaking.

He heard a rumble coming from the earth and his plate toppled off his lap. What the . . . ? The whole front yard seemed to be moving.

Slowly, Jake unclenched his fists and, just as his mum walked back outside, the ground shuddered to stillness.

A banquet had been laid out in honour of Andy's home-coming. The lazy Susan was laden with steamed chicken feet, pigs' trotters in vinegar and an array of his favourite dishes.

Andy leant back and patted his stomach. He couldn't eat another thing.

His mum had been holding tightly on to his arm from the moment he'd sat down. 'The thing that really worried me was when they found your supplies on the path.'

'That's right,' said his dad. 'We knew there was no way you would throw away your *nai nai's xiaolongbao* dumplings.'

'And my poncho!' added Nai Nai. 'Only crazy person do such thing.'

'I thought a murderer had to have attacked you,' said his mum, shuddering at the thought.

Andy patted her arm. 'It was nothing like that, Mum.'

'So what *was* it like?' piped up Viv, who had been watching him intently. 'You still haven't told us exactly what happened.'

'It was . . .' How could he put it into words? 'It was kind of amazing, actually.' Now that he'd said it, he realised it was true. He loved his family, but a part of him missed fending for himself, tackling demons and – well, having a girl who liked him.

Nai Nai whacked him hard across the head with the back of her hand. 'Amazing? You stupid boy. You nearly die. Your family nearly die from worry. Not amazing.'

Andy rubbed his head.

Nai Nai shook her finger at him. 'From now on I walk you to school, I walk you home. You not leave my sight.'

Andy sighed. This lunch was too much. He pushed his chair back. 'I'm going to the bathroom.'

Nai Nai's chair screeched back too. 'I'll come with you.'

'Mum,' his dad cautioned, shaking his head.

Andy burst into the restaurant's toilets. He felt like he was suffocating. He turned on the tap and splashed his face and neck. That was better. What he wouldn't give to dive into the cool water of the river right now. All the way in – not just up to his waist.

He reached over and turned the tap off, but the water kept flowing. It streamed out of the tap and then shot straight up towards the ceiling, where it swirled around in an elegant pattern. Andy stared at it in amazement before it fell back down with a splash, drenching him from head to foot.

Sam's family stared at him in utter disbelief. He was sitting at the head of the table, shoving food in his mouth as he filled his family in on the previous two weeks.

'And you had another son called Sammy who was a total tool, and get this – this is way weird . . .' He turned to Mia, who was sitting beside him, a concerned expression on her face. 'You were going out with him. And your best friend was that goth chick, Ellen.'

'Yeah, right . . .' said Mia slowly, pulling on her cardigan.

'Honey,' his mum said gently. 'We think the trauma of what you've been through –'

'It was trauma, all right. Starving to death, having no family, no girlfriend –'

'Sam, what we're thinking is that maybe you should see someone,' said his dad.

Sam stopped mid-chew and looked at them. 'You think I'm crazy?'

'Nah,' said Vince.

'Just completely certifiable,' said Pete.

'I'm telling you the truth!'

'OK,' his dad said calmly. 'But maybe you should also tell your truth to someone else.'

Sam took a deep breath. The studio portrait of his family, which was hanging on the wall, caught his eye. There he was, smiling confidently, and surrounded by his brothers and his parents. There was no sign of Sammy anymore. This was Sam's house. *He* belonged here.

So why were all the people he loved most in the world looking at him like he was crazy?

Mia stood up suddenly. 'Thanks for lunch, Mr and Mrs Conte. But I have to go.'

Sam grabbed her hand. 'Wait a minute. Where are you going?'

Mia looked around and then spoke quietly to Sam.

'Maybe later you and I could meet somewhere private and have a chat?'

Sam took those words in. *A chat.* He knew what that meant in girl-speak. He wasn't dumb.

Mia extracted her hand. 'I've got to go.'

Sam watched her disappear down the steps. Through the window, he could see the washing line in the corner of the garden, spinning in the breeze.

All this time he'd been waiting, wanting to be with Mia, and now, just when he was ready to be the best boyfriend in the world, she was going to dump him.

The washing line picked up speed, spinning faster and faster. It was strange. There didn't seem to be a wind outside, but it spun around in a frenzy, the sheets and towels on it flapping wildly, until they flew right up into the air and landed in a heap on the grass.

'I can't believe you dumped me for a jock, a nerd and a moron.' Ellen shook her head in disbelief at Felix.

He grinned. 'I know. What was I thinking?'

His mum banged out of the back door, carrying two salads. His dad was fiddling with the barbecue.

'I don't know how you could've possibly survived out there for two weeks,' Felix's mum said as she piled food on to his plate.

'Oh, we ate berries, and Andy knew about weeds. And Sam had a Mars bar.' He fiddled with the bottom of his shirt as he spoke.

'Well, you're as thin as a rake. Come on, eat up.'

Ellen looked at Felix carefully as he shovelled salad into his mouth. She leant over and whispered in his ear. 'You always fiddle with your shirt when you're not telling the truth.'

Did he? Felix put his fork down. Ellen knew him better than anyone. It was so good to see her again.

'Well?' she said. Her forehead crinkled up, the way it did when she was determined to get something out of him.

'I missed you,' Felix blurted out. He hadn't meant to say it out loud, but there it was. Seeing Andy with Ellen had driven him nuts. And that hadn't even been the real Ellen. *This* was the girl he'd really missed.

Ellen looked a bit taken aback. She looked down at the tablecloth. 'Yeah. I missed you too.'

Felix looked around. His dad was busy with the barbecue and his mum was buttering bread rolls at the other end of the table. He reached under the table and grabbed Ellen's hand. 'No,' he muttered. 'I *really* missed you.'

For a moment, she didn't react and then, to Felix's enormous relief, she squeezed his hand back.

'This thing's empty,' Felix's dad declared, throwing the gas lighter down on the table. 'I'll get some matches,' he said, and walked towards the house.

'Give me a go,' said Felix. He smiled at Ellen, who smiled shyly back.

Felix picked up the gas lighter and clicked it. His dad was right, it was empty. He walked towards the barbecue and a flame burst out from the grill.

What the –? Maybe his dad hadn't realised he'd lit it?

But as he dropped his head, the flame disappeared. Felix stared at it. He lifted his head and the flame rose again. He dropped his head and the flame dropped. Felix grinned. This was mad. He could control fire?

His dad reappeared. 'Thanks, mate. That's great.' He dumped a plate of sausages on to the grill.

'Oscar?' his mum called. 'Lunch is nearly ready.'

'I'll go find him,' said Felix.

Oscar was sitting in his wheelchair on the front porch, drawing in his sketchbook.

'Mum says lunch is nearly ready.'

Oscar looked up. 'Damn, I was hoping that now you're back she'd only force-feed one of us.'

Felix sat down next to him.

Oscar looked sideways at him. 'You know for two weeks, all they've talked about is you.'

'That must've been hell.'

Oscar grinned. 'Actually it was great. No one could care less about me, for a change.' His expression shifted. 'They thought you might've run away because of . . . you know.

What happened.'

'That's not why,' Felix said quickly.

Oscar looked determinedly at the decking, as if he was trying not to cry. 'None of that matters, Felix. 'Cause without you here . . . everything kind of sucked.'

Felix swallowed hard. 'I'm sorry.' He put his arm around his brother. 'I won't go away again, I promise.'

Oscar wiped his eyes and handed Felix his sketchbook. 'Here. While you were away, I drew these. They sort of made me feel better.' He wheeled his chair inside.

Felix smiled and opened the book. Inside was a hand-drawn comic, starring him, Jake, Sam and Andy. He turned the first page. There they were, running through the woods, battling aliens and other monsters. Felix laughed, and then something in the comic caught his eye. He looked closer. What was that around his neck? He stared at it.

Oscar had drawn an exact likeness of the talisman.

But that wasn't possible. Oscar couldn't have known what the talisman looked like.

'It's not over yet,' a voice whispered.

Felix looked up. A breeze had blown up out of nowhere and the trees in the front garden were swaying gently. There was no one there. He shook his head and went to go inside.

'It's not over yet,' came the whisper again.

He turned around sharply. 'Who's there?'

A woman stepped out from behind the elm tree. Her eyes

were as hollow as empty wells and her pale face was stony.

Felix stared at her. He knew that face. He would never forget it.

'Felix,' Alice whispered, and the sound of his name carried like a sigh on the wind.

Behind him, the screen door creaked open.

'Felix?' He turned to see Ellen standing at the front door. 'Are you OK?'

Felix looked back at the elm tree. There was no one there. 'Sure.'

Ellen grinned. 'Come on. Your mum's dying to propose a toast to her long-lost son.'

As Felix went to follow her, the voice came again.

'Felix.'

Felix spun around. He waited for a moment, listening carefully, but the only sound was the murmuring of the wind. He must be imagining things.

He went inside, letting the screen door slam behind him. As if in response, the leaves shivered on the elm tree and the whispering wind danced its way up the branches until it reached the power lines, where it began to vibrate with a gentle hum.

acknowledgements

Writing the novel for *Nowhere Boys* has been such a pleasure, made all the greater by working with the Hardie Grant editorial team. Thank you, Hilary Rogers and Beth Hall, for your incredible patience, your expert guidance, and your unwavering faith in me as an unminted novelist.

I would like to thank my parents, David and Yvonne McCredie; Anna Howard for all her support; my wonderful husband, David Pledger, for living with this world for so long and never tiring of it; and my own adventurous boys, Cassidy and Rafael. I would particularly like to thank Cass for his early editorial skills and his passion for this story.

I am indebted to all the writers who wrote episodes of series one: Roger Monk, Craig Irvin, Rhys Graham, Polly Staniford, and Shanti Gudgeon. Your ideas and clever dialogue have been integral to making the series spring to life as a novel.

To the Nowhere Boys themselves, Joel Lok, Dougie Baldwin, Matt Testro and Rahart Sadiqzai: you were fabulous to work with, fabulous to watch and having you all in my head as I wrote this novel was a joy.

To all the folk at Matchbox Pictures, particularly the exceptional producers Michael McMahon and Beth Frey, thank you for your support of this project.

Most of all however I would like to thank Tony Ayres for creating *Nowhere Boys*. Thank you, Tony, from the bottom of my heart, for taking me with you on the *Nowhere Boys* journey and for entrusting me to turn your brilliant, adventurous and unique series into a novel.